DARK PRINCESS

KNIGHT'S RIDGE EMPIRE #11

TRACY LORRAINE

1

CALLI

The deep rumble of an engine is the first thing I'm aware of when I come back to.

My body aches and my head is fuzzy as I lie there, my heart picking up speed with every second that passes.

My dad is going to be so pissed.

Probably not the most helpful of thoughts while I'm locked... I assume in the back of a van, but there you go.

He told me to wait. He told me that he'd come.

Did he know this was likely to happen?

Does it even matter?

Pushing my feet against the floor, I fight to sit up, but I soon realise it's pointless. With my hands tied behind my back and whatever is in my system making my thoughts hazy, my body won't cooperate the way I want it to.

Rolling onto my front to relieve my aching arms, I let out an almighty scream of frustration.

By some miracle, I manage to drift back off to sleep once more with the gentle rocking of the van as I'm driven fuck only knows where.

My only saving grace is that my phone is in my pocket. Dad can track me. They'll find me. And when they do, whoever took me is going to be fucking dead.

Of course, that's assuming I don't get the chance to do it myself first.

I might not be trained like Stella, or have the experience of a life in Lovell behind me like Emmie, but when it comes down to it, I've got Cirillo blood running red-hot through my veins. I refuse to bow down to whoever thinks they're smart enough to do this.

"You failed," Stefanos states, his voice cold and hard.

"I couldn't remember any of it."

Silence floats up from the kitchen to where I'm stopped on the stairs.

Mum, Dad, Uncle Damien and Auntie Selene are away, so we're playing at Alex and Daemon's house. Or at least we were, until I excused myself from Alex's room to get drinks.

The boys are all playing some dumb zombie game on the Xbox, and I'm bored out of my mind. Well, all the boys but Daemon. He hasn't come to find us since we got back from school.

It makes me sad to think he'd rather be alone than

play with his friends. But I can't say I'm surprised. He's always been like that.

"Alex didn't fail," Stefanos continues. "When your grandfather hears about this, he'll—"

There's a loud crash before Daemon appears in the hallway, but he doesn't see me. He doesn't look up at all, too intent on running for the door.

"Nikolas," Stefanos booms, forcing me into action as Daemon pulls the door open and rushes outside.

"Daemon, wait," I call once I'm free from the house, but he's already halfway across the garden, his much longer legs eating up the space as he flees.

My feet pick up speed as he disappears into the trees, into their den.

His angry shout hits my ears before there's a loud bang and another cry, this time one of pain.

Slipping into the shadows, I gasp when he appears in front of me, tears streaming down his cheeks, blood covering both his knuckles and his chest heaving with exertion.

"Leave me alone," he barks. But I do the opposite. I step closer.

His eyes widen in shock and a warning growl rumbles deep in his throat.

"I'm not scared of you, Daemon. Just let me help."

I jolt awake and instinctively try to crawl away from a bang somewhere close to me. I can't see a damn thing thanks to whatever they pulled over my head when they snatched me.

My heart races and my hands tremble behind my

back as deep male voices filter through the side of the van.

"Oh my God. Oh my God," I whimper.

I have no idea where I am, who took me—although I can hazard a guess to that one—or what they want with me.

I just have to keep banking on my phone still being in my pocket and still being on.

They'll come for me, I know they will.

There's another bang that forces my heart into my throat and sends a tremor of fear rocking through me, turning my blood to ice.

A door slides open and light finally filters through the bag over my head, although it's not enough to allow me to see anything but the fabric in front of my face.

My skin prickles, aware that whoever is standing there is watching me closely before the van dips with their weight and I'm dragged across the floor and lifted out.

The fight I was missing when they first grabbed me emerges and I kick and scream, doing anything I can to hurt someone, to attract some attention.

My foot collides with something hard before a deep, terrifying voice grunts something I don't understand.

"*Figlio di puttana.*"

I gasp as confirmation of who's taken me sounds out loudly around me.

"Get the hell off me," I scream, continuing to thrash about.

"Enough," an accented voice booms before I'm hauled to my feet and shoved forward.

The scent of the ocean hits me and when I focus, the sound of seagulls squawking in the distance makes my brow crease.

If I had to guess where they'd bring me, then I'd have said some dark and dirty warehouse in the middle of nowhere. Not the bloody beach.

But then I guess I don't really know how the men around me operate, seeing as I've spent my life shielded from this part of reality, let alone those of our enemies.

Nothing is said as I'm led… somewhere.

The grip on my arms is tight once more, fingertips digging into the sore spots from behind.

Anger burns red-hot in my belly, but what the hell am I meant to do about it? Without my arms, my sight, I'm pretty fucking useless.

So I continue to allow them to push me forward and hope that I'm able to figure out another way out of this once I'm put wherever they want me.

I think of Dad, of Nico, Theo, Daemon. They'll freak out the second they realise I've gone and they'll raise hell to get me back, I know they will.

Chances are that I'll be back in my basement by sunset like this never happened.

I hope.

I stumble through a doorway before the light dims

and the sound of the crashing waves and gulls lessens until I'm released into a room, whatever is binding my wrists is removed, and a door slams behind me, a lock engaging not a second later.

In a rush, I reach for the bag over my head and pull it free.

I blink a couple of times as my vision clears, not believing what I'm seeing.

I'm in a bedroom. A really nice bedroom.

"What the hell?" I whisper, taking in the huge, low bed covered in pristine white sheets. All the furniture is whitewashed wood, there are shelves with trinkets on, and a couple of ornaments.

I stand there in the middle of it all in disbelief.

This is... this is someone's house.

Why the utter hell would the Italians bring me here? I'm sure the last thing they really care about is the comfort of the Cirillo princess.

Why aren't I in a dark and damp cell being tortured?

Why am I—

There's a loud bang from somewhere outside the door and I startle.

This room might be nice, but I can't forget the past... however long.

They abducted me. Drugged me. Threw me in the back of a van and brought me to... somewhere a lot more pleasant than I was expecting, but still. That is not the point.

Walking toward the doors, my chin drops when I

find that there isn't a garden outside, but the actual fucking beach.

Clearly, we're still in England, because I'm not staring at golden sand and the deep blue ocean. But even still, it's really damn pretty.

There's not a person in sight, just endless blue sky and sea.

It only adds to my confusion.

There is furniture, a huge firepit, and everything anyone could need to enjoy that insane view. It kinda reminds me of the last few days, only instead of the woods surrounding me, it's the coast instead.

Spinning around, I take in the room once more before walking to the other door to find a modern bathroom with a huge walk-in shower much like the one in my basement.

Images of my time in there with Daemon fill my mind and a pang of loneliness hits me.

"Shit," I hiss, wondering what's happening at home right now.

How much time has passed? Do they all know that I've vanished? Are they already out there looking for me?

I use the toilet and then head back into the bedroom. I check the doors that lead to the beach, but unsurprisingly, they're locked.

Unable to find a clock or any kind of clue as to what time it is other than the quickly descending sun over the horizon, I crawl onto the bed and curl into a ball.

When I wake and drag my heavy eyelids open once more, the room is dark and silent, but unease ripples down my spine as if I'm being watched.

I hesitate, unsure if I really want to turn over and discover what my latest reality is.

Sucking in deep breaths through my nose, I prepare to pull up my big girl pants and channel my inner bad-arse.

But I don't get the chance, because the person waiting for me loses patience.

"I know you're awake."

His voice rocks through me, making my heart fracture in my chest.

"No," I breathe as disbelief floods my veins.

"Calli, it's okay. It's—"

"No," I bark, finally flipping over and pushing to my knees. I stare my captor dead in the eyes, thankfully showing no signs of fear.

Why would I, when I've never feared him in the past?

Betrayal hits me so hard that I actually sway as if it was a physical blow.

"No," I repeat, unable to come up with anything more eloquent as shock renders me useless.

"It's not what it looks like," he argues, standing from the chair he'd pulled close so he could watch me sleep like a creep and holding his hands up in surrender.

"It's not what it fucking looks like?" I squeal, not accepting a word of it.

I jump to my feet, refusing to be at a height disadvantage with him. Not when I've clearly been at his mercy since the second he grabbed me.

My eyes leave his for a beat and I notice a glittery rock thing on the shelf beside me. Before I know what I'm doing, I've got it in my hand and I'm throwing it full force at his head.

"I trusted you. I fucking trusted you."

He doesn't even try to protect himself as the rock flies toward his brow and my stomach lurches when it finally makes contact. His skin splits, blood immediately pooling at the wound before it trickles down his face.

I want to feel guilty. But I refuse to. I refuse to feel anything but hatred toward him for doing this.

Jumping from the bed, I move on instinct as I fly toward him, my hands curled into fists. I hit anywhere I can, letting my frustration bleed out of me in a way I've never really experienced before. I've never been a violent person, but right now, all I want to do is hurt him, force him to feel just an ounce of the pain that's shredding my insides right now.

"How could you do this to me?" I scream, my enraged voice not even sounding remotely like my own. "I trusted you. I thought you were different."

He lets me go wild, leaving his arms hanging

limply at his sides as I rain hell down on him. Or at least, in my head, that's what I'm doing. I'm sure the reality is very, very different.

The second he notices that I'm exhausting myself, he reaches for my wrists, lifts them above my head and slams my back against the wall.

His nostrils flare and his chest heaves as he stares down at me.

His face is nothing but a mask. One that I'm more than familiar with. I've witnessed my dad, brother, and the rest of the guys pull theirs on enough. Like this, nothing outside of the task at hand matters. Nothing but being the one who survives, the one who wins, matters.

And it fucking terrifies me.

Because the person he needs to beat right now is me.

"Please." The word falls from my lips as a plea and I hate it.

I want to be strong. To stand up to the monster staring me down like I know Stella or Emmie would.

But I can't. Despite the cold mask staring back at me, I remember exactly what's hiding beneath it.

A door slams somewhere else in the house, I notice for the first time since I woke up that the bedroom door is open.

If I weren't so intent on hurting him, then I could have run.

Not that I'm sure I'd have got very far.

Footsteps pound closer and my heart rate increases as I attempt to tug my wrists free of his grip.

"Please," I whisper. "Just let me go. I-I don't know what you—"

My words are cut off when a shadow appears in the doorway, my body trembling with fear that one of his less-friendly buddies is about to join us and make this whole situation so much worse.

But then the shadow reveals himself and relief floods me.

"Daemon, oh my God."

But when he stops in the doorway, his eyes darting between me and the man glaring down at me, any hope I had dies.

2

DAEMON

"**I**'m not here for trouble, I fucking swear to you," Antonio fucking Santoro says, lifting his hands in surrender.

Refusing to accept his words, I keep my gun trained on his head and wait. Although, I must admit that I'm impressed. The last time I saw him, it ended with one very serious threat about where my next bullet would land if he showed his face around me again.

"It's Calli," he confesses. "She's in trouble."

"What?" I roar, fear rolling through me and making my hand tremble, something he can't miss. "Where is she?"

"I don't know. I just came from my uncle's. I... uh... overheard something I shouldn't have."

"Why the fuck should I believe a word you're saying?" I growl.

"Because I'm standing here at the end of your gun,

willingly giving you intel that will likely get me killed," he says without so much as a waver in his voice.

My chest heaves as I stare at him, trying to decide if he's telling the truth or not.

"They're going to go after her."

"Ricardo wants our businesses. Why would he suddenly—"

"He wants retaliation for killing our guys. For shooting his nephew," he states, lifting a brow at me. "An eye for an eye."

My head starts to spin.

"He thinks she's going to be an easy target."

I shake my head.

"No," I breathe.

"And I hate to say it, but he's right. Evan doesn't have enough protection on her. We need to do something."

"We?" I ask.

"I might be the enemy, but she's not." Desperation and fear that I more than recognise darken his eyes.

"Fuck," I bark, lowering my arm. "Fuck."

Taking a step back, I tuck my gun into the back of my trousers.

"Come with me," I say, striding away from him and back to my car.

Pulling the back door open, I nod for him to get in, confident that he'll be well enough hidden by my dark windows.

"If you're fucking lying to me, I'll personally carve

you up and deliver you back to your darling uncle in pieces," I warn, leaning in after him.

"I fucking swear to you, I'm not lying. I want her safe, just as much as you do."

"She's going to get you killed."

He shrugs one shoulder. "She's worth it, don't you think?"

"Motherfucker," I snarl, slamming the door on him before resting my hands on my car and hanging my head.

I suck in a handful of calming breaths before I slide back into the driver's seat and pull my phone out, opening up the tracking app to see where my girl is.

If some Italian cunt gets their hands on her before—

No, just fucking no.

I sit out the front of the house, staring at the light coming from the windows.

I didn't want to leave. But there's fuck all inside, and if we're really doing this, then if nothing else, we need some fucking food.

I probably should have sent him. Hoped that he'd get lost and just never reappear again. But I know that wasn't how my luck was going to go.

The only bit of luck I can claim having right now was that we got to Calli before Ricardo and his men.

I have no clue how quickly they were going to act, but the fear in Ant's eyes as he delivered what he'd overheard told me that they weren't going to hesitate for long.

Which meant we couldn't wait.

I needed my girl safe, and if that meant going to extreme measures and siding with the enemy for a bit, then I was okay with that.

For her. Always for her.

The burner phone in my pocket rings, and I damn near jump out of my skin as it rips from every speaker surrounding me.

"Boss," I say the second Evan's call has connected.

"Everything good?" he confirms.

"Yeah. She's safe. And will be for as long as the threat is out there," I confirm.

"And you're still refusing to tell me who your rat is?" Suspicion is more than evident in his tone.

"What did your snakes say? Anything different?"

"No. They've got a hit out on her," he says, his voice cracking with concern.

"Then you need to trust me."

"You're not even meant to be working. When your father—"

"I'm not working. I'm studying. And so is Calli. Safely."

"I swear to fucking God, Deimos. If you fuck this up and she—"

"Nothing is going to happen to her. She's safe. No one knows where we are."

"I'm aware," he mutters, his irritation clear that I've even refused to tell him our location.

Both Ant and I have our trackers off. I killed off Calli's the second we got her, and we drove up here in a van with fake plates on.

The only way anyone is going to find us is if that Italian fuck inside squeals.

And if he does, there's going to be zero chance of me sparing his life for a third time.

"I'm trusting you, Deimos. Look after my girl."

"You've got my word, Boss."

I cut the call before turning the phone off, and the second I'm out of the car, I drop it to the ground and crush it beneath my foot.

I'm not leaving anything to fucking chance here. There is no way any other Italian motherfucker is getting anywhere near my girl.

Grabbing the bags from the boot, I head toward the house, my eyes shooting everywhere as my paranoia gets the better of me.

Silence greets me as I head toward the kitchen and try not to panic when I don't find Ant where I left him.

Dumping the bags, I go in search of him. My heart rate increases with every step I take and I don't see or hear any evidence of them being here.

By the time I'm halfway through the building, I'm damn near running.

I shouldn't have fucking left him here with her.

I fucking trusted him, and if he's—

All the air rushes out of my lungs as I turn the corner and find him pressing my angel against the wall, staring down at her as if she's his.

Her eyes widen in relief as she stares at me, doing her best to free herself from Ant's hold.

"Daemon, oh my God," she breathes. The sound of her voice sends goosebumps racing across my skin.

My fingers curl, the weight of my gun tucked into my waistband becoming more and more apparent.

"Let her go," I growl, my eyes locked on the side of Ant's head. My brows pinch when I find a small trickle of blood running down his cheeks as he continues to stare down at her as if she was made for him.

She fucking wasn't.

When he doesn't move, my hand takes on a life of its own, and in seconds, I have my gun once again trained on his head.

"Daemon," Calli warns. "Don't."

"Then he needs to back the fuck up," I bark, pointing my gun in the direction I want him to go.

The second he releases her, Calli jumps in front of him, protecting him.

"Put it down," she demands.

"Are you fucking kidding me?" I hiss. "You're protecting him?"

She stares at me in disbelief.

"Put the gun down, Daemon," she growls, her angry eyes holding mine, demanding I follow orders.

After a couple of seconds and a silent death threat at Ant, I finally lower it. But I don't tuck it away, preferring to keep it at my side just in case.

He might have been on our side when he came to me for help with this, and I might trust him to keep her safe, but I don't fucking trust his intentions beyond that.

He wants her. I didn't need to see him pinning her to the wall to have that confirmed. The image of him between her legs in his room a couple of weeks ago has never left me.

Finally, she steps away from Ant and closes the space between us.

My entire body aches as her scent fills my nose.

She stares up at me, her eyes dark and tired. Her skin is pale and her hair a mess.

She looks fucking beautiful.

My fingers curl as I fight my need to reach for her.

My heart thunders as I wait for what she's going to do.

For a second, I'm clueless. Totally fucking lost as to where her head is at with all this. But then her hand twitches at her side and I know exactly what's coming.

The sting of her slap makes my breath catch, but I don't react other than that.

"You fucking arsehole," she sneers, snatching her hand back when I try to hold it against my face.

"I won't apologise for protecting you, Angel."

"You're serious, aren't you?"

I shrug, standing by the decision Ant and I made to make our abduction look realistic.

If the Marianos were hunting her, if they saw us, then we needed them to believe we were on their side.

If they knew we'd snatched her to take her to safety, then they'd be out for blood.

Mainly Ant's.

"I want to go home," she demands, still holding her ground in front of me.

"Not happening. We have everything you could need here."

"Here? Where is here?"

"It doesn't matter. It's safe. No one is going to touch you here."

"No one?" she asks, tilting her head to the side. "Because it seems to me that Ant already has."

"Careful, beautiful. I've let you have your fun with Ant, with Alex. My patience only extends so far," I growl, closing the space between us.

Ant's eyes bore into the side of my head, jealousy rearing its ugly head inside him. But fuck it.

He has to know that I care about her. And hell, he's already holding enough of our secrets right now. What's one more?

She gasps and Ant takes a step forward when my fingers wrap around her throat.

"I apologise if we were too rough with you, Angel. If we scared you. But something tells me that you wouldn't have come willingly if we pulled up in a van and told you to get in the back."

She swallows nervously, her pulse thundering against my fingers.

I don't need her words. I can read her answers in the depth of her eyes.

"Get out," she breathes.

"Ang—"

"No," she cries, shoving me in the chest, forcing me to back up. "You don't get to do this, Nikolas," she taunts. "You don't get to hide from me, to control me. To take my decisions away from me, even if it is in your fucked-up need to protect me."

My lips part to respond, but I quickly realise that I have no answer that she'll even consider accepting right now.

"Come on, man. Let's give her some space," Ant says, siding with her and walking toward the door.

"You haven't eaten. You need food."

"I'll live," she sneers, taking a massive step back, making me drop my hand and remove my touch from her.

Hate pours from her. And while I might despise that it's directed at me. I still refuse to back down.

Being here, her not knowing where here actually is, is the right thing to do right now.

"I know you don't understand," I whisper. "But everything I'm doing is to protect you."

"You're right," she hisses. "I don't understand. And do you know why? Because no one trusts me with the truth. No one thinks I can handle it."

"No, that's not—"

"Is that what you thought while you covered me in your blood in my shower?" Ant's breath catches behind me at her words, but fuck him. I couldn't give a shit if she forces him to listen to every single thing we've done together. It'll just help prove to him who she belongs to. "Did you do it because you think I'm weak?"

"No, I don't think—"

"Then tell me the fucking truth, Daemon. About everything. This is bullshit."

Something on the floor catches her eye. She reaches down to get it a beat before something collides with the wall right beside my head.

I glance down as the crystal hits the carpet with a soft thud.

"Get the fuck away from me. I'm not interested in a word that comes from your lips until it's the truth."

"I've never lied to you, Angel."

"You lie to everyone every goddamn day of your life, Nikolas Deimos."

She turns her back on me, cutting off our connection.

"Come on. We'll leave your stuff out by the door, Calli. We'll be in the kitchen if you're hungry."

"You should leave, Ant. Being here is dangerous. If anyone finds—"

"I know what I'm doing, Calli. And Daemon is right. Your safety is the most important thing here."

"If that were true, you wouldn't have been spending time with me. You knew as well as I did the danger we were putting ourselves in."

"What's going on has nothing to do with us."

A growl rips from my throat at his words.

"But if it weren't for us, you might not be having such a pleasant time of it right now."

"Pleasant?" she spits, spinning back around and glaring pure death at him. "You think being drugged—again"—she cuts me with a look—"thrown in a van, and brought here against my will is my idea of a pleasant time?"

"It could be worse, I assure you."

"Whatever," she scoffs, turning away from us once more.

"Angel?" I breathe when Ant slips away as she requested.

"I'm not interested. Just leave me alone."

3

CALLI

He stands behind me, staring at me, silently begging me to turn back to him for the longest time.

But it's going to take more than the magnetic pull that's always between us to make me cave this time.

He's gone too far.

I was mostly for jumping on the crazy train with him. But this...

This is fucking insane.

I'm at risk. That may well be true.

The Italians are after me in retaliation. That's not all that hard to believe.

But he could have talked to me. He could have cornered me in that alleyway and explained.

If he did it well enough, I might have even agreed to be thrown in the back of a van.

He didn't need the theatrics to keep me safe.

If he'd done what I've been craving from him for

days—hell, for months—and just talked to me, opened up, told me the truth... then I'd have been putty in his hands.

But no.

He had to go all psycho devil on my arse.

But eventually, he must realise that I have a stubborn streak that can rival his, and he backs away without another word.

Once I'm confident that he's gone, I spin around, finding the bag I'd taken away sitting on the floor by the door.

My body aches as I move, exhaustion and the lingering effects of whatever he pumped me with making my movements sluggish.

Pulling the zip, I look inside, not having a clue what to expect.

What I find makes me fall on my arse in shock.

I'm sorry, Angel.

I need you to trust me, because a world without you in it isn't a world worth living in.

All the air rushes from my lungs at his words. Tears fill my eyes, and a lump so huge I struggle to breathe around it climbs up my throat.

Reaching into my bag, I pull out his note—accompanied by an origami bat, of course—and my iPad as I fight to keep my emotions in check.

I fail, mainly because the second my eyes land on his messy scrawl once more, an ugly sob erupts from my throat.

Confusion, frustration, and betrayal all war within

me. But mostly, it's my need for him that wrecks me. It's how badly I want to rip that door open and bury myself in his arms that makes me sob like a baby.

I shouldn't need him this badly. I shouldn't want him after all the things he's done. But that broken, scared boy has latched on to something deep inside me and I can't let him go.

With the note still clutched in my hand, I crawl onto the bed once more and just give in to the tears that still demand to spill over.

I take a step forward, and Daemon immediately takes one back. It's as if he's scared of me, all the while trying to ensure I'm scared of him.

It makes my head spin. But no matter how many times I try to figure this boy out, I never manage it. He's too confusing. Too... different from the others.

Give my brother, my cousin, a games controller or a football and they'll be happy for hours.

But nothing seems to make Daemon happy. In fact, everything seems to make him sad.

He's sad at school, at home, when he's playing with my brother.

I don't know why, but I want to see him smile.

He's so cute when he does. It makes his eyes light up like they're made of silver, and he's got these two dimples that are usually hidden by his scowl.

"You need to leave," he says, his voice quieter, weaker than I'm used to, and I hate that his dad has the power to do that to him. To strip him of his confidence and make him run away.

So what if he failed a test?

It happens to all of us from time to time.

And it's not like the boys in our family don't have other things to do. Our fathers are always on their cases. Forcing them to exercise, to train, whatever that means.

I'm excluded from all of it. Not that it bothers me too much. From what I've heard, it doesn't sound like much fun. At least they have each other, though. I'm always alone.

The girls at school don't want to be my friend. Not really. They want to be friends with them. And as soon as they've got close to them, they forget I exist.

It's fine. It's not like I want to be friends with them either. All they care about is clothes and how they look.

I want a real friend. Someone who gets me.

Someone like Daemon.

"Let me help," I say, taking another step toward him.

"I don't need any help," he scoffs, turning away from me. Hiding from me.

"What test did you fail? I can help you study."

"It was nothing. Just a dumb test."

"Then you'll pass it next time, right? Let's just make sure you smash it. Prove him wrong."

It takes a couple of seconds, but eventually, his eyes find mine.

His tears have stopped, but they still cling to his eyelashes.

"I'll test you and we can practice," I tell him, more than ready to argue if he even thinks about disagreeing.

I'm just about to try again when he nods.

"I'll go and get some paper," I tell him. "And tomorrow, you'll ace that test."

A small smile twitches at his lips.

"Don't go anywhere," I tell him as I move back toward the exit.

He shakes his head. "I'll wait for you." I'm at the door when he speaks again. "As long as it takes."

I wake with a start, my fingers curling around the paper that's still in my hand.

Blinking, I find that there's sunlight streaming through the still-open curtains, but I'm still very much in the same house, wherever it is.

Rolling onto my back, I stare up at the ceiling and focus on keeping my breathing steady.

I've got so many questions, so many thoughts and fears racing through my mind. But I'm not sure if I'm brave enough to voice them all.

I have a feeling that the truth is going to be even more terrifying than everything that's spinning around my head right now.

Movement outside my door makes me jump, but it's not enough to force me to move.

The sound of the ocean outside teases me, and I can't help but wish I could throw the door open and really enjoy it, just pretend that I'm on holiday and able to really relax and enjoy myself.

Closing my eyes, I let my imagination wander and allow myself to think about it just being the two of us here. Just me and Daemon, or more so, Nikolas. I want the boy beneath the mask, not the soldier who hides the incredible person beneath.

But is that even a possibility? Has he spent so long hiding that boy that he's going to forever remain buried, just teasing me with glimpses of what could be?

I let out a heavy sigh as I think about the parts of yesterday I can remember.

Was what they did really necessary?

Misguided or not, I trust them. Both of them.

And despite my anger, deep down, I know that they did what they did for a reason.

I just wish they hadn't.

I wish they felt that they could have talked to me, explained, and not just acted on impulse and fallen back on the brutality they're usually forced to use.

But would you have believed them? Would you have followed orders and taken their words seriously?

Eventually, my need for the toilet forces me to roll out of bed and pad toward the bathroom.

Despite having seen it the day before, my eyes still widen at the sheer size of the room.

Wherever they decided to bring me, it's not exactly lacking luxury.

My eyes linger on the bath, trying to imagine what Daemon might look like with his arms resting over the roll-top and bubbles coating his skin.

It's an image I possibly will never get to see in reality. Not while he keeps hiding from me, anyway.

Forcing my sadness down, I continue forward. It's

not going to help me here. I've got to focus on my anger and my need for answers.

Shock rocks through me when I come to stand at the basin and find what looks like a brand-new pink toothbrush and tube of toothpaste waiting for me.

Spinning around, I look into the shower, my eyes widening when I find my usual bottles of shampoo waiting for me.

Did they plan this?

From what they said yesterday, I assumed this whole thing was a spur-of-the-moment abduction. But...

No.

I refuse to believe that Daemon and Ant would have colluded and come up with this.

Why the hell would they ever work together if the threat they talked about yesterday wasn't true?

They wouldn't.

The fact that they're both in the same house and haven't killed each other is something of a miracle.

The second the hot water of the shower rains down over me, washing the stench of that van from my skin, I begin to feel a little stronger. Like I might just be able to go out there and stand my ground.

I need answers.

I deserve answers.

I'm done with the days where I let everyone sugarcoat everything and give me watered-down versions of the truth just to protect me.

I'm no longer content with living on the periphery

of my life.

I'm Callista Cirillo, and I have just as much right as everyone else in my family to know what's happening around me. Even if it is dark. Even if it is brutal, terrifying.

After rummaging through the bag Daemon packed for me, I pull on an outfit that I hope will give me some courage, blow-dry my hair until it's perfect, and spend an inordinate amount of time on my make-up.

If I'm intending on going up against these two control freaks, then I need to look my best and feel my best, despite the aches in my body from my less-than-desirable journey here or the fuzziness of my head.

Smoothing my hair down once more, I head for the door.

I curse myself when my hand trembles as I reach out.

You're stronger than this, Callista.

You're better than them.

I pull the door open with a flourish and storm out, ready to go up against them and demand some answers.

But I don't get very far when my foot catches on something and my heart jumps into my throat as my top half keeps moving and my legs don't.

"What the—"

"Shit," a deep voice barks as I begin my heart-stopping descent toward what looks to be solid oak floors.

There's movement beneath me a beat before I hit

the floor. Hands wrap around my waist and I'm caught, suspended a few inches from what was inevitably going to be a broken nose.

"What the hell are you doing?" I snap the second I'm placed back on my feet and find myself staring into a pair of tired, dark grey eyes.

Pain flickers through them. But it's so fast, I start to wonder if I imagine it as his mask falls into place.

"Were you sitting outside my room like a creep?" I sneer, my heart barely slowing its erratic pace now that I'm toe to toe with him again.

I was hoping I might have had a few more minutes at least before I had to face him—them. That I might even be able to sneak up on them, overhear a few things that might just come in useful.

I was not expecting this.

"Just keeping you safe, Angel."

"Bullshit," I spit. "If that were the case, you'd have just come in and handcuffed me to the bed."

Heat blazes in his eyes as I say those words, and I can't help the clench of my lower muscles from the image that pops into my head.

"I'm trying to give you what you asked for," he confesses.

"The truth? Gotta be honest, D," I say, stealing Alex's nickname for him, "you're doing a really shitty job of it."

"Protecting you," he growls, closing the space between us.

His words hit me like a ton of bricks. I hadn't

forgotten the reason I woke up here. Not even a little bit. But hearing him say those two words was a reality check I didn't really need.

"I'm gonna need more than that, devil boy."

Spinning on my heels, I attempt to walk away from him, but unsurprisingly, he's not having any of it.

His fingers wrap around my wrist a second before I'm tugged back and slammed against the wall.

All the air rushes from my lungs as he grabs my jaw in his unforgiving grip.

"You don't get to turn your back on me, Angel. That's not how this is going to work."

His lips slam down on mine, the length of his body pressing against me.

It takes all the self-control I possess not to kiss him back.

But as his lips move against mine, I remain motionless while my heart thrashes in my chest.

"Angel," he groans before tugging my bottom lip into his mouth and nipping at it to get me to react.

The sound of a coffee machine down the hallway hits my ears before the scent of fresh beans fill my nose.

To my surprise, he releases my wrist and I manage to press against his chest.

He allows me to push him back and he removes his lips from mine.

Instantly, I feel his loss, but I slam a door down on all of those feelings and shove away from the wall, my eyes holding his the entire time.

"It's going to take more than a kiss, Daemon. You want me on board with this stupid plan, then you know what you need to do."

Turning my back on him, I follow my nose until I find a kitchen and Ant standing at a coffee machine.

He does a double take when I storm in, his eyes immediately dropping down my body.

I place my hands on my hips, my irritation levels with both of them at an all-time high.

Footsteps close in behind me as I quirk a brow at Ant.

"Nice... uh..." he stutters as Daemon steps up behind me. "Sweatshirt," he finally finishes.

"Thanks. I made it myself," I sneer. "Coffee, please. Strong."

Pulling out a chair, I drop into it with zero class or care. Crossing my arms across my chest, I stare at the wall as they both stand at opposite ends of the kitchen, looking utterly out of their depth.

If the situation weren't so dire, it would be hilarious.

Finally, Daemon clearing his throat drags my attention to him.

"He's right. Nice shirt."

I glance down at the text written above my tits and smirk.

Not your average princess.

I did the design for Stella and Emmie, but it seems to suit the situation right now.

I glower at him as the coffee machine jumps into

action.

Silence rings out between the three of us, the air crackling with tension as we all bite back the things we're desperate to say.

After a couple of minutes, Ant delivers me a perfect cappuccino that would put any barista to shame.

"Hungry?" he asks.

"What do you think? You snatched me when I was buying snacks. Where are they, by the way?" I ask, not willing to give up my chocolate stash.

"I've got it," Daemon says, walking deeper into the kitchen.

"You worried I can't cook, Deimos?" Ant grunts.

"I don't give a fuck if you can tap dance while doing it. Calli is mine, and I have every intention of ensuring she's looked after properly."

"Did you decide that before or after you injected me with whatever you pumped my veins full of yesterday?" I hiss.

"All I care about is keeping you safe," he says so seriously it makes my chest ache. It doesn't mean I'm going to roll over, though.

"I need to talk to my dad about your access to drugs. You're fucking lethal."

"Only when it's necessary."

Not having any sensible words to say back, I just throw my hands up in exasperation.

"Does my dad know about any of this, or have you left him, all of them, at home, freaking the fuck out?"

"You have nothing to worry about, Angel."

"How reassuring," I mutter as he pulls bacon and eggs from the fridge.

"Trust us, Calli," Ant urges.

Daemon gives him a double take over his shoulder.

"Trust me," he pleads.

"I might have if you'd just talked to me. I'm assuming my dad knew something was going on, which is why he jumped off the deep end when I said I was going to the shop?"

"We've been on high alert for a while, keeping a close eye on you all. But then Ant came to me yesterday with new intel," Daemon confesses. He does it through clenched teeth, but I still count it as a win.

"I overheard my uncle talking about their plans. They want you in retaliation for the men your Family have killed recently."

"Great." I fall quiet, my thoughts running at a million miles an hour around my head. Daemon grabs a pan and Ant watches silently while resting back against the counter, sipping on his coffee.

Both of them look exhausted, and I wonder if either of them got any sleep last night. Obviously, it's not an unusual occurrence for Daemon, but I'm not aware of Ant having issues.

Guilt tugs at my insides that they're both wiped out because of me, feeling the need to protect me like this.

I love it and hate it in equal measures.

4

———

DAEMON

I keep my focus on the pan in front of me and allow myself to drown in the scent of the frying bacon as Ant moves closer to Calli and drops down in the seat beside her.

For the longest time, nothing is said and I'm able to breathe easy.

But then the deep rumble of his voice floats through the air and every muscle in my body tenses.

Glancing over, I find him leaning into her space, studying her as if he owns her as he speaks.

His voice is too low to hear what he's saying, but it doesn't matter. His body language says it all, and it's like a fucking knife to the chest.

The bacon is forgotten as I watch them. Their familiarity, the easy way they talk and react to each other.

Jealousy bubbles up inside me until I'm barely able to contain it.

My fingers ache to reach for my gun in my waistband, to put an end to the way he's looking at her as if she's his everything.

She's not.

She's mine.

I don't realise the growl that rips through the air is mine until they both turn to look at me.

Calli's expression hardens in anger while Ant just shakes his head as if he's amused by my reaction.

Leaning in closer, he whispers something in Calli's ear.

My fists curl as he taunts me and I push forward, closing the space between us all and more than ready to drag him away from my girl should he overstep the mark.

His eyes find mine, mirth dancing within them, which I'm equally as impressed by as I am fucking mortified.

The need to paint this room red with his blood burns through me. He should not be amused by it in any way. Most would be terrified if they had little choice but to look into my eyes while I was feeling quite so unhinged, but it seems that Ant may just have bigger balls than I gave him credit for.

I mean, he has been seeing our princess behind all our backs for months, so clearly, he's got something about him.

Possibly just stupidity.

I guess only time will tell.

"Don't you need to fuck off?" I bark.

"Daemon, don't—" Calli starts, but she's soon interrupted.

"You fucking know I do," Ant growls back at me. "Could you give us a minute?"

One of my brows lifts as I remain exactly where I am.

"Whatever you have to say, you can say it in front of me."

Calli jumps up from her chair, glaring at me. "You're being a—"

"It's okay," Ant says calmly, standing with her. "He's allowed to freak out and get all possessive when he sees you with me."

"Damn fucking right I am," I hiss.

Calli looks between the two of us with a scowl.

"Would you like me to get a tape measure so you can both measure your cocks, or did you just want to piss all over me like the overbearing dickheads you are?"

"That's not necessary," Ant says calmly.

"Damn right it's not," I agree. "And anyway, we both know I'd win. You do seem quite fond of the size of my cock after all."

A growl rips from Calli as Ant's eyes widen in shock. It's the first time I've acknowledged out loud that I'm more than a soldier protecting his princess. Not that I think for a second that Ant hasn't worked it out.

It's the reason he came to me yesterday with this intel, after all. Well, that and anyone else wouldn't have believed him and would possibly have blown his brains out the second he got close.

"Daemon," Calli growls.

Ignoring me, Ant turns his attention to the girl vibrating with anger in front of him.

"Take this," he says, digging something out of his pocket and passing it to her. "The only number saved is to my burner. If you need anything, need an escape from that psycho, then—"

"She won't be needing that," I say, snatching it from between the two of them and stuffing it into my pocket.

Calli glowers at me, but she doesn't say a word.

"Do you have to go?" she asks, emotion cracking her voice before she looks back up at him.

More shreds are ripped from my heart as I watch the way her expression softens when she looks at him.

"Yeah. They're going to notice I've gone soon, if they haven't already."

"What happens if they find out what you did?"

"You don't need me to answer that, sunshine," he whispers.

A sob catches in her throat.

"Stay. We'll protect you. We'll—"

"I can't. I've done what I needed to do. You're safe."

She nods. "Th-thank you."

"Always. I knew a future for us was never in the cards, but it was fun pretending, huh?" he asks, his hand slipping around the side of her neck.

Watching him touch her sends a surge of rage through me. It takes everything I have to stay put and not rip him from her body.

"I'm so sorry," Calli whispers weakly.

"Me too. In another life, you could have been it for me."

Twisting his fingers in her hair, he presses his lips to her forehead as she cries.

They stand in silence, completely still for the longest time.

"Please," Calli pleads when he finally releases her. "Be safe."

He smiles at her, the tears tracking down her cheeks breaking his heart just like I'm sure they are mine.

His eyes shoot to me briefly before he turns back.

"Give him hell, yeah? He deserves it."

A sad laugh falls from Calli before he takes off through the house.

I take a step to follow him, to have the final say, but Calli's pained cry rips through the air and I quickly turn her way.

Part of me expects her to push me away when I wrap my arms around her, but she doesn't. Instead, she collapses into my body and sobs against my chest.

Pain slices through my heart as her cries echo around the kitchen long after Ant slams the front door behind him.

My hold on her doesn't falter as her tears soak through my shirt.

"Shhh, Angel, it's okay."

Her fingers twist in my shirt, holding me to her as if she's scared I'm about to walk out too before she looks up.

My breath catches in my throat at the pain that's written over her face from losing him again.

The longer she stares up at me, the more my heart races at the thought of her wanting him over me.

I hate it. I hate that my mind goes there, but it's been ingrained in me all my goddamn life.

I'm second best.

Always.

"It never could have wor—"

My words are cut off when she stretches up on her tiptoes and presses her lips to mine.

Relief floods my veins as she kisses me, her fingers releasing my shirt in favour of slipping beneath it and dragging her nails down my abs.

"Angel," I groan into her kiss.

"Take me away," she begs. "Make it all go away."

"Fuck," I grunt into her kiss as she pushes her hand beneath my waistband in search of my cock. "I love it when you're bad."

"Daemon," she moans as I lift her from the floor and lay her out on the table before me.

The scent of the bacon beginning to burn on the stove doesn't even register as I kiss down her neck.

In only seconds, I'm stuffing her knickers in my pocket and spreading her wide before me.

Capturing her lips once more, I brush my fingers

between her folds, a loud, desperate groan rumbling deep in my throat as I find her dripping wet for me.

"Fuck. I'm addicted to you, Angel."

"Please," she whimpers as I tease her entrance. "Please just... yes," she cries when I push two fingers inside her.

Her muscles clamp down around my digits, making my cock jerk in excitement, knowing exactly how it feels to be sucked deep inside her body.

Her back arches off the table and she grips the sides as I drive my fingers inside her in a way I know she likes.

"You're so fucking beautiful, Angel. You bring me to my fucking knees."

"Knees. Yes. I want your mouth," she begs.

Ripping my eyes from hers, I look between her legs, watching as my fingers disappear inside her.

Unable to deny her anything, I drop to my knees and press the flat of my tongue against her clit.

"Nikolas," she cries, her hips rolling in an attempt to fuck my face.

My cock aches behind the confines of my trousers, desperate to be set free, to push inside her, to claim her, to mark her.

Her fingers twist in my hair, holding me tightly against her as her moans and cries for more get loud and louder.

The table rocks beneath us as she writhes, one of the mugs that was sitting on top of it smashing to the floor. But if she hears it, she doesn't react. She's too lost to the race to the end to be aware of anything else happening around her.

"Come for me, Angel," I demand, my deep voice vibrating through her.

"Yes, yes," she cries, her grip on my hair tightening until I'm sure she's about to pull some out, but I don't stop her. I can't. I fucking need this just as much as she does.

In only two seconds, her body finally quakes as she screams my name.

My chest swells hearing it, reminding me that she's still here. That watching him walk out might have wrecked her, but she didn't chase him. She fell into me. She sought support and comfort in me.

She wants me.

"Fuck," she pants, finally releasing her hold on me and pushing up on her elbows.

Lifting her foot, she presses it to my chest and gives me little choice but to back up.

The second I've released her, she slides off the end of the table and stands, staring down at me on my knees before her.

"It's going to take more than a mind-blowing orgasm or two. Thanks though," she says coldly before turning her back on me, grabbing an apple from the side and disappearing down the hallway.

The slamming of her bedroom door rattles through me as my entire body slumps in defeat.

5

___

CALLI

I fall onto the bed and stop fighting the pain that wants to bubble out of me.

From the very beginning, Ant and I knew that it wasn't going to work between us. Neither of us is stupid enough to believe a miracle was going to happen. But at the same time, we were both happy to enjoy what we had and try not to worry about what was going to happen next too much.

But watching him walk away just then... Knowing that he's going back to his uncle, the rest of his family, when they might know, or even suspect what he's done... It wrecked me.

I don't want him hurt because of me. Because he was trying to be a good friend, trying to protect me.

I have no idea how long I lie there with my pillow soaked with my tears when his footsteps get louder outside my door.

Guilt tumbles through me for walking away from

him like I did. But he's hurt me, lied to me, freaking abducted me. And now I'm stuck here—wherever the hell here is. And I have no idea what's going on other than the fact that everyone I love could currently be in trouble. Or worse.

He hesitates outside the door for the longest time. I start to think he's going to take a seat on the floor out there again and just wait.

But after a few more minutes, the sound of the door opening hits my ears before he lets himself in.

I keep my eyes closed and my breathing steady, too intrigued to see what he's going to do while I'm sleeping to open my eyes.

I also know that if I do that, it's going to end in an argument that I really don't have the energy for.

The apple I stole on the way out is currently sitting on the bedside table, and my belly aches, it's so empty. But my stubborn streak is stopping me from getting what I need.

Well, for food, anyway. Apparently, my inner whore doesn't listen to my hard-headed side, because she threw her legs wide open to get what she needed.

I've sat back for months and watched my friends lose their minds over guys and sex, and I didn't get it.

Now I do.

Now, I totally understand the meaning of dick drunk, and just how fucking magical they can be.

His loud sigh rips through the air as he looms over me.

I'm plunged into darkness as he steps in front of

the stream of sunlight that was warming me through the French doors.

My fingers twitch to reach out to him, to drag him down with me and find out what's going on.

But I hold myself back, wanting to see if he'll give me anything willingly.

"I hate seeing you sad," he whispers, his fingers brush down my cheek softly, and I impress myself with my lack of reaction. "I hate that you're hurting. And I wish I was enough to make it all better."

My heart shatters for him, but I remain still, silently begging him for more.

With another sigh, he moves once again, the warmth of the sun returning to my skin before the bed dips behind me.

"He wasn't good enough for you, Angel. I just fucking wish I was, because someday soon, I'll be in your position right now, watching you walk away from me."

His arm wraps around my waist as he lines his front up with my back and holds me tight.

"I know you're never going to feel the same. I came to terms with that many years ago," he whispers. His lips brush against my neck and sends a shudder of desire through me. "But you're my everything."

I just about manage to catch my sob before it erupts.

He holds me tighter, breathes me in and just lies there with me.

The minutes slip past and I start to think that I

should probably give myself up and confess that I'm actually awake when a soft snore fills the room.

My eyes pop open in shock.

I mean, he looked wrecked when I found him earlier. It was more than obvious that he didn't get a wink of sleep last night. He needs this desperately. But still, I'm shocked that it happened so fast when both he and Alex have told me just how much he struggles to rest.

Carefully and painfully slowly, I turn myself over so I can see him.

"You are good enough, Nikolas," I whisper. "I just wish you weren't so scared to show me just how incredible you really are."

I drop a kiss on the tip of his nose, my anger and frustration from earlier melting away as I take in his peaceful, relaxed face.

He looks so much more like Alex when he's sleeping. It's a weird kind of head-fuck. When they're awake, despite looking practically identical, it's easy to tell them apart. Their auras are totally different, for a start. But when their eyes are closed and everything is calm, all of that melts away.

I lie there beside him for the longest time, studying his features and silently telling him all the things I think he needs to hear but equally isn't ready for.

He's been beaten down all his life. I've heard some of it, but I have no doubt that it was worse behind closed doors.

Yes, he might have been born the weaker, smaller

twin. But in the grand scheme of things, that means nothing.

The person lying before me is a man. A beautiful, complex, dark, incredible man who's overcome more than I think he's probably even aware of.

He's defied everything his father and grandfather expected of him. It might have been fuelled by their cruel words and disappointment, and I might wish he would open up a little more. But I also understand that after a lifetime of trying to be someone you're not, trying to hide the broken parts, how hard it must be to trust someone with the parts everyone else has deemed unworthy.

I get it, I really do. But I'm also desperate to smash down those walls and really get to find out who the boy hiding behind the façade is.

Eventually, my hunger pangs get so bad that I start to feel light-headed and weird, and I have little choice but to slide out from beneath his arm and do something about it.

The kitchen is tidy once again when I step inside. The evidence of the breakfast Daemon started cooking and then massacred when I basically demanded he eat me instead has been disposed of, the lingering smell of burned bacon the only clue it ever happened.

Pulling the fridge open, my eyes widen when I find it fully stocked with everything we could need and then some. It seems someone has intentions of us being here a while. My heart races at the thought of being stuck here with Daemon. Things could certainly be worse. I grab some butter and cheese and set about making a sandwich. I'm not much of a cook. Jocelyn has tried to teach me over the past couple of years, but it's just really not my thing. Not like I think it might be Daemon's. My mouth waters as I think about that breakfast he made for me in his flat.

I pause with the bread halfway to the board.

How exactly did I go from being locked in his flat, to locked up... here?

And why was my first thought filling my belly with him passed out in bed and not escaping?

Because there isn't actually anywhere else you'd rather be right now than with him.

I focus on the task at hand, my body acting on autopilot as I fill my plate and carry it out of the room with the intention of finding out a little more about where we are.

I might have only been in the bedroom that seems to have been allocated to me and the kitchen, but both of those alone have been enough to clue me in to the fact that we're somewhere fancy. And as I step into a huge living room with floor-to-ceiling views of what seems to be the private beach beyond, that's only confirmed.

"Wow," I breathe. The view from my bedroom seems that much more breathtaking from here.

I don't bother walking toward the doors that lead out to the decking and the sand beyond. I already know they'll be locked. Instead, I head toward the huge white sofa and curl my legs beneath me and start eating.

My plate is empty in an embarrassingly short amount of time, yet my stomach still growls for more as I abandon it on the cushion beside me.

Finding a clock sitting on one of the shelves, I find that it's almost lunchtime.

I'll have been gone twenty-four hours soon. Are they out looking for me? What do they think has happened? Or don't they even know?

Daemon said that Dad knows. Has he covered it all up? Does he trust Daemon to keep me here? How long is all of this going to be necessary for?

A million and one questions float around in my head as I sit staring at the waves crashing against the shore.

I lose myself in my thoughts for hours, and it's not until my third visit to the kitchen that an idea hits me.

I stand before the white curtains tucked into the corners of the room. The thought of closing them and hiding that view seems like a crime, but I can't deny that the rope ties around the middle don't inspire me.

Walking over, I run my fingertips over the soft fabric as images of them being used in another way fill my mind.

A smile twitches at my lips. I have no idea if it will work—probably not, to be fair. But I'm willing to try my luck.

I make quick work of untying them and carry them back to the bedroom I left a few hours ago.

Silently, I slip inside, finding Daemon still fast asleep, only he's helped me out somewhat by rolling onto his back.

I stand there for a few seconds, just watching his chest rise and fall. One of his arms has been thrown over his head, his lips are parted, and his eyelids flicker.

I almost change my mind and walk back out again, seeing him looking so peaceful. But I tell myself that if he's ever going to sleep like a normal person, then he really doesn't need to sleep all day.

Twisting the rope in my fingers, I close the space between us and look between the bed, my soon-to-be bindings and his wrists.

I'll be the first to admit that I have no idea how I'm going to pull this off. But I figure that I'll only regret not trying.

To my utter shock, Daemon doesn't so much as stir as I move his arms and slip the rope over his wrists.

I secure my knots the best I can and just hope that it'll be enough before I lift his trouser leg, plucking his pocket knife from its hiding spot and crawling on top of him.

I may not have forgotten that he'd stolen my knickers earlier, but the second the fabric of his sweats connects with my sensitive skin, I'm more than aware of the situation.

Shamelessly, my hips roll over his crotch, and I smile as I feel him growing beneath me.

"Calli," he mutters in his sleep, his arms pulling against his binding.

My heart jumps into my throat and my stomach knots as I watch him start to come to.

Have I just made a massive mistake?

"Angel," he groans, his hips bucking from the bed. "Did you need something?"

"Yeah. A few things actually."

I know the moment he fully comes back to himself. His entire body freezes beneath me before he tries to move his arms from above his head.

"What the—" His eyes fly open in shock and they instantly find mine.

A wicked smile curls at my lips as I twist his knife in my hand.

"Calli?" he warns, his sleepy voice less than scary as he licks his dry lips.

"You know," I say, dropping my eyes from his to his Cirillo knife. Each soldier is issued one when they officially join the Family. "I've always wondered why I was never good enough to own one of these."

"Y-you're—"

"If you tell me it's because I'm a girl, then I might put yours to really good use sooner than I was intending," I growl.

"I-I wasn't going to say that."

"Good, because it's bullshit. Stella has one. And I wouldn't be surprised if Theo has given Emmie one too."

"They're both trained to use it."

"Right," I mutter. "Once again, I'm too much of an innocent little princess to do something as bad-arse as learn how to use a knife to protect myself. You know, our situation right now would be very different if I'd had even a small amount of the training you've had over the years. It's almost like my dad wanted to make a target out of me."

"No," Daemon argues. "That's not why—"

"I'm not some delicate flower who's content being locked away, Daemon. I'm more than capable of being a useful part of this family instead of a burden."

"You're not a burden, Angel. But trust me, being locked away with you is certainly no hardship."

I roll my hips against him, and a growl rumbles up his throat.

"So what did you want with me?" he asks, his eyes dilating with desire. Clearly, he's forgetting that I'm pissed with him.

Fine by me. Two can play at this game.

6

DAEMON

I suck in a sharp breath as she flicks my knife open, and I swear to fucking God, the sight of her with it pointing toward me only gets me fucking harder.

"Angel, w-what are you doing?" I growl, my voice rough with desire.

"Finally taking control," she states confidently. Leaning forward, she presses the flat of my blade against my cheek, the cool metal doing little to cool my skin. "You see, I think I've been pretty patient. I thought I'd proven myself to be trustworthy. Yet you still keep hiding shit from me," she seethes.

My pulse hitches as she drags the blade down to my neck.

"I-I t-trust you," I whisper, cringing at how quickly I'm losing grasp of my control.

Her eyes hold mine as she shakes her head sadly.

"You seem to say all the right words, Nikolas. But your actions speak louder."

"N-n-n—"

"Just look around," she says, throwing her free hand out and gesturing around the room. "I don't even know where we are. I barely know the reason we're here. I've no clue what's happening at home, where everyone thinks I am. Yet I'm meant to blindly trust you? A guy who has drugged me. Twice. Ignored me for months. Locked me up both in his flat and now here. And yet he still refuses to let me fucking in."

I stare at her with my chin dropped. I've always known there's more to Calli than everyone thinks there is.

But knowing it and seeing it are two very different things.

"I'm so fucking hard for you right now," I force out, keeping my voice steady.

Thrusting my hips up, my cock aches as her breath catches and her eyes shutter for a beat. But she quickly recovers and her jaw locks up in frustration.

"We're not going there," she snarls. "I've got a point to make, and you're not going to make me forget it with your big, magical dick."

I can't help the smirk that twitches at my lips.

"Magical?" I ask, losing the fight with my amusement, feeling my mask slipping away as I stare up at this girl who's owned me for far longer than I'm sure she'll never be able to grasp.

"Not the point I'm trying to make," she mutters, her cheeks heating from her admission.

"So what was the point of tying me up and putting me at your mercy then, Angel?"

I can't deny that if anyone else had done this to me, I'd be freaking the fuck out.

Being restrained, losing control. Neither is something that I'm good with.

But it's Calli.

I might have been holding out on her, but really, I know there's nothing I won't give her. Even my fears.

I tug at my wrists, impressed with how she's trussed me up.

After years of training, I'm pretty sure I could slip them pretty easily, but for now, I'll let her have her fun.

"I want inside you, Nikolas."

"Pretty sure that should be my line," I quip.

A growl rumbles deep in her throat.

"You're infuriating."

"And you're sexy as fuck and grinding what I suspect is your still-bare pussy down on my cock."

The deep pink of her cheeks tells me that I'm right.

"Did you want me to have easy access for round two, beautiful?"

"No, I—"

"Show me," I demand, my eyes dropping to her spread thighs. My mouth waters, knowing what's hiding behind her short skirt.

But she denies me.

"I know what you're trying to do," she says, her eyes dropping from mine in favour of the knife in her hand as she lightly trails it down the centre of my chest.

My heart rate picks up as I realise her intentions with that thing. Curling my fingers into a fist, I try to keep my fears locked down.

It's just Calli.

It's just Calli.

I don't realise I've closed my eyes until my name falls from her lips.

They pop open, immediately finding her blue ones staring back at me.

Anger still darkens them, but it's what I find beneath that, that makes my breath catch.

Hope.

It's something she shouldn't feel when it comes to me.

I've been nothing but a disappointment my entire life, and I have no reason not to believe that at some point, she'll realise that as well.

I'm not sure I'm strong enough to keep her from seeing it anymore.

Pulling my t-shirt from my body, she presses the edge of my knife against the fabric.

It instantly parts, showing her just how sharp the blade she's playing with as if it's nothing more than a toy is, and she gasps in realisation.

"You could kill me with one wrong move,

beautiful. Some days, I'm sure it would be better for everyone if—"

"Stop," she demands. "Stop that right now."

I nod, my lips falling closed.

"I'm not them, Nikolas. I don't have unrealistic expectations for you." I have to bite down on the insides of my cheeks to stop myself from telling her that she does. "I don't want you to be anything but the person you are. I'll take the broken and cracked bits. I'll take the dark, the painful, and the tortured. What I don't want is to be kept on the periphery of your life like you keep everyone else despite constantly telling me that I'm yours. Because if I'm yours, then you're mine too. And if you're mine, I want every single piece of you."

With her eyes still locked on mine, she slices straight up the centre of my shirt, easily splitting it in two and revealing just some of the ugliness I try to hide.

"Calli." Her name falls from my lips as a plea as I fight with the devil inside me that wants to do anything in its power to stop this from happening.

To stop her from seeing the real me.

My eyes close, needing to cut myself off from her silent begging to allow her in, and she lets out a pained sigh.

I'm doing exactly as I said I would. I'm disappointing her, and it fucking kills me.

Pain slices right through my chest, as if she pushed my knife straight between my ribs.

She shifts over my hips, her weight lifting from my body, and I swear to fucking God, it would have been easier to deal with if she'd pushed her hand into my chest and ripped my heart clean out.

I swallow down the roar of agony that wants to rip from my throat, and I force my eyes to stay closed, knowing that I won't be able to watch her walk away from me.

But then...

"Fuck," I hiss when the soft brush of her lips tickles my collarbone.

My eyes fly open and I stare down at her hovering about me, her lips pressed to my skin and her eyes on mine.

"Show me," she begs, her eyes glassy with emotion. "Let me see him."

My heart races so hard, it thumps against my ribs akin to that of a tennis ball hitting a wall over and over.

"Angel," I groan as she shifts, dropping her lips to the top of my longest scar.

"You don't scare me, Nikolas. Nothing about you scares me."

I'm pretty sure my heart stops beating altogether as she finally rips her eyes from mine, lowering her lips before kissing a line down my scar.

"Fuck," I moan as she drags her tongue back up, and she doesn't stop until her lips find mine. But she doesn't kiss me. She just stares down into my eyes, her breath rushing out over me and making my mouth water for a taste of her.

"Where are we, Nikolas?"

It takes a few seconds for my brain to fire correctly to be able to form words.

"M-m-my g-grandparents' place. M-my mum's p-parents."

"Where does everyone think I am? We are?"

"Y-y—" I suck in a breath, steeling myself for a beat. "They think your mum booked you a place out of town so you can focus."

"How long are we going to be here for?"

"I don't know, beautiful. Until I know it's safe for you to be back. I fucking swear to you, I won't do anything that will put you in danger. Ever."

She nods in understanding, her nose brushing against mine.

"Where do they think you are?"

"Where do they ever think I am? Hiding. Sacrificing my soul to Satan."

The pillow beneath my head shifts and she lifts up a little so she can look at me properly.

"They just want you to be a part of them, you know that, right?"

I shrug one shoulder. "I'm sure they'd barely notice if—"

"No," she snaps forcefully. "You need to get this bullshit out of your head. They care, Nikolas. They've always cared. They've just... they've tried to be what you need. But I don't think you know what that is any more than they do."

"I need—" I quickly cut myself off, a knee-jerk reaction to hold myself back despite all of this.

Calli growls in warning, and if I weren't currently bleeding out beneath her, I might laugh at her attempt to scare me. But as it is, I'm pretty fucking terrified right now.

"I need to be accepted," I say, jerking my eyes away from her as shame burns through me.

"See, this is what you don't get," she says softly, her fingers grasping my chin and turning me back so I have no choice but to look at her. "They all accept you. The only person who doesn't is you."

"And what about you?" I ask, my head spinning with everything she's saying to me. It's not a surprise. Deep down, I know all this shit. But knowing that she sees it too, that she can peel back all my bullshit layers and know exactly how I'm feeling is mind-boggling.

"I wouldn't be pushing this hard if I didn't care, Nikolas."

"Why are you?"

She sits back, her fingertips trailing over my bare chest, making a violent shudder rip through me. No one has touched my skin here for... a long fucking time.

"Because..." she says, teasing me and making me wait.

Her eyes drop from mine, and I watch as she takes in that long scar she kissed before her eyes flick to the others—some she's aware of, some that must take her by surprise.

Her fingers delicately trace over each and every mark.

Disgust bubbles up inside me.

I fucking hate them. Despise them.

Each mark is more evidence of everything I was told growing up. That I'm weak. Not good enough. A liability. Useless.

My eyes study her as she memorises my body as if she's scared I'll never show it again. To be fair, she might not be far off the mark there. Silently, I beg her to finish what she was about to say, but I fear she's not going to.

After all, this hasn't been about her opening up. It's been entirely about her cracking me open and finally getting to see all the torture and ugliness that I hide within.

Her fingers tease the indents of the V that disappears into my trousers, making a moan rumble deep in my throat, and my cock jerk beneath her before she curls her fingers under the waistband as if she's about to drag them off me. But she never does.

"Angel," I beg, hating how weak and desperate I sound. I just fucking hope she realises that there isn't another person on this earth who would ever hear me begging like this.

"Where are the keys, Nikolas?"

I hesitate, but it's pointless as she shifts lower, feeling the bulge in my pocket. She pushes her hand inside and pulls them free, hanging them from her finger between us.

Not content with just that though, she pushes her hand into my other pocket and fishes both our phones out, along with her underwear I stuffed in there earlier.

"Calli," I growl.

"Time to put your money where your mouth is, Nikolas."

"No, wait," I cry pathetically when she climbs off me and stands beside the bed.

Pocketing her finds, she shimmies her knickers back into place and looks into the mirror, checking her make-up.

I watch her teasing me with my cock aching behind the confines of my trousers, desperate for her to come back.

Spinning around, she pins me with a look that is full of confidence and strength, and it fucking floors me.

Walking back toward me, she snatches my knife that I didn't notice she'd discarded on the bed beside me.

Her eyes drop down my body, her attention stopping on each scar, but she doesn't say anything as she flicks my blade away and tucks it into her pocket.

I swear there and then that I'm going to go against Evan's orders and get her one of her own.

She looks too fucking bad-arse not to have one. Even if she only ever uses it in the bedroom.

"Does anyone else know where we are?"

"No."

"Can I talk to them?"

I nod. "Through wi-fi."

"And where might I find the code for that, devil boy?"

My lips twitch at her nickname for me. I shouldn't like it. But hell, there's a lot I like that I probably shouldn't when it comes to Callista Cirillo.

"You're already connected, Angel."

She reaches out, and I expect her to untie me, but that's not her intention. Her hand lands on my rough cheek, and she stares down into my eyes until I swear she can see right into my black and tarnished soul.

Her thumb rubs across my mouth, and I ache for it to be her lips.

"You're worthy, Nikolas. So fucking worthy."

Before I get a chance to even think about a response to that statement, she's grabbed her iPad from the side and she's gone, closing the door behind her.

7

CALLI

My heart thrashes in my chest and my hand trembles as I pull the keys free once more and begin the task of finding out which one works on the door before me.

"Come on," I beg when the first two don't fit.

Thankfully, the third one is the one, and in only seconds, I'm sliding the huge door open and finally sucking in some fresh air, stepping out into the warmth of the spring sun.

My hands tremble and my chest heaves as I walk over to the double lounger and drop down.

I ignore my iPad and the phones in my pocket. Right now, I don't have it in me to talk to anyone else.

My mind is reeling from my time with Daemon in that bedroom.

I squeeze my eyes closed, and the image of his scarred chest and stomach comes back to me.

My own stomach knots at the pain he's obviously endured.

I knew about the operations he had as a kid. It was no secret that he was born with a hole in his heart and had more than a few surgeries to get everything corrected in his early years. But I wasn't expecting the rest. The angry, rough wounds. The burns.

Red-hot tears fill my eyes as I try to even consider what he might have been through.

All the guys have been in more than a few fights over the years, and at some point, they've all been hurt badly enough to end up in the hospital, or at least to have Gianna pay them a visit to patch them up.

But I've never heard of Daemon getting hurt that badly.

I guess that shouldn't really be a surprise, seeing as no one tells me anything. But something tells me that no one else knows either. And that just makes my heart ache.

A lone tear escapes, dropping down my cheek as I think of that poor little boy who was told again and again that he wasn't good enough.

I might be totally naïve to what really happened, but I see it in him. I see his pain. I see his belief in the words that were spat at him as a child.

The only person who has any kind of understanding about what he's been through is Alex. But even still, I suspect he doesn't really know either.

Reaching up, I swipe the tear away angrily.

I don't want him to think I'm pitying him.

I want to be strong for him. I want to stand by his side and hold his hand, show him that everything he's always felt is bullshit.

But I can't.

The sight of him, the things he said about himself...

A sob rips from my throat, the sound of it banishing that of the ocean just a few metres away.

Folding my legs before me, I drop my head into my hands and somehow manage to shed a few more tears. Only a few hours ago, I'd have claimed that I'd run them dry.

My insides, mostly my heart, feels like it's done three rounds with Tyson Fury by the time my sob fest begins to subside.

With the afternoon sun burning through my black sweatshirt, I cross my arms across my body and drag it up over my head.

There are no other properties to be seen, and with only Daemon inside tied to the bed, I'm not too worried about anyone watching me sunbathing in just my bra and skirt.

I fall back against the lounger with a sigh and tilt my face toward the sun, desperate to feel more of its soothing touch. The heat wraps around me like a warm hug, and I stretch my body out, needing the emptiness that comes from drifting to that easy place inside my head. It's the same place I go when I'm drawing, but I don't have the energy for that right now. I just need... nothing.

The tears staining my cheeks have barely dried when a shiver runs down my spine and my nipples pebble against the lace of my bra.

Reaching my arms above my head, I wrap my fingers around the cushion and arch my back.

"It seems I underestimated your skills, devil boy," I purr, keeping my eyes closed and my face toward the sun.

"I can say the same thing, Angel. Nice knot work."

His footsteps get louder, and the anticipation of him being close tingles beneath my skin.

"I was a Girl Guide, you know," I say with a smirk. "I'm assuming you didn't learn your escape artist skills in the Scouts?"

"It will probably come as no surprise to you, Angel, that I'm not really a fan of group activities."

"Shocking," I mutter, finally lowering my chin and cracking my eyes open.

My breath catches when I find him standing at my feet, amazingly still shirtless, and staring down at me as if I'm about ten seconds from being devoured. Or killed. And quite honestly, as he stands there with the sun shining around him, looking like the devil himself, I don't really care which route he chooses.

"Whenever we used to go and stay at our grandparents', my father's parents, our grandfather would set us challenges," he explains. "I'm sure most kids would get some kind of hide and seek to enjoy. But not the Deimos twins."

I gasp loudly when his hands wrap around my ankles, parting my legs so he can press his knees between them.

"He used to have this shed in the garden. Well, he called it his shed. Alex and I named it his torture chamber."

I'm so lost in his eyes, in the pain oozing from him as he tells me this story, that I flinch violently when his hands skim up my calves.

His eyes widen in horror, and he rips his touch from mine.

"No," I cry, sitting forward and wrapping my fingers around his upper arms, dragging his hands back. "Keep going," I urge.

He nods, shifting forward as his eyes search mine, desperately trying to find something that will tell him I don't want this.

"I want everything," I whisper.

"I learned nearly almost everything I know in that shed," he continues, making my heart pick up speed.

I might not know the details, but I've heard enough to know that Daemon's skills lie in torture.

My stomach turns over at the thought of what his grandfather could have done to those two little boys in that shed.

"He'd tie us up and leave us in there to escape," he says before my imagination can run too wild. "And the whole time, he'd have videos playing of all the things he could have been doing to us while we were stuck there."

"Jesus."

"Alex hated it."

"He doesn't like blood," I whisper.

"He'd refuse to watch. Instead, he'd lose himself inside his head. Singing whatever song he could come up with to drown out the cries of the men on the screen."

He crawls closer, spreading my legs wider, but his eyes never leave mine.

"I, however, watched every second of those videos. I studied the reactions of the victims. I learned what made them talk and what didn't. And all the while, I figured out how to get us both out.

"While you were all practising for maths and spelling tests, I was learning how to escape, and coming up with even more terrifying ways to make grown men cry, because I promised myself that one day... one day, I was going to tie him to that chair and make him suffer in all the ways he'd force us to endure."

My breathing is beyond erratic when he's finally right in front of me, his hands resting on either side of my hips and his nose barely a breath from mine.

"H-he had a heart attack, didn't he?"

His eyes darken for a beat.

"Yeah. Motherfucker died before I got the chance to show him just how beautifully he'd trained me."

Silence falls between us, only the sound of a squawking gull in the distance audible.

"Stop waiting for me to run, Nikolas," I warn. "I can handle your darkness."

"I'd have done it, you know." I nod. "I had it all planned out."

"I'm disappointed you didn't get the chance. He deserved it."

He laughs, but it's full of anger and hatred.

"You have no idea, beautiful."

"So give me one. Tell me," I urge, finally lowering my arm and cupping the side of his face.

He nods in agreement, but no words fall from his lips for the longest seconds. And when they do, they might not be the ones I wanted, but they're a pretty close second. "One day," he promises.

"Okay. I'll take that."

"Fuck, Calli. This is... y-you a-are—"

"I'm here. I'm safe. I'm..." I hesitate with the next part, aware that I'm possibly about to dive into something utterly insane, but at the same time knowing that, really, I jumped in a while ago. Halloween, to be exact. "I'm yours."

All the air rushes past his lips, tickling over my face as his hand wraps around the back of my neck and his lips crash against mine.

His hands slide up my thighs, pushing my skirt higher so he can grip my arse, lifting me until I have no choice but to feel his hardness beneath his trousers.

Wrapping my arms around his shoulders, I hold

myself against him, loving the feel of his hot skin against mine as our kiss continues.

He licks into my mouth as if he'd die without it, his fingers flexing against the softness of my arse as if he's holding himself back.

Ripping my lips from his, I kiss along his jaw until my lips are brushing against his ear.

"I'm still so fucking mad at you," I confess.

"Feels like it," he mutters lightly.

"You're a controlling, possessive, jealous, contr—"

"You said controlling," he points out, grinding me harder against him.

"Pain in the arse."

He squeezes me harshly.

"I think you love it."

A loud, whore-worthy moan rips from my throat as he hits my clit perfectly.

"Fuck, Angel. You've ruined me."

"I think there's only one of us doing any corrupting around here, devil boy."

"True," he confesses, his lips brushing mine in the most teasing of kisses.

"But you've introduced me to the dark side, and I'm not in a rush to go back."

"I've turned my angel into a devil."

"Only for you," I breathe. "It can be our little secret."

"Fuck, I wish I could keep you."

My lips part to comment, but instead of saying the words that are on the tip of my tongue, a shriek of shock rips from my throat as he flips onto his back and settles me over his waist once more.

"I want to watch you come," he growls, fuelling the fire whose flames are already burning me from the inside out.

I shake my head, my cheeks blazing.

"I want you."

"You'll get me," he promises. "But the next time I take you, there's going to be nothing between us."

I lean forward and rest my hands on his chest, either side of the long scar that runs down the centre.

"There doesn't seem to be now." I roll my hips over him and his jaw clenches.

"I'm not good at doing the right thing, Angel."

"Fuck the right thing, devil boy. For once, just take what you want, what you deserve, what you—"

I yelp when his fingers twist in my hair tight enough to send pain shooting through my skull as he drags me forward. He fumbles between us as his lips claim mine in a wet and dirty kiss, and in only seconds, my knickers are dragged to the side and the head of his cock presses against me.

"Fuck me, Nikolas. Fuck me like you own me and you're never going to let me go."

The roar that rips from his throat as he thrusts up inside me is something I'll never forget.

His fingers tighten on my hips as he takes control of our movements, dragging me down onto him so that there's nothing between us.

"Fuck, that's deep," I moan as he forces me to circle my hips. "Fuck."

"You feel that, beautiful? You feel how fucking perfectly we line up? You were made for me, Angel. All." Thrust. "Fucking." Thrust. "Mine."

8

DAEMON

"Don't go," Calli pleads sleepily, her grip on my waist tightening as I attempt to slide out from beneath her.

I knew she wasn't actually asleep. The patterns she was drawing with her fingertips on my chest and over my abs was evidence enough of that. But she's relaxed, and I don't want to ruin that.

I've ripped the rug out from beneath her enough recently, I just want us to... be.

I want this time together. No. I crave this time together like a fucking junkie.

I have no idea how long I'm going to get to pretend like this for, but I want it for as long as I can get it.

"I need to take a piss." I lean down and kiss the top of her head. "You should come too."

She tenses for a beat before looking up at me with a small grin.

"I know I ripped your armour in two and managed

to dig a little further inside, but don't you think watching you pee is a little overkill?" she asks, her brow lifting.

Twisting around, I fall over her, my body engulfing hers in my shadow.

Her eyes drop from mine in favour of my mouth as her tongue sneaks out to wet her lips.

Fuck. I love this look on her. The innocent girl has been well and truly left behind, and in her place is this sexy woman who gazes at me as if she'll never get enough.

I wish I could fucking bottle it and keep it forever, because I already know that I'll never find it again. Calli is my girl. My only girl. I could spend a lifetime looking, but I already know that I'll never find anyone who compares. No one that even comes close.

"I mean, yeah, if watching gets you hot then feel free."

"Ew no, I—"

"But you should pee after sex," I state, smiling as both her brows hit her hairline.

"Oh?"

"Yeah. You could get an infection if you don't."

Dropping a kiss on her nose, I push to my feet. She reaches for me, her fingertips brushing my cock as I stand and making it jerk in excitement.

"So you'll screw me senseless bare without checking I'm on birth control. Multiple times," she adds. "But you're concerned about—"

"I know you're on the pill, Angel. And I won't do anything to risk your hea—"

"How? How do you know I'm on the pill?" she demands, sliding to the edge of the lounger. Her skirt rides up around her hips, teasing me with the lace that's covering her. The thought of that fabric being damp and covered in my cum that's dripping out of her makes my dick harden instantly. Something she doesn't miss as the fabric of my sweats begins to tent.

Ignoring it, she jumps up onto the lounger so we're eye to eye. "How, Daemon?"

"I've seen your medical records."

"Y-you've seen my medical records?" I parrot.

I shrug, not seeing the issues with that. "I'd offer you mine," I say, "but you're looking at them." I hold my hands from my sides and stand back, offering myself up to her once more despite the tight knot in my stomach that move causes.

Her eyes drop and my skin tingles with her attention exactly where I don't want it. Although, it's not as bad as it would be if anyone else were studying me so closely.

"Did you even get these looked at?" she asks, jumping from the lounger and closing the space between us.

My entire body jolts when she touches the ugliest scar on my side. It's almost three inches long and was courtesy of some motherfucker with a serrated knife two years ago. I didn't even see the fucker coming, I sure as fuck felt it.

I shrug, because what can I say? It's obvious I didn't. I just patched myself up and prayed he didn't hit anything vital. I threw back a couple of sleeping pills with a bottle of whisky I stole from Dad's office and just hoped for the best.

I woke two days later with one motherfucker of a pain in my side, but I was alive, so fuck it.

"Never do that again, Nikolas. Promise me," she begs, her thumb remaining on the scar while the rest of her fingers wrap around my side, tugging me closer. And the sap that I am, I go to her.

"What? Get stabbed? I'll do my best, Angel."

"Well, yeah. But if you get hurt, you need to get it looked at."

"I survived," I mutter.

"And what if you didn't? What would I have done then?" she asks, tears quickly filling her eyes.

"Not had your soul darkened by me," I mutter, cupping her cheek in my hand.

"No. That's not—"

"Come on." I take her hand and drag her into the house.

She stands, silently leaning against the door frame of the bathroom in the master bedroom I put her in when we arrived, and I can't help but smile.

"I thought you didn't have a thing about watching," I shoot over my shoulder.

"You're beautiful, you know that?"

A bitter laugh falls from my lips.

"That's about the furthest from the truth that you can get, Angel."

"Bullshit," she spits as I tuck myself away and flush.

I get caught in her mesmerising blue eyes as I step toward the basin.

"Stop looking at the world through rose-tinted glasses, Calli."

Her lips purse in irritation.

"I can see things perfectly clearly. Don't treat me like they do," she seethes.

"Then stop romanticising this." I gesture to myself. "Our lives are ugly, messy, brutal. There's nothing beautiful about me or any of the things I do."

"You are to me."

My lips part to argue once more, but how can I when she thinks she's right?

"Yeah, and look what I've done to you. I've tainted you with the devil."

I step in front of her and grasp her chin between my fingers, staring down into her pure, innocent eyes.

She trembles in anger, but she doesn't say a word as I take my fill of her.

"Clean up. I'm going to make dinner."

All the air rushes out of her lungs as I release her and march through the bedroom and down the hall to the one I reluctantly claimed for myself. Or at least the room I dumped the clothes I bought when I went shopping yesterday. Not that I'll sleep. I won't be able to anywhere in this place unless I have Calli right by my side.

Memories flood me as I step into the room with the two single beds. The image of Alex bouncing on the one closest to the window fills my mind, and I can't help but feel lighter. He was always so full of life. He still is, despite everything we've both lived through. But he was like the fucking Duracell bunny whenever we got to stay here.

I used to think it was the constant treats that our grandmother used to give us, or maybe even the beach. But now I realise he was able to break free of the shackles that tied us down at home. Clearly, his weren't locked quite as tightly as mine.

I grab my phone, my need to reach out to him burning through me, but I quickly remember that Calli still has it.

Blowing out a long breath, I reach into the bag of clothes and pull out a white t-shirt and snap the tag off.

The second we had her in the van, my only focus was getting out of town, and there was no way I was hanging around long enough to pack a fucking bag for myself.

We got the necessities and then hightailed it away from danger as fast as we could, stopping on the edge of the city to switch the plates out and cut their ability to track us.

No fucker was going to follow us here. And no Italian cunt was going to get their hands on my girl.

Movement at the other end of the hall catches my attention, and I get to the door just in time to see her slip back outside with her iPad in hand and, sadly, now wearing a top.

My lips part to say something, but I decide against it.

I told her I trust her, and if she's about to go and call Stella or Emmie, then I need to follow through on my words.

Calli isn't stupid. Far from it. She knows the seriousness of this situation, and I have to believe that she'd rather be here with me than at home, constantly looking over her shoulder.

I make my way to the kitchen and pull the fridge open, assessing my options.

Cracking a can of Coke, I mentally run through the dishes I'd planned when I bought all this food and make a decision.

I learned to cook in this kitchen. I spent hours with my grandmother while Alex was out in the ocean, trying to surf and other random shit with our granddad.

Our mum's parents might have been the most incredible grandparents any kid could wish for, but that didn't stop me second-guessing my granddad at every step. I was so used to the sick and twisted motherfucker who had a hand in making our father that I was dubious of his intentions. It was stupid, but I couldn't help the inkling of fear that trickled through me whenever he was nice.

I wish it was different. I wish I'd made an effort to push through my fear, because I know I missed out. I'd listen to him and Alex talk about what they'd done, the things they'd discovered on their explorations of the bay and the huge rock pools beyond with huge smiles on their faces and wish things were different.

But they weren't, and I was a pussy who was happier in the kitchen with Gran, cooking up a storm for when they got back.

It was the kind of mindless activity I needed while I was out of town and away from the judgement and torture of those we'd left behind. Here, I could almost rediscover the kid I should have been. The one hiding behind his weaknesses, his scars, his fear. But not quite.

I lose myself in the food prep, falling back into old times as I find everything where it always used to be.

After they both died, Mum was going to sell this place. She probably should have. But I visited her not long after she left Dad, and I cracked when I found the paperwork sitting on the coffee table.

Without a word, she reached out and ripped the house details up in front of my eyes.

It's probably the single most meaningful thing anyone has done in my life.

No one can understand just how much this place means to me, just how much solace it offers me.

It's the only place where I could be the kid I deserved to be. It was a judgement-free zone where I could just be me. Gran didn't care if I cooked in silence, if I let the demons I wanted to leave behind cause havoc within me. She didn't care that most of the time I wanted to hide, to sit in a dark room in silence, and she didn't tell me that I was wrong to sit up and watch the waves crash against the beach while the moon was high in the sky.

She just let me be me.

Just like Calli does...

I feel her the second she steps into the room. My skin prickles and my balls ache for her, despite only being inside her a few hours ago.

Fuck. It's never going to be enough with her.

I don't stop what I'm doing as I fill the chicken breasts before me with the cheese mixture I made and wrap them both in parma ham. It's a dish I used to look forward to whenever we came to stay here. It didn't take Gran long to notice just how quickly I demolished it, and she ensured she made it for me every time we stayed. Mum tried to replicate it at least once a week for me, but she never quite got it right. Or it might just have been the place that was wrong. Not having the sound of crashing waves or the scent of the sea in my nose ruined it.

I place them both onto a baking tray before turning back toward the potatoes that are sitting on the side, waiting for attention.

"Did you want something, Angel?" I ask, my voice soft and calm.

I don't want to argue with her. I don't want to piss her off, or risk her resenting being here with me. But

I'm also aware that we've got differing opinions on things, and I'm sure they're going to bite us both in the arse more than once during our time here.

"Um..." She hesitates and I smirk, shooting a look over my shoulder and finding her staring at me as if she's about to jump me. "You put a shirt on."

"Y-yeah, well, I didn't much fancy adding to the patchwork of scars while we're here. Actually," I quickly correct, "if you want to start brandishing my knife again, I might just reconsider."

Her lips open and close a couple of times.

"I won't hurt you, Daemon," she says eventually.

Ignoring the dinner for a moment, I spin around and rest my arse back against the counter.

My eyes drop down the length of her, taking in her crop top with a crown on the front, the curve of her waist, her short skirt and then her sinful legs that I crave to feel wrapped around my body.

"You need some sunscreen, beautiful," I point out when I finally make it back up to her eyes, ignoring her previous comment.

"Bit late now, the sun is going down," she points out.

I glance over her shoulder, noticing that she's right and that the sun is quickly sinking toward the sea.

A smile pulls at my lips as a wicked image floats into my mind.

"What?" she asks hesitantly.

"Just imagining getting you ready for being in the sun tomorrow."

"What do yo— oh." Her lips form a perfect circle as her mind catches up with mine. "I was considering a little naked sunbathing."

My temperature spikes at her words.

"I can get on board with that, beautiful."

"Huh," she mutters, eyeing me suspiciously.

"What's going on in your head right now, Angel?"

"I'm just surprised, is all."

"About what?"

"That you're not freaking out about a seagull getting a glimpse of my tits."

A laugh rumbles in the back of my throat.

"Don't worry, I've got plenty of ammo for any little fucker who looks at anything he shouldn't. Your body is mine, Angel."

Her nipples pebble against her tank at my words.

"You like that, don't you? You like knowing that you'll be lying there in the sun and I'll be on my knees for you, unable to look away from your beauty."

"Daemon," she half warns, half moans.

"You have no idea the power you hold over me, do you?"

She chews on her bottom lip as she studies me across the room.

"I need you to do something for me," she finally blurts.

"Anything."

A sly smile curls at her lips and her eyes sparkle with achievement.

"What's going to happen if you don't pass your exams?" she asks simply, throwing me for a loop.

"Uh..."

"And don't even think about lying to me, Nikolas."

I hesitate, not wanting to confess this to her, but I don't have a choice. I promised to let her in, and I have every intention of doing so.

"Dad's s-stopped me w-working, and if I don't p-pass then..."

"Then," she urges, finally stepping farther into the room. She steps right up to me and holds my face in her hands. "Then what?" she whispers when I don't respond.

I swallow, not wanting to force the words out, but she's not going to let me hide from this.

"Then he's going to enrol me at Knight's Ridge full time in September and make me do it all again."

Her eyes flash with shock. "And stop you working?" she guesses.

I nod, pain slicing through me at the thought of having to give up the one thing I'm good at in life.

"So that's why you're having all the extra tutoring."

"I'm not going to do it. My grades are shit. And even with two more years, I doubt I'll manage it. I wasn't made for school, Calli. I was made to torture and maim and terrify our enemies."

"You're going to pass those exams, Nikolas," she promises me, determination shining bright in her eyes.

"Angel, I can't. I just—"

"Do you trust me?" she asks, cutting me off.

"Fuck. You know I do. But I don't trust myself."

Releasing my face, she takes a step back, making me crave her touch the second I lose her heat.

"I propose a deal," she states.

"Go on."

"I'll help you with your exams, if you—"

"What the hell could you ever want from me? All I can offer you is orgasms," I scoff.

"Wrong. You can offer me so much, Nikolas. But there's one thing I want, no... need." My brow quirks at her. "Okay, two, because I might just take those previously mentioned orgasms as well."

I can't help but laugh at her.

"Anytime, Angel. All you've got to do is as—"

"I want you to train me," she says confidently, cutting me off.

"Y-you want me to—"

"Train me. Teach me everything you know. Help me be able to protect myself in a way the rest of you can. I'm so fucking fed up of being the weak link in the group. I want to hold my own. Hell, I want to be a part of it. I'm fed up of— ARGH."

9

———

CALLI

My heart pounds as Daemon pins my body between the hardness of his and the cold wall of the kitchen.

He's got my hands pinned behind my back as he breathes in my ear, sending a delicious shiver racing down my spine.

"What are you doing?" I pant, sounding nothing but like a shameless whore as I try to grind my arse back against him.

"Just seeing how much work I've got to do. A lot, it seems," he whispers in my ear.

"Am I too big a challenge for you, devil boy?"

"Never. I love breaking in a virgin," he growls.

"I bet you say that to all the girls."

"There is no other girl but the one pressed against me."

My heart melts at his words.

"You believe me, don't you?" he asks, his voice full of emotion and honesty. "The girls I have been with before, they're nothing. They meant nothing."

"Nikolas," I moan, tugging my arms against my bindings.

"That was brave of you earlier, you know. There aren't many people out there who I'd let tie me up like that. And anyone else who tried wouldn't still be breathing."

"Oh God."

"That makes you hot, doesn't it? Knowing how deadly I am."

I swallow harshly, not wanting to give him an answer, despite the fact that we both know it.

Holding my wrists in one hand, his other brushes up my arm, his fingers quickly circling my throat.

I gasp when his hold tightens enough to make breathing hard.

Heat floods me at the possessive move and my eyes shutter.

"Tell me, beautiful," he demands, his voice dark and deadly as he proves just how dangerous he is. He could kill me like this—I'm sure with little effort. And that knowledge does funny things to my insides.

"Yes," I whimper. "It makes me hot."

"What does?"

"You. W-what you're capable of."

A growl rumbles in his throat and his weight presses harder against me.

"You're thinking about the shower, aren't you?"

I nod, unable to deny it.

"You loved it, didn't you, my filthy little angel?"

He releases my hands and my fingers immediately wrap around his wrist, pulling his grip from my throat.

I stare at the red wound that stretches across his palm.

"That's going to be my favourite scar, beautiful. Every time I look at it, I think of you."

"You're right-handed," I whisper, and he immediately laughs.

Not wanting to miss that smile that's curling at his lips, I spin around. He gives me the space I need before leaning into me once more.

"Yeah, Angel. I'm right-handed." His lips brush my ear. "And I think of you every time I wrap my hand around my cock."

I gasp, his words hitting me right between my legs.

"Keep that in mind until later, yeah?"

He's gone before my brain has a chance to catch up with his movements, and I sag against the wall.

He chuckles as he watches me, his erection more than obvious behind his sweats. The sight makes my mouth water. But that's nothing compared to when he shoves his hand beneath the waistband. His eyelids drop as he squeezes himself, but he doesn't take it further.

"You're no fun," I sulk.

"Angel, I'll be all kinds of fun once I've fed you

properly. You've got a habit of ruining my meals, and I refuse to let you go hungry. Now, either sit and watch or go and do whatever you were doing."

"I think I'm good watching. Maybe you can teach me a thing or two in here too."

"I'll teach you whatever you want to know."

I grab the drink I'd first come in here for from the fridge and pull out a chair to watch him at work.

"Your phone is ringing," I say as he's plating up our food. Pulling it from my pocket, I find Isla's resting bitch face staring back at me. "It's Isla."

"Decline it. I'll message her later."

"Fair enough." I hit the red button and place it on the table top so he can have it back.

"That was incredible," I say, leaning back in my chair and placing my hands on my swollen belly.

The most incredible smile lights up Daemon's face at my praise. It makes happiness and contentment swell within me.

I should still be mad at him. I guess I am deep down, but it's easy to forget the reality outside of this house, of this little slice of heaven I've found myself in with him.

"More?" he asks, lifting the bottle of wine he put into a cooler between us.

If I didn't know any better, I'd think we were in

some beachfront restaurant. The food was that good, and the view... well, I'd happily look at a contented and relaxed Daemon any day of the week.

"Are you trying to get me drunk, Mr. Deimos?" I quip.

"Damn right I am. Not that I think it's necessary to have my wicked way with you." He winks, and I feel it right in my clit.

"Are you trying to say I'm a whore?"

"No, Angel. I'm just telling you that you're mine."

My lips part to respond, but my iPad starts ringing on the chair beside me.

"Shit," I hiss, reaching for it and finding a FaceTime call from Stella.

"Answer it. Let them know you're still alive and kicking," Daemon says, filling my glass.

"But—"

"I'll go clean up. Be good," he warns.

"When aren't I?" I ask, pretending to be offended.

"It's not you I'm worried about, Angel. Stella is the troublemaker."

"Fair point."

I wait until he's collected up the plates and is almost inside before I swipe the screen and wait for the call to connect.

"Holy shit, where are you?" Stella gasps the second her eyes lock on the view of the ocean behind me.

I can't help but laugh. "Paradise."

"I was pissed when I heard your bitch of a mother shipped you off, but now I'm kinda jealous."

"Things could definitely be worse."

"Bit extreme though, don't you think?"

No, not really. "Mum's always been one to go to the next level. I can't even really be pissed. I'd planned to lock myself into my basement for two weeks. I get to do that sitting out here."

"But you're so far away," she complains, making me wonder if she does know exactly where I am.

"I'll be back before you know it. And it's not like you don't have anyone to keep you company back there. How's everyone?" I ask, concern twisting up my insides.

The Italians might be after me, but I'm not naïve enough to think that they won't turn their attention elsewhere once they discover I've been well and truly hidden.

"Everyone's good. The guys are all pretending they're studying, but mostly, I'm pretty sure they're watching porn and getting drunk."

"They're in Nico's flat then," I mutter, reaching for my wine.

"Oh, check you out."

"Check who out?" a familiar voice asks behind the screen somewhere.

"Calli is in heaven," Stella says as Emmie drops beside her, passing a bottle of cider over.

"Sea, sun..." Emmie says, studying me and my surroundings. "She's missing something."

"Jesus, do you two ever think of anything but sex?" I ask, my cheeks heating, knowing that the end of Emmie's statement isn't far from the truth. And as if he's listening, Daemon chooses that moment to reappear.

"It's almost criminal not to make the most of that beach," Emmie mutters.

"I'll keep that in mind. Maybe I'll find a local to make use of. Have a little holiday romance."

A deep growl rumbles in his throat as he grips the top of the door frame. His shirt lifts up, giving me a delicious shot of those deep V lines that disappear into his sweats.

Darkness clings to him just from my bullshit words, and it makes my heart rate pick up.

"Damn, that would be hot. Have you seen any of the locals?"

"Not yet. There was a guy working out down by the shore earlier. If he comes back, maybe I should talk to him."

My eyes flick between the screen and the angry guy staring at me like he's about to charge any minute.

"Hell, yes. You need to do it tomorrow and get us photos."

"Not sure Seb and Theo would be happy with that."

"Ah, don't worry your pretty little head about that," Stella says with a laugh. "We've got plenty of ways to prove to them that it's only their cocks we want."

"Right... well... How's... things with the Italians?" I ask, risking another look up at Daemon.

"We're all on high alert. The guys reckon they're going to try and hit us soon. But it's all good. We're ready."

I stare at the two of them, my heart in my throat at the prospect of them being in danger.

"I hate being so far away when shit's getting real."

"You're in the best place. Enjoy the peace. Hell knows, if we knew where you were, we'd come and hibernate with you."

"You wouldn't cope without the boys' cocks," I point out, much to Daemon's amusement.

"Who needs a boy's cock? I've got a more-than-willing one that's all yours in return for mind-blowing orgasms," a deep, familiar voice offers down the line.

Panic squeezes my chest, my eyes shooting up to Daemon, who immediately releases the door frame and storms outside.

He gestures for me to sit forward, and I do without any argument, ensuring my body fills the screen.

"We don't want your cock, Alexander. I've heard it's rotting from all the trash you've stuck it in."

"I'll have you know that my— Baby C," he announces happily after pushing his way between Stella and Emmie on the sofa. "Where are you? I miss you."

"I've been gone a day," I say, rolling my eyes at him.

"A day too many. I had to sleep on my own last night. I miss my cuddle buddy."

Both Emmie's and Stella's brows rise at that.

"Don't," I warn them both before they start. "Nothing happened in the tipi."

"Not with him, anyway," Daemon scoffs quietly.

I shoot him a death glare as he paces back and forth across the decking as if Alex is going to jump through the screen and find us here together.

"I'm breaking her down. She'll be begging for it sometime soon."

"Whatever you say, Deimos."

"So, where are you at? Is that the sea I hear?"

"Uh... yeah. Mum booked me this insane place. It's incredible."

"Aren't you lonely? All you gotta do is shoot me your location and I'll be right there, baby girl."

"Ew, don't *baby girl* her," Emmie complains with a shudder. It's what her dad calls her stepmum, something none of the guys let her forget too often.

"I'm good. Thanks for the offer, though."

Alex stares at me through the screen and my stomach knots. I swear he can see more than he should be able to.

"So what have you been doing? Too much studying makes Calli a boring girl. And we all know she deserves to party."

"I'm good, honestly. I need the peace to just study."

"But it's so much fun when we do it together. You know you love our naked study sessions."

Daemon's palms land on the table with an angry thud, making everything on top of it, including my iPad, rattle. He glares at me, silently begging for me to confirm that's not true. I'm not sure why it's necessary; we both know he's watched our study sessions from his little hiding spot outside my basement.

"What the hell was that?" Stella asks, her brows pulling together.

"Nothing," I say in a rush. "I kicked the table leg. It's wobbly as hell."

The girls buy it, but Alex looks suspicious as fuck.

"Shit," he says, pulling his phone from his pocket. "I gotta get back up there. I just came down for the beer Seb said was in the fridge."

"Yeah yeah," Stella mutters. "Clean us out, why don't you."

"I promise to send him back to you good and wasted."

"Told you they were up there watching porn."

"We do some twisted shit, Princess. But gang bang porn watching ain't one of them."

"I'm not sure if I'm relieved or disappointed," Emmie says, taking a pull on her cider. "If it were to happen though, you'd all be naked with your cocks in your hands, right?"

"Jesus," Alex mutters, moving closer to the screen.

"Do you think that you might even give someone

else a hand? You know, if they needed an extra bit of encouragement?"

"Calli, this is all your fault. You loaned her that book," Stella laughs.

"I am not getting involved in this."

"What book?" Alex asks.

"Just go back up to your boys. I'll see you soon, yeah?"

"Fine," he sighs, looking a little disappointed to have to go. "Just call me if you need me, yeah? I hate the thought of you being sad and lonely."

"I promise I'm fine." I risk a look at the raging bull that's still staring at me with anger and dark promises in his eyes.

"If you say so. Speak soon, baby C. Love you." He blows me a kiss before disappearing.

We chat for a few more minutes, but Daemon's burning stare becomes more and more unbearable, and in the end, I tell them both that my dinner is ready and hang up.

"Tell me he's lying," Daemon growls from his position, looming over me with his chest heaving.

"Of course he's freaking lying. You already knew that though, didn't you?"

His brows pinch in confusion.

"How?" he growls, rounding the table to get to me.

In a rush, I push the chair out from behind me, preparing to run from him.

Fear and excitement licks at my insides and my temperature spikes.

"Where is your hiding place, Nikolas?" I take a step back for every one he takes forward.

"M-my hiding... oh," he laughs, a devilish smile lighting up his face. "In the trees," he admits.

My chin drops at his confession.

"You climb a tree to spy on me."

"Yep. Took me fucking ages to find the right one too," he growls, continuing forward.

My body aches for his touch, especially while he's in this dangerous mood. But I don't let myself give in.

Not yet, anyway.

"You're crazy."

"Yeah," he agrees, combing his fingers through his hair, his eyes raking over every inch of me.

My head spins a little from the wine, but it's nothing compared to the effects his hungry gaze has on me.

"I found the perfect one, so that even when you close the blinds, I can still see through the little window in the door."

My chin drops and I gawp at him.

"Do you not have any boundaries?"

It's obviously a rhetorical, but that doesn't stop him from answering.

"When it comes to you? No. Zero. Zilch. You're mine, Calli. And even when you didn't know it, I did. I've always known."

"What if I never found out?" I ask, although I don't think I'm going to like the answer.

"Then... nothing. I'd have continued watching you, protecting you."

"Why?" My heart aches, knowing that he's telling the truth, and I don't like what that reality could have looked like for him.

"Because I couldn't not," he explains like it makes total sense.

"That's insane. What if I met someone, fell in lo..." I trail off at the pain that shoots through his eyes at my words.

"You will. One day, that will happen."

I'm barely able to breathe as his eyes hold mine, the darkness in them consuming me.

It's not until he's standing right before me, his warm breath cascading over my face, that I realise I've stopped moving.

"N-no, it won't. Nikolas, I'm—" Right before my eyes his dark, impenetrable mask slams into place and I swallow down the words that are right on the tip of my tongue.

"Strip," he demands, his voice leaving no space for argument.

I don't move. I'm frozen to the spot, locked in his pained stare.

His movement doesn't register, but the flash of moonlight on the smooth side of his knife sure catches my eyes.

"Daemon, what are you—" My words are cut off

with a gasp when the blade slices through my top, and only a second later, it makes quick work of my bra too.

My breasts spill free a beat before the sting of the small cut he gave me registers.

"Fuck," he grunts, his eyes locked on the small bubble of blood that appears.

"It's okay, it's—"

He drops to his knees before me, and his tongue hits the skin just beneath the cut before he drags it up, collecting the blood.

"Holy fuck, devil boy," I pant, my nipples hard as glass as his tongue pushes into the little cut, making me wince.

His fingers make quick work of the button on my skirt before he drags it and my knickers down my legs, leaving me standing bare in the middle of the beach.

Sitting back on his haunches, he stares up at me in awe, his fists clenching on his thighs as if he's holding himself back from something.

"Run," he growls, but my head is spinning and I barely register the word.

"What?"

"Run. And if you're sensible, you won't fucking stop to let me catch you."

My heart lunges into my throat before I take a step back. The cool evening air whips around me, making my skin erupt in goosebumps and sending a violent shiver down my spine. Although that could be courtesy of the danger that emanates from the boy on his knees before me.

"Three," he starts, and I back up again. "Two."

"Nikolas." His nostrils flare at the sound of his name falling from my lips.

"One."

A shriek rips from my lips and I take off as he jumps to his feet to follow me.

I don't look back until my feet hit the freezing water of the sea, and when I do, ripping his clothes off as he strides toward me, his long legs eat up the space much faster than I anticipated.

10

DAEMON

Calli's excited shriek fills the silence around us as she races into the water.

She should be scared. Most grown-arse men are terrified, looking into my eyes when I go to that dark, destructive place inside me. But not my angel.

Somehow, she sees more than anyone else does.

It's fucking terrifying. It's exhilarating. It's... fuck.

The water laps at my calves as I race into the sea after her, but I barely feel the cold. My sight's set firmly on my girl as she attempts to escape me.

"Holy shit," I gasp when my balls hit the water, the temperature situation suddenly more than obvious.

It's soon forgotten though when I finally wrap my arms around Calli's waist and haul her back against me.

"Didn't run fast enough, Angel," I growl in her ear,

continuing to walk us farther out, the water hitting my waist.

"Maybe I never really wanted to escape." She reaches behind, her fingers twisting in my hair and holding me close. "Maybe I like being your prisoner, devil boy."

A deep growl rumbles up my throat a second before I surge forward, submerging both of us in the freezing-cold water.

Spinning her in my arms, I position her so that when we surface once more, her legs are wrapped around my waist and her pussy is right where I want it.

"Oh my God," she splutters, wiping the water from her face. "It's fucking fre—" My lips capture hers, cutting off her words as my fingers dig deeper into her arse, pulling her closer.

I push my tongue past her lips, seeking out her own and letting myself drown in her.

My anger ebbs away with each brush of her lips against mine, her light banishing some of my darkness.

Thoughts of her with someone else, with Alex... they drag out a possessive, psychotic part of me that even I'm slightly terrified of.

It was bearable before I'd had a taste of her.

But now she's mine, even if it is only for a short time, I'm not sure I'm going to survive watching her walk away which she will inevitably have to.

I'm not good enough for her.

Evan and Nico will never let this happen.

They have a plan for her, and I know for a fact that I'm not a part of it.

I just need to take what I can. Give myself enough memories in the hope that it will be enough when the time comes.

Pain slices through my chest, but then she rolls her hips against me and I'm dragged back to the here and now, reminded that at this very minute, I've got exactly what I've always wanted in my arms.

"Fuck, Angel. You're everything," I groan into our kiss as the water continues to lap at our shoulders.

Releasing one hand from her arse, I slip it between us, pressing the head of my cock against her entrance.

"Nikolas," she moans as I slip inside her easily.

"Dirty little angel," I groan, her heat surrounding me and bringing my entire body to life.

Her grip on my hair tightens, and she lets out the most incredible lust-filled moan as I drag her down so she's fully seated on my cock.

"Tell me you've not been studying naked with my brother," I demand against her lips.

"Of course I haven't. The only person I've been naked with is you," she says between gasps as I slowly pull out of her.

"Liar."

"W-what?" she asks, her brow creasing in confusion.

"Alex has seen you naked. So have all the others."

"No they... skinny dipping," she says on a sigh.

Holding her up with one hand, I wrap my other around her throat, my eyes bouncing between hers.

"I don't like others seeing what belongs to me, Angel."

"N-no one was l-looking," she stutters as I up my pace.

"I hardly think that was the case."

"Fuck... I'm not interested in Alex."

Her eyes hold mine, allowing me to see the honesty within them.

"Why?" I urge, needing to hear her say it.

"B-because I want YOU," she cries as I slam into her as hard as I can.

"Fuck yeah," I bark into the night. "FUUUUCK."

My hips piston in and out of her as fast as I can with the force of the waves trying to drag us out to sea.

I claim her lips, my tongue plunging into her mouth, mimicking what's happening beneath the surface.

"Can't get enough of you, Angel."

"Nikolas," she cries, spurring me on.

"Addicted. Never want to let you go."

"So don't. I'm yours."

"Fuck." If only that were true.

My grip on her throat tightens as my balls begin to draw up, losing my fight even with the coldness desperately trying to get its claws into me.

"Come for me, beautiful. I want to hear you screaming out my name so the universe knows you're mine." *At least for now.*

"Nikolas," she breathes, her eyes wide, as if she's in awe of me. It's a head fuck, because it almost makes me think that I could be something. Someone. But then I thrust my hips and remember that it's just my cock she's reacting to. As her pussy clamps down on me like a vice, I let all those toxic thoughts fall from my head and allow myself to drown in her. My angel, my everything.

"Louder," I demand, gritting my teeth to try and hold off my release.

"Nikolas," she cries, but it's still not enough for me.

"Tell the fucking world, Calli. Who do you belong to?"

"You, Nikolas. YOU," she cries, her cunt squeezing me impossibly tight as her body quakes. "Oh my God," she screams as her orgasm crashes over her. Wave after wave of pleasure washes through her, dragging my own out of me.

"Fuck, Angel. Fuck. Fuck. CALLI," I boom, my voice echoing in the dark night sky.

My cock jerks violently inside her as pleasure banishes the last bit of darkness that was trying to engulf me.

Releasing her throat, I wrap my arms around her, holding her tight to my chest, reminding myself that right now, she's mine. She's here and she's all fucking mine.

I've just got to pray that it's not all over too fast.

Her hot breath races across my neck as I soften

inside her. But as aftershocks from her release make her pussy contract, it's not long before I'm gearing up for round two.

Unfortunately, Calli's body seems to have other ideas as she trembles against me.

Threading my fingers into her hair, I pull her face from the crook of my neck and watch as her teeth chatter.

"Shit, beautiful."

"I-I'm o-ok-kay."

"I made a vow years ago that I would always look after you."

Holding her tighter against me, I walk us out of the water. Ignoring our clothes, I stride up the sand, both of us dripping in seawater as we step into the house.

She climbs me like a spider monkey, and I can't help but wonder how long I could get away with carrying her around like this.

Spotting a bottle of my granddad's favourite whisky in the unit we pass, I reach out for it and continue toward the shower in the master bathroom.

Her lips trail up and down my neck as we move, and a growl rumbles deep in my throat when she sinks her teeth into me.

"Devil," I murmur.

"I wonder where I got it from," she mutters lightly as I place her arse on the counter and reluctantly release her.

A groan of disapproval rips from her throat and

she quickly reaches for me, her fingers digging into my upper arms.

My heart melts as I stare at her trembling before me. Her cheeks are bright red, her lips swollen, and her nipples hard enough to cut glass.

But then I glance lower and my breath catches in my throat at the sight of my cum dripping out of her swollen cunt.

Fuck. I did that.

"Here," I say, twisting the top off the whisky and passing her the bottle.

But she makes no move to take it from me.

"It'll warm your belly. Trust me." I wink, lifting it to my lips and swallowing down a couple of shots before passing it back. Heat licks down my throat before settling in my belly exactly as I promised her it would.

This time, her fingers brush mine as she takes the bottle.

"Good girl."

I drop to my knees before her, barely noticing the bite of the tiles.

"Ugh, fuck. That's gross," she complains after swallowing a hit of whisky. "How do you drink this— oh Jesus. Daemon." Her cries fill the room as I push her knees wide and drag my tongue up the length of her cunt. "That's... you're..."

Just to prove a point, I drop lower, tonguing her entrance, tasting both of us.

Her eyes flare with heat as she watches me with lust-filled eyes.

"Drink another," I demand, rolling my eyes up the length of her.

"But it's—" Her words falter when our eyes connect. Instead of arguing, she just lifts the bottle to her lips, swallowing another mouthful before her face twists up in disgust when the burning alcohol hits her throat. "Ugh."

"Trust me," I murmur before slipping my hands around her arse and dragging her closer to the edge.

The bottle slams on the counter before her fingers curl around the granite as I damn near pull her off the thing in my need for more.

My tongue finds her clit again and I circle it until she's crying out my name.

"Fuck, I love making you scream," I say, pulling away and staring up at her as I push two fingers inside her.

"So why are you stopping then?" she pants, her eyes blown with lust and her chest heaving.

"Good fucking question."

I curl my fingers inside her as I suck hard on her clit, and in only a few minutes she's screaming, filling the silent house with her cries.

The second she's done, I stand, slam my lips down on hers and lift her from the counter. She groans when she tastes herself on my tongue, but she doesn't pull away.

I had every intention of getting the shower ready

for her to help her warm up when we first got in here, but that all goes to shit as I march behind the screen and turn the dial, allowing us both to be blasted with ice-cold water once more.

"Oh my God," she cries, ripping her lips from mine.

"I'll keep you warm, Angel."

Slamming her back against the wall, I quickly adjust our position before thrusting inside her.

"Oh God. That's—"

"Hot. Incredible. Mind-blowing. Amazing," I offer.

"I was going to say sensitive, but yeah, all of the above," she says with a laugh.

"I can go all night, beautiful. Just imagine how it'll feel then."

Whatever her response was going to be is cut off when I claim her mouth once more.

I fuck her like a savage, my hands not knowing where they want to grip, my teeth and lips marking every patch of skin they connect with as her moans for more and my grunts of pleasure mix.

It is fucking everything.

But it's still not enough, and I'm pretty sure it never will be.

She clings to me as I lower her back to her feet, not trusting her legs to hold her up.

Happiness engulfs me as I stare down at her big blue eyes.

"Hey," she says shyly.

"Hey, beautiful," I whisper, unable to speak for a moment as the magnitude of having this time with her presses down on me.

Her eyes focus on mine as her teeth sink into her bottom lip as she studies me.

"What's wrong?"

My heart races with all the things I want to say to her, with all the promises I want to make her but know that I can't.

"Don't hide from me, devil boy," she warns.

Swallowing down the emotion clogging my throat, I tell her just a little bit of what's currently swirling around in my head.

"I wish we could run away and just be the two of us. Forever."

"Nikolas," she says, cupping my face in her hand and giving me the cute, puppy-dog look that melts my heart every single time.

"Don't, Angel. Don't pretend like this is real," I beg.

"But it is," she argues. "I want this."

A smile curls at my lips as I allow myself to believe for just a few seconds that it could be possible.

But then another shiver rips down her spine and I'm reminded of what we were doing in here in the first place. I drag her under the torrent of hot water falling from above.

"You need to warm up," I say, running my hands over her sinful body while my lips find her neck, allowing myself to drown in thoughts of this lasting outside of this beach house.

It's a pipe dream, one I know that is going to slip through my fingers the second we're called to return back home.

11

CALLI

A scream rips from my throat and my eyes fly open, but I don't get a chance to actually see anything because something covers my head, cutting off my vision.

"Get off me," I scream, my body thrashing, my arms and legs flailing in the hope that it might be enough to fight off whoever it is.

But it's futile.

In only seconds, my body is pinned back against a solid one and a pair of arms wraps around my own to stop me from fighting.

Panic floods me, dragging me into its ugly clutches and stopping me from reacting in a way that might help me out of this situation.

I'm dragged across my room as my legs continue to try and make contact with him in the hope of... something. But I fall still when realisation hits me.

If someone has got in here and has me, then what's happened to...

"DAEMON," I scream, my previous panic blinding me as I think about them getting to him first. "DAEMON."

A low growl rumbles from the arsehole behind me when my foot finally collides with his shin, but the second the sound hits my ears, I still.

"You fucking prick," I squeal, barely able to force the words out through my shock.

Suddenly, everything I failed to notice the second I was ripped from bed hits me. His scent, the way his body fits against mine. His fucking boner against my arse.

His deep chuckle behind me only infuriates me more.

"What the hell are you playing at?"

Suddenly, he spins me around, and with one quick shove of my shoulders has me falling to the sand we're now standing on with a disgruntled thud.

I just manage to rip the sack off my head before he lands on top of me, pinning my hips into the sand and falling on his hands that drop on either side of my head.

He stares down at me, his eyes full of mirth and a smirk on his lips that makes me want to forget all about being annoyed at him.

His smile is my ultimate weakness, right alongside his vulnerability, and I think he knows it. Damn him.

"Thought we should start your training."

"By abducting me from my own bed?" My chest heaves with his proximity and that amused glint in his eyes, something he doesn't miss as his eyes drop to where my hard nipples are pressing against his shirt that he demanded I sleep in last night.

"What? It's cold," I hiss.

His laughter fills the air once more and my skin erupts in goosebumps.

"Sure. Does that affect how wet your cunt gets too, beautiful?"

My teeth grind at his words.

"You're cute."

"I'm not. I'm pissed."

"Exactly. You're cute when you're pissed."

"I am not, I—" My words are cut off as his lips find mine.

I restrain myself for a good twenty seconds, but I'm powerless to resist him when his tongue pushes deeper into my mouth and he growls out my name.

He kisses me until I've melted for him, completely at his mercy and desperate for more before he turns the tables on me once more, somehow managing to flip me beneath him and pin my arms behind my back, rendering me useless.

"Yeah, okay. You've made your fucking point," I hiss, missing his lips more than I'm sure is healthy. "Now teach me how to fix it."

He leans over me, his hard cock grinding against my arse as his burning breath races down my neck, making me shiver beneath him.

"I'll teach you anything you want, beautiful. And I'm really hoping you make it hurt."

"Psychopath," I mutter, much to his amusement. "That's meant to be an insult."

"Remember who you're talking to, Angel. Pain and torture is almost as vital to me as air and water."

"Then show me how to make it hurt, devil boy."

As if I'm nothing more than a rag doll for him, he scoops me up and plants me on my feet.

"Show me what you've got then, beautiful," he says, holding his hands out to the side to give me an easy shot.

I harden my glare as I run my eyes down his tempting body.

He's hiding behind his black armour again, and I don't like it.

"I'm not putting you on your arse until I'm wearing underwear," I state confidently, as if there's even a slim chance of me being able to do that.

"You look perfectly dressed to me."

"You look overdressed to me," I counter.

"Fine." He smirks, reaching behind him to pull his shirt from his body. "We even?" he asks.

My eyes drop to his chest, eating up the inches of toned skin before me.

Each of his scars makes my heart ache for him, and the mystery behind most makes my head spin with possibilities.

Especially the burns.

"This way, when I get you back under me, I get easy access to what I want most."

His arrogant smirk makes my fists curl, a move he doesn't miss.

"Come on then, Angel. I want to see that fire you hide inside. I know it's there. I've seen it."

I stare at him as he prowls closer.

"I want to experience how you really feel every time you realise you've been kept in the dark. I want to know how useless you feel every time we tell you to stay home, when we lock you up like a useless little princess and keep you wrapped in cotton wool."

"Daemon," I growl, anger licking at my insides, my blood beginning to heat.

"You want to break free, beautiful? You want to show your dad, Nico, all the guys, that you're not someone who should be overlooked? You want to prove your worth, show that you're as capable as Stella and Emmie?"

A growl of anger erupts from my throat as I fly at him.

I'm not totally useless. The girls have been teaching me the basics for weeks. I can throw a punch, and I could probably take a weak opponent down at this point. But I don't have any intentions of going up against someone weak. I want to take on the strong, the powerful and the most formidable men in our city. I want to take down the devil and then watch him morph back into the guy I'm falling for faster than I thought possible as he stares at me with pride and awe in his eyes because he realises for real that I'm not just some innocent angel sent to make little Cirillo heirs.

My fist lands on his ribs and a grunt falls from his lips as his eyes widen in surprise at the force behind it.

His hands lift on instinct, protecting his body, but I quickly work around them.

"You going easy on me, Devil?" I taunt when he makes no move to strike back despite the fact that my knuckles are raw and I've got sweat rolling down my back.

The sun has barely risen above the horizon, but I'm melting. The air around us is a beautiful shade of orange as everything begins to come to life.

"We're training you, not me."

"Then I need a real opponent, not a pussy who's too scared to go all in."

"You calling me a pussy, beautiful?"

"Yeah, I am. Big, bad mafia soldier too scared to go up against the princess." We both know it's bullshit—there's nothing about me that terrifies him—but it's fun to pretend as he stands there, taking my beating.

He laughs, and it captures my focus on the briefest of moments, allowing him to take control.

His fist finds my stomach in the lightest punch I'm sure he's ever thrown in his life.

"Pussy," I hiss, returning his hit with an uppercut to his jaw.

A savage roar fills the air before he finally lets go of the shackles holding him back and we really start going at it.

"Oh my God," I pant after a good fifteen minutes of sparring. His arms are around my body, much like when he dragged me out of the house this morning, as sweat pours from me and my hair sticks to my face.

"Get out of it," he demands.

"I can't," I pant, my entire body trembling from the exertion.

"Stamp on my foot for a start, beautiful. If it's hard enough, my grip might slip. Then go for the balls. Quickest way to take a man to his knees, but I guess you already knew that."

"I'm not kicking you in the balls," I argue.

"You should after the way I've treated you," he confesses darkly in my ear.

"Maybe. But it's still not happening."

"Fine. We'll pretend, but only because I need my D fully functional. It's the only thing I'm letting you off with, though."

"Fine."

I stay still for the longest time in the hope that he loses focus as the sun climbs higher in the sky and the gulls begin to emerge for a day of squawking and stealing food wherever they can find it.

When I sense him relax a little with his chin resting on my shoulder, I lift my foot and slam it down as hard as I can without any shoes on.

His gasp of shock rips through the air and his arms loosen enough for me to spin. I don't lift my knee, although I can't deny that I'm tempted, just to see how this might play out if I took it more seriously. Instead, I slam my fist into his stomach, causing him to bend over —I think the move is to humour me, because I can't imagine it actually hurt—giving me the time I need to pull the knife I know is hiding in his pocket.

I flip the blade open as he stands to full height once more and pride flares in his eyes.

"Fuck yes, Angel," he says with a wide smile, his chest heaving and his skin glistening in the morning sun.

Heat courses through my veins as he looks at me as if I'm an entirely different person for a few seconds.

I'm so lost in his eyes that I don't realise he's moved until his knife is ripped from my fingers and I'm lifted into his arms.

"You're fucking perfect, Calli," he tells me a beat before he captures my lips and walks me... somewhere.

He lays me down, and when I open my eyes I find only the clear, blue sky above me.

He drags my legs around his waist and slides his hands up my thighs, taking his t-shirt with them until he's dragging it over my head, leaving me sprawled on the outside table bare.

Pushing up onto my elbows, I watch as he shoves his sweats down and grasps his hard cock.

"Watching you with a knife gets me so fucking hard, Angel," he confesses as he rubs the head of his cock through my wetness and thrusts inside.

My body trembles but I stay exactly where I am, watching as he claims me in the most primal way.

"Gonna make the most brutal princess out of you yet, beautiful. Every motherfucker is gonna be terrified of you," he promises, and I drop back to the table, handing myself over to him completely.

After we gave all the seagulls soaring above us a morning they probably won't forget in a while, we headed inside to wash the sweat and sand off, although I can't deny that that wasn't before we continued our workout against the tiles, just like the night before.

I'm discovering that I have a whole new love for taking showers these days, and the view I'm blessed with in the form of Daemon's body is only part of it.

He made us both a full English breakfast before he finally conceded to letting me help him study.

I figured that seeing as we had nowhere to go, he was going to have a hard time refusing my help, but to my surprise he was more than willing to accept it, as long as I did the session in my underwear. Something tells me that Alex's taunting about naked studying has stuck in his mind. But while it might not be my usual choice, I'm powerless to refuse his request, especially when I know accepting my help is already pushing his limits.

So I stripped down to my underwear and he dragged me to sit between his thighs on the sofa, seeing as the sun had decided to slip behind a thick layer of cloud while we were losing ourselves in the shower.

Unsurprisingly, with the right encouragement, Daemon was more capable than he's ever given himself credit for.

Yeah, he might struggle academically, but he's nowhere near as useless or stupid as he thinks he is. He just needs to focus and be provided with the right inspiration... like the best blow job he's ever received if he gets all the answers right.

I mean, it's not really a hardship. And it's certainly more fun than the study sessions I've had to cancel with Jerome this week.

By the time the sun began to sink once more, we curled up on the outside loungers in a tangle of limbs and just relaxed as the clouds moved across the sky and music drifted from inside the house.

It was heaven. And I never wanted it to end.

But, as much as I might pray that it won't, the knowledge that we're only on borrowed time in this little bit of paradise we've carved out for ourselves is never far from my mind.

At some point, it's going to be safe to return, and I really don't know how that is going to look.

Daemon has commented more than once about not being able to keep me, and while it rips my heart to shreds each time he says it, I'm not brave enough to broach the subject.

I know what I want. I want to fight for this. For us. For him.

But something tells me that he's not going to agree, and it's going to shred my heart to pieces to hear him say it. So I keep my words stuffed inside for now, because I want to enjoy this while we have it. The time for the harsh reality we're going to face will come faster than I'm ready for, I have no doubt.

But for now, we can pretend.

12

CALLI

Something startles me, and I wake with my heart racing and panic taking hold just like I have since the other morning when Daemon woke me by scaring the ever-loving shit out of me. But each time, there isn't even a noise that drags me from my sleep. It's just my subconscious trying to fuck with my head.

And each time it's happened, he's been right here beside me. Usually awake, watching me and totally chilled, making me instantly relax.

I roll over, searching for my personal bodyguard, but all I find is cold, empty sheets when I slide my hand over.

Opening my eyes, I blink against the darkness, looking around for clues as to where he is, but I find nothing. Well, not until there's a voice somewhere down the hall.

Swinging my legs out of bed, I reach for Daemon's

shirt that was abandoned on the floor before we tumbled into bed naked together however many hours ago.

My body aches in the most delicious way from both our daily training sessions and our sexcapades afterward.

I've always been active, doing gymnastics and cheerleading, but Daemon's workouts hit a little differently.

We've been here five days now, and I hate that every morning I wake, I can't help but wonder if today is the day it all comes to an end.

Daemon's been in touch with my dad a couple of times, and each time they talk, I'm just waiting for the news that we need to go home, but it hasn't happened yet.

A part of me is desperate for it never to happen.

Fuck school. Fuck real life. We'll just stay here and carve ourselves out a future where it's just the two of us and no enemies who want to come between us.

But I know that's not our reality.

We have to go back. Mostly so Daemon can smash his exams and reclaim the life he's desperate for.

As much as his job terrifies me, I know it's who he is.

I can see the fear in his eyes every time we talk about exams or the future, because he really believes that he's going to have everything ripped away from him.

I've tried to tell him that Damien and Stefanos

will change their mind. There's no way they want to go through the next two years without Daemon on their team, but he's convinced that they're serious. That it's pass these exams or nothing. And I won't lie, I'm terrified of what will happen if he fails. There's a darkness in Daemon that even I've not managed to unlock yet, but I worry that him failing will force him to fall head first into it.

Leaving the lights off, I head out of the room in search of my man.

There's another noise that seems to come from the kitchen, so I head that way with only the light of the moon to guide me.

I find him dressed in black, crouched over a bag and rummaging inside, and my heart jumps into my throat that something might have happened, that he's going to sneak out while I'm sleeping.

"What are you doing?" I ask, panic gnawing at me.

He jumps up in fright, but I'm faster than him. I rush forward, crashing into his chest with such force he stumbles back into the wall. Reaching up on my tiptoes, I slam my lips down on his, one hand fisting his shirt and holding him tight against me while the other drops lower in a pathetic attempt to convince him to stay.

His shock makes him hesitate for a beat, but the second my fingers brush his cock, his lips move against mine and he quickly hardens in my hand, a groan rumbling deep in his throat.

"Don't leave me," I beg into our kiss.

Suddenly, the room is illuminated around us, the spotlights from above burning into my eyes and making them water.

But before my brain has a chance to figure out what the fuck is going on, I'm dragged backward by my shirt and pinned to another hard body.

"What the—"

"What the fuck are you doing?" Daemon growls, the promise of imminent death oozing from each word as my eyes finally focus.

"Oh shit," I gasp, staring at the owner of the body I just molested.

"Bro, I did nothing," Alex says, holding his hands up in surrender.

My chest heaves and my head spins as I stand there between the two of them, Daemon's arms locked around my waist as if he thinks he needs to physically hold me back from his brother.

"You're hard," Daemon points out, and of course my eyes fucking drop.

"Oh my God, Daemon, that's—"

"She touched it. What the fuck did you want it to do? Shrivel up into my body? Jesus."

"You touched... I swear to God, I'm going to fucking—"

"Daemon, no," I cry when he releases me and surges toward Alex, his fists curled and his shoulders set, ready to fight.

I manage to jump between them just in time.

My hands land on Daemon's bare chest, and I stare up into his dark, haunted eyes.

"It's okay," I whisper. "I thought he was you. It was dark, and I panicked because I thought you were leaving. I had no idea he was here."

As I talk, I watch him calm down. The fury that was swirling around him like a storm only seconds ago begins to fade, and as I slip my hands up to his face and brush my thumb across his bottom lip, his body begins to relax.

"You kissed him." The emptiness of his voice shatters my heart.

"Because she thought I was you, dipshit," Alex says, reminding me that he's standing right behind me. "Anyway, surprise!" He pushes from the wall and pulls out a chair. "I thought it was about time I interrupted your sex fest."

My eyes widen as I stare at his amused face.

"What? You really thought I didn't know? Jesus. How stupid do you think I am? Fuck."

Getting back to his feet again, he marches toward the fridge and yanks the door open, searching for something.

Daemon uses the moment of privacy to his advantage. His fingers grip my jaw and I'm pushed back against the wall.

His nostrils flare as he stares down at me, danger flickering through his eyes that makes my nipples pebble beneath his shirt and the muscles south of my waist clench. Reactions that I only now realise were missing when I kissed Alex. I knew the second our lips touched—hell, when I got in his personal space and he smelled different—that things weren't right, but my panic at being left here took over my rational thinking and I acted on impulse.

Something I'm now wholeheartedly regretting.

The fridge closes, but I'm locked in Daemon's stare and unable to look away.

A chair scrapes across the cold floor before Alex must sit down, but neither of us turns to look.

"What? You want me to pretend I'm asleep so you'll kiss her? Fuck me, Bro. She turns you into a right pussy, you know that?"

Tension crackles between us as Alex's words float off to nothing.

I start to think Daemon isn't going to react, but then his hand drops from my jaw in favour of my throat and he uses his grip to drag me into his body, slamming his lips down on mine.

"That's better. Nothing like live porn when you haven't seen any action for weeks," Alex mutters, but his words barely register as Daemon's weight falls on me and I'm once again crushed against the wall. His hand slips from my waist, hiking my leg up around his hip, making me gasp when we connect.

He kisses me until I'm breathless, my body aching for more as his hard cock grinds right against my core.

"Fuck," Daemon hisses, ripping his lips from mine and burying his face in the crook of my neck.

"Don't stop on my account. It's not like I haven't listened to it all before."

"You're a motherfucker, A."

"That was one time, man. And Calli doesn't need to know about it."

"Oh my God," I breathe, barely able to believe I've found myself in the middle of this. "Excuse me, I need... a minute."

Thankfully, Daemon releases me and allows me to slip from between him and the wall.

I keep my eyes on the floor as I rush out of the room, but despite not looking at him, his attention burns into my skin as I run for the hallway and hide around the corner.

"What the fuck are you doing?" Daemon barks, his voice vicious and leaving no room for bullshit.

"Missed you, man. Just wanted to make sure you both really were okay." I can't see them, but I can imagine Alex relaxing back in his seat, resting his ankle on one knee and shrugging like he literally gives no shits about turning up here in the dead of night and risking his life by sneaking in.

Leaning against the wall, I wait for Daemon's response.

"How'd you know we were here?"

"I asked Mum if she knew where you'd fucked off to when you didn't return to your flat last week. She said she didn't," Alex confesses in a rush to bail Gianna out of the shit. "But I knew she was lying.

Then, when I saw Calli on that video call, I figured it out pretty fast."

"Fuck's sake," Daemon mutters, his voice sounding closer.

"I gave you five days, man. You can't be all that pissed. You've had plenty of time to act out all your dirty fantasies with your princess." I can't help but smile at the teasing lilt in Alex's voice.

"What are you talking about?" Daemon grunts.

"Oh, fucking come off it, man. I know you. I see you. Your very first hard-on was for that girl out there and you know it."

Daemon might have said similar words to me in the past about me being the only girl he's ever seen, but hearing those words from Alex... hearing that his brother has known all this time... Well, it hits differently.

"Fuck off. At least I wasn't rubbing one out over the housekeeper."

"Dude, Helena was fucking banging and you know it."

"She was old enough to be our grandmother," Daemon shoots back, amusement starting to enter his tone.

"Nah, man. She might have had grey hair, but there was no way those perky tits belonged to a grandmother."

"Fucking hell," Daemon mutters.

"Anyway, back to the issue at hand."

"There is no issue."

"Bro, you've been fucking our innocent little Calli for months." My eyes widen and my chin drops. "And the fact that Evan and Nico will want to put a bullet between your eyes when they find out is a fucking issue in my book."

"I haven't been fucking her for months," Daemon argues.

Alex laughs. He actually fucking laughs.

Anger licks at my insides and I'm about to storm inside to put him right when he speaks again.

"You always underestimate me, man. Which is fucking hypocritical if you ask me, because you think everyone does it to you. You think I don't know, that I don't see things?"

"What are you talking about?" Daemon scoffs, clearly getting pissed off with his brother's antics right alongside me.

"Oh, I don't know, Batman. Why don't you tell me?"

I'm standing in the doorway before I've even realised my legs have moved.

"You knew. All this time, you knew."

Just as I suspected, he's sitting there, giving no shits, as if this is a normal fucking conversation.

He nods. "I saw you dancing together. Made sure big bro was distracted by shoving a willing pussy in his direction." I cringe at his words, but also, I can't be anything but grateful. I just assumed that everyone was having too much fun and not paying us any attention that night. Clearly, I was wrong, and more than a little drunk.

"You knew he took me upstairs and you never said anything this whole time. It's been months."

Alex just shrugs, looking innocent as fuck.

"I figured it either didn't go as Daemon had hoped, or—"

"How the fuck would you know what I'd hoped for?" he grunts, but Alex just rolls his eyes at his brother.

"Well, I didn't think you were dragging her off for a fucking Scrabble duel, man," Alex mutters lightly. "Or I thought it did go to plan, and I knew you wouldn't want me sticking my nose in."

"Whatever gave you that idea?"

"Well, when you both ignored each other like it never happened, I assumed Calli shot you down and wasn't interested. But then as time went on, I saw glances between you when no one was looking. It was nothing really, but at the same time, it was something."

"Why didn't you say anything? For weeks, you've been openly flirting with me, yet you knew that I was..."

"Fucking my brother?" He shrugs once more. It seems to be becoming his favourite move. "I wanted one of you to open up, to admit what was going on. But clearly, neither of you trusts me so..."

His words fade to nothing as hurt washes through his grey eyes.

My lips open to respond as guilt burns through me.

"I need you to know, baby C. If Daemon was with anyone else right behind my back—literally—then I'd have joined the party. But you..." he says, pushing to his feet, "you're it for him. And no matter how close you think we might have got to anything happening, it never would. Even if Daemon changed his mind, you've been his since we were kids. You just didn't know it."

My mouth is gawping open as Alex moves toward me, his face emotionless once more, reminding me of the guy who's also been stunned into silence behind him.

"Excuse me, I need..." He doesn't finish that sentence. He just marches deeper into the house before a sliding door slams, leaving Daemon and I alone once more.

The silence that hangs between us is so heavy, it presses down on my shoulders as I stare into his dark eyes.

"Calli, I—"

"I need the bathroom," I say like a pussy, and bolt toward the bedroom, quickly closing the door behind me.

I use the toilet on autopilot, but I didn't really need it, and it's not until I'm washing my hands that his knock comes.

"Angel, are you okay?" he asks softly. So softly it makes my heart fracture.

I stumble back, my arse pressing against the counter and my hands still wet as I replay those few moments in the kitchen.

I kissed the wrong one. I should have realised sooner and stopped.

They're like night and day different. How didn't I fucking notice before I freaking groped him?

How far would he have let it go if Daemon hadn't dragged me off him?

"Shit," I hiss, embarrassment washing through me.

"Angel?" His deep voice rumbles through me. My skin prickles with his proximity, but my shame stops me from looking up from the white tiles beneath me.

His feet appear before he's standing right in front of me, the heat of his body warming me instantly.

"Hey, it's okay," he says softly, obviously able to sense that I'm balancing on the edge right now.

His hand cups my cheek and he lifts my head, forcing me to meet his gaze.

My breath catches at the dark and intense look in his eye.

"I kissed him," I whisper, but as much as I might want to look away, I can't. He's ensnared me, and I'm powerless to sever it.

His jaw tenses and his Adam's apple bobs with a harsh swallow, but he doesn't say any of the things that I know are right on the tip of his tongue.

"I know. But it's okay."

My brows pinch as I stare at him.

"I know it was a mistake, beautiful. If you'd wanted Alex, you'd have had him by now."

Fair point. He's sure given me enough chances to take things further with me.

"Yeah, I know, but—" *I thought you'd be freaking the fuck out right now.*

Deep down, I can see that he is. The promise of pain and blood swirls in his eyes, but this is Alex we're talking about. If it were anyone else, I've no doubt he'd already be bleeding out on the kitchen floor.

"Who do you belong to, Angel?" he grits out, voice cracking with pent-up rage.

"You. Always you."

Dipping his head, he brushes his lips over mine in the gentlest of kisses.

"Aside from you, Alex is the most important person in the world to me."

"What about Isla?" I ask, aware that the two of them are close.

"Close third," he confesses. "But in an entirely different way to you."

I nod in understanding. I can only assume—or hope—that he feels about Isla as I do Alex.

"You're mine. And I'd do fucking anything for you. Both of you."

I nod again, silence stretching between us as I run the events of the past thirty minutes through my head.

"He knew. All this time... he knew. That's..."

"Yeah," Daemon agrees. "I shouldn't be surprised. He's always been a bit of a sneaky fucker."

"Oh?" I ask, grasping that little thread that might reveal some secrets and tugging.

He chuckles, shaking his head softly. "Not now. But I think you should go and talk to him."

"Me?" I ask, rearing back in surprise. "No, I think you should probably—"

"Trust me, Angel. It needs to be you."

I suck in a deep breath, unsure if I'm going to be able to face him after feeling him up only minutes ago.

"I'm going to need to put some knickers on," I say, making my favourite lazy smile appear on Daemon's face.

"Yeah, that would be ideal. My restraint is only so good."

"You wouldn't hurt hi—" I quickly stop myself, knowing full well that he would. He has recently because of me, so there's no reason why I should think he wouldn't do it again. "Okay, so you would. But it's not necessary."

"I know. That's why I'm here with you right now and not pounding him into the sand."

"How very brotherly of you," I quip.

To my surprise, he takes a step back when I push from the counter, ready to pull up my big girl pants—literally—and go and talk to Alex.

I stop when I get to the door and look back.

"Where were you when he came in?"

"Out on the beach," he says, but dread sweeps

through me when his eyes drop as the words fall from his lips.

"What's wrong?"

"N-nothing. I just h-had..." He sucks in a deep breath. "Nightmares." He quickly shakes his head. "It's nothing."

"No," I say with enough strength in my tone that it makes his eyes widen. "It's not nothing. Not if you're suffering because of them." Closing the space between us, I wrap my hand around the back of his neck and reach up on my toes, kissing him hard. "You're going to tell me about them. You're going to share the weight," I tell him between kisses, not giving him a chance to argue with me.

"What are you doing to me, beautiful?" he growls.

"Hopefully making you feel good and helping you sleep."

I give him a beaming smile before walking out of the room to find some knickers.

Daemon watches me from the bedroom doorway with a soft encouraging smile on his lips as I walk through the living room toward the doors that will lead me to where Alex disappeared.

I have no idea why he thinks I need to be the one doing this when he's Alex's other half, but I trust him to know what Alex needs.

I find him sitting on the wooden stairs that lead directly onto the sand. But despite knowing that he's been joined by someone, he doesn't react.

The cool night air whips around me, making me

wish that I'd grabbed one of Daemon's hoodies, but it's too late now. I don't want him to think I changed my mind about talking to him.

"Hey, can I sit here?" I ask, although I'm already lowering my arse to the top step beside his.

"Sure," he rumbles, glancing over at me. It's pretty bloody dark out here, but I don't miss the emotion that fills the depths of his grey eyes.

"You okay?"

A sad laugh rips through the air.

"What are you talking about, baby C? Of course I'm okay."

"You know, you two aren't all that different," I tell him. "You both lie about how you're really feeling in the hope no one digs too deep."

"I'm not lying, Cal. I really am okay." He turns to me, his thigh bumping mine as he rests back against the railing. His eyes catch on something in the house, and I can only imagine that Daemon is standing in the shadows in the living room like a creepy, possessive psycho. "You're good for him, you know?"

"I'm not sure I—"

"You are. You have this calming effect on him. You always have."

"Why did you never tell me?"

His eyes find mine in the darkness once more.

"Why didn't you ever tell me?" he counters.

"Touché."

Ripping my eyes from his, I stare out at the dark

ocean before us and watch the water as it glitters in the moonlight.

"It was just one night. One drunken, stupid night that at the time meant... everything. But the second it was over, it was like it never happened.

"I wasn't meant to find out who it was. He..." I hesitate, feeling stupid for admitting all of this but compelled to do so now that the truth is out.

"He..." Alex prompts.

"He never took his mask off. I didn't know... I didn't know who he was."

Alex's eyes widen as a mixture of shock and pride appears on his face.

"You fucked a stranger in a mask on Halloween?"

"No, we didn't..." I drop my head into my hands, hearing just how ridiculous this all sounds now I'm finally saying it all out loud. "It never got that far. The shooting started and he ran. I only found out it was Daemon because he shed his mask as he disappeared into the trees."

"Were you disappointed?"

"W-what?" I ask, my head twisting to look at him so fast I'm surprised I don't pull something.

"Were you disappointed when you found out it was Daemon?"

My chin drops as I realise that he really is asking that question.

"Honestly, I had no idea who it was. Nothing he'd said or done gave me any clue that it was him. It was obvious that whoever was hiding behind that mask knew exactly who I was and that they shouldn't be anywhere near me. But I'd had too much to drink and my brain wasn't firing as it should.

"When he looked back though, and reality hit, it made a lot of sense."

"In what way?"

"He kept saying things like he shouldn't be touching me, that I deserved anyone but him, that I was going to regret letting him near me. Crazy shit that is totally untrue."

Alex nods, deep in thought.

"Daemon is... complicated."

I can't help but laugh. "You really don't need to tell me that, Alex. You think that everything that led up to us being here has been all rainbows and unicorns? It's been... well, everything you'd probably imagine of your brother. Dark, twisted, painful, but perfect, in its own fucked-up way."

"Jesus, Calli." He scrubs his hand down his face, rubbing at his rough jaw.

"You might think that I'm good for him, but he's exactly what I need, too. The perfect bad influence in my perfectly protected life."

"It's funny," he says with a laugh. "I always knew there was more to you than you let everyone see. But I never thought it would be enough to put up with him. Me maybe, Toby possibly. But you really have gone all in with the devil worshipper."

"I don't like to do things by halves." I shrug.

"Clearly not."

Turning away from him once more, I stare up at the clear, star-filled sky as memories from the kitchen not long ago come back to me.

"I'm sorry about... about jumping you and... yeah, well, that." I wave my hand in the general direction of the house behind us.

"Don't ever apologise for that. Most exciting thing that's happened to me in days."

"Jesus."

"Seriously, it's been boring as fuck without you both. And yeah, you might have left me aching for another stroke of your hand, but hell, at least you've both finally admitted the truth."

I drop my head into my hands and talk into them.

"I can't believe you knew what we were doing last week and didn't say anything. We were right freaking there, Alex."

"Trust me, I know how damn close you both were."

"Why? Why did you just lie there?" My head spins with the thought that he just listened to us. He could have got up, walked out, called us out there and then, but he didn't. He just... laid there.

"Daemon's been through so much shit, Cal. It might have driven me to insanity that he couldn't be honest with me and tell me what was going on with you, but ultimately, I want him to have all the good he can get. And that's you. You're his good, and I was scared that he'd stop allowing himself to have it if I knew the truth."

The tears fill my eyes with every word he says. I always knew that Alex cared for Daemon, that he'd do anything for his other half, but knowing it and hearing it are two very different things.

Lifting my hand, I wipe a tear from my cheek when one finally drops.

"Aw, Calli, I wasn't meant to make you cry."

"You're not. Well, kinda. But it's good. Daemon has no idea how lucky he is to have you on his side."

"Yeah he does," the man himself says behind us.

13

DAEMON

"Shift up," I say, nudging Calli's arse with my foot.

She immediately slides over and I join them.

"I brought beer," I say, holding a bottle out for each of them.

Alex takes his while his other arm rests over Calli's shoulders before his hand clamps down on mine.

"Love you, man," he says, making my breathing falter as my eyes collide with his.

The second Calli slips her beer from my hand, I automatically wrap it around her bare thigh, needing the connection with her and totally forgetting that we have an audience.

"You can say it, you know. It won't make you any less scary to admit you love him too."

"And it won't make you weak to say the same thing to your girl, either."

"When exactly did this turn into a therapy session?" I mutter, ripping my eyes from Alex's and taking a pull on my beer.

"It's far from that, man. It just fucking normal when you're hanging out with family."

"Family," I mutter.

"Yeah, I mean, if you're gonna steal Calli as yours, then I guess I can cope with her being my sister-in-law."

The beer I'd just poured into my mouth sprays from my lips in shock.

"What the hell have you been telling him, Angel?"

Both of them look at me seriously for two seconds before they fall about laughing.

"Don't worry, devil boy. It was nothing to do with us getting married, so you can chill."

Pain twists up my insides as my heart damn near rips in two.

"I'd marry you tomorrow if I could," I confess.

You could hear a pin drop in the seconds that follow my statement.

Needing to break it, Alex finally barks out a laugh. "You lot are all fucking insane, you are aware of that, right? It's like everyone moved into our building and suddenly turned middle-aged. We're eighte—"

"No we're not," I point out.

"Ugh, whatever. I'm just reminding you that we're not thirty either. All this serious relationship and marriage shit is giving me hives."

"Nah, I think that's just jealousy because everyone

but you is getting laid. Ow," I complain when he hits me upside the head. "Tell me I'm wrong." I stare at him with my brow quirked, waiting for him to try to spit some bullshit at me, but it's not his deep voice that fills the air next.

"You'd marry me?" Calli asks, disbelief laced through her tone.

"I told you, beautiful. If I could keep you, you'd be it for me."

"You can keep me," she says, her brow wrinkling in confusion.

"Uh... I should probably leave you to this."

"Don't go," Calli says quickly, reaching for Alex's hand before he stands to his feet.

"Uh..." He looks between the two of us like he doesn't quite fit, and I hate it.

I nod, and he relaxes a little, although his shoulders are still pulled tight with tension.

"You know this can't last, Angel. Your dad, Nico... this—me—is not what they want for you."

"Fuck them," she barks, surging to her feet and standing on the top step so she's looking down on me. "That's bullshit and you know it. I don't give a fuck what they want for me. I'm done with letting them control my life."

"Cal," I sigh, pushing to stand.

"No, don't do that. Don't just give up because you think it's going to be hard. Will they be happy? No, probably not, and there's every chance Nico will break at least one bone in your body but—"

"Pfft, he can try," I snort.

"Really? You gonna pull the 'I'm the scarier soldier' bullshit right now?"

I hold my hands up in surrender and take a step forward.

"Calli, you can't really think that we can go home and just continue like we have been here." It breaks my heart to say it, but it's true.

Evan and Cassandra, and Nico, will never accept this. They want a good, safe, solid Greek boy for their princess, and I'm none of those things. I'm a liability, the one who's never quite good enough, the one who'll end up dead and leave her alone. And plus, why would they ever want my DNA? I'm not good enough to even work for them right now, let alone help provide them some heirs.

"Well, no, but we can figure something out."

Darkness begins to seep through my veins, all the insecurities that I've battled with all my life threatening to drag me under.

"I'm not good enough for you," I whisper, the words tearing my heart to shreds.

"Bullshit. You're everything."

"She's got a point, man. The only reason she's safe right now is because of you," Alex says, defending me.

"It won't make a difference. They won't accept me. This," I say, gesturing between the two of us, "has an expiration date. I've known that all along. That's why I had every intention of never acting on how I felt for you. But I was weak. I caved. So now I just need to take everything I can get before you're stolen from me."

"No," she cries. "Tell him," she demands, her eyes finding Alex's over my shoulder. "Tell him he's talking shit."

"I... uh..." I imagine him rubbing the back of his neck as he tries to come up with something to pacify her. He knows I'm right. He knows they won't accept us being together. "I think that maybe we should all calm down. None of this matters right now. While Calli is at risk, the only thing we need to be focusing on is keeping her safe."

"He's right," I breathe, hoping it's enough to calm her down.

I step toward her, half expecting her to back away from me, but to my surprise, she does the opposite and collapses into my body, her arms locking around my waist as she holds me like there's a risk I might just disappear.

Movement to my right catches my eye, and I look up, finding Alex watching me. He smiles sadly, understanding and sympathy etched into every feature.

A violent shiver rips through Calli's body and I hold her tighter, letting her steal my warmth.

"We should go inside," Alex encourages, gathering up our bottles and heading into the house, leaving us alone.

"Come on, Angel. You're freezing," I say into her hair as I gently push her forward.

We make it halfway to the doors when her hands slide up my chest, stopping me from going any farther.

She tilts her head up, her tear-filled eyes capturing mine. The emotion, the sadness within them makes a lump climb up my throat.

"You're more than worth it, Nikolas. I'd give anything to keep this, keep you."

"Fuck," I breathe. Unable to find any other words to come back with, I dip my head and capture her lips in an all-consuming kiss.

We're still lip-locked as we stumble into the living room.

"Ugh, I need to get laid," Alex complains as I drop onto the other end of the sofa with Calli in my lap.

"You should," he mumbles against my lips. "It's fun."

Alex snorts a laugh. "Who knew fucking the devil would be fun?"

"Fuck you, man. You don't need to question my skills."

"True that. I've heard her moaning your name, *Nikolas*," he taunts, wiggling his brows as Calli kisses my jaw and down my neck. "Never thought I'd see you let someone call you that, man."

A growl rumbles deep in my throat when she sinks her teeth into my neck.

"It's Calli. She can do whatever she likes," I say, looking down at the girl in question.

"What have you done to our innocent princess?"

he mutters lightly, staring at her with his puppy-dog eyes as if she's stolen a part of his heart, too.

"Showed her the dark side, Bro. She loves it."

"You're bad, devil boy," she mutters, nuzzling my neck and holding me tight. "Oh God." Her moan rips through the air, baffling the fuck out of me for a second before I follow the length of her bare legs and find her foot in Alex's lap and his fingers digging into the arch.

Jealousy burns through me, but the ache in my cock watching him with her and the way she holds me and kisses my neck softly as he does it is stronger.

"That feel good, Angel?"

"Hmmm," she moans.

Alex's eyes catch mine, a little hesitation flickering through them at whatever he first reads in mine.

"Don't stop," she moans.

I nod at him, and a contented hum vibrates up her throat.

Silence falls between us as we both stare at the girl in my arms.

It's only minutes later when her breathing begins to deepen and she fully relaxes in my arms, falling into a deep sleep.

Dropping my lips to the top of her head, I press a kiss there, breathing her in while wishing that everything she said to me out on the decking was true.

But I can wish all I like. I know it's never going to come.

Shoving that harsh reality down, I look up at Alex, who's watching her with tired eyes.

"How did you get here?" I ask, a harshness to my tone that hasn't been there since finding my girl attached to him in the kitchen.

"I drove," he mutters, rolling his eyes like I'm an idiot for even asking.

"I swear to fuck, A, if you were followed then—"

"I wasn't. Why the fuck do you think I turned up in the middle of the night? No one knows I left, and the car is stolen."

A smirk pulls at my lips.

"What?"

"Been a while since we went out boosting, huh?" I ask, memories from our younger years flooding me.

Hopping around the city, boosting cars with your twin brother probably isn't the kind of happy childhood memories most kids have, but they're ours all the same.

"Yeah. It was kinda dull doing it alone."

"Needed the Batman to your Robin?" I ask, a quiet laugh rumbling in my chest.

"Nah, we both know I'm Batman. You were always the sidekick. And, I'm more Spiderman anyway." He shrugs as if it's obvious.

"Of course you are," I mutter.

"Seriously, though, no one followed me. I have no way of being tracked. I'm not a dumb-arse."

"I know, I know," I concede when he gives me a disappointed look. "I just... I need her fucking safe, man. The thought of the Italians getting a hold of her..." Fear so fucking strong grips me in its unyielding claws just from the thought alone. I'm more than aware of the things I've done to their men, and it fucking terrifies me, thinking about how they might retaliate with my girl.

"It won't happen," Alex states confidently. "I know you'd die over letting them take her. And that ain't fucking happening either."

I nod, unable to find a response to that. While everyone else around me seemed to doubt and question my skills and ability at every turn, Alex never has. I always just assumed that was because he heard everything that was said to me and he felt the need to try to smother some of it with his own differing opinion. And while I know some of that might be true, I also know that he sees more in me. If nothing else, he encouraged me to at least try every time someone tried to write me off.

"How did you find out about this, anyway? You weren't meant to be working, yet you turned up with the juiciest intel?"

I look between my twin and my girl, the truth bubbling up on my lips.

"You can trust me, Bro. With this," he says, gesturing between the two of us, "and with whatever went down. I've got your backs. Both of you."

"Calli was seeing Antonio Santoro," I say quietly.

"What?" Alex roars, making Calli fidget in my lap as he wakes her.

"Bro, seriously?" I mutter.

"Sorry."

He waits with a million and one questions right on the tip of his tongue until she's settled once more and I give him a nod.

"She was seeing Antonio Santoro," he parrots.

"Yeah. Has been since she met him at that party last year."

"Jesus." He scrubs his hand down his face as he processes that little nugget of information. "How the hell did you find out?"

I blow out a breath, really not wanting to go back there. "The night we raided their warehouse, I found her in his bedroom."

Alex's chin drops. "That's where you fucked off to that night," he whispers, like it all makes sense. "And why you shot him."

"That was an accident. It was meant to be his head."

Alex holds my eyes. "That's bullshit, right here."

"What? That I should have blown his fucking head off? Unlikely."

"You don't have accidents with guns, D. You want someone dead, you make it happen. You chose not to because of her."

"Yeah, okay, maybe," I concede, knowing damn well that it's true. "Anyway, it's a fucking good job I didn't, because he was the one who came to tell me that they'd put a hit out on her." His brows lift. "So we beat them to it."

"H-he knows you're here?"

"Yeah," I force out. "He won't squeal. He cares about her." I wince.

"Wow, Bro. You're putting her safety in the hands of an Italian. She has fucking changed you."

"Trust me, I know what you're saying. And any other Italian wouldn't stand a chance. But the way he looks at her, man. Fuck." My heart rips in two just thinking about the love that was in his eyes, the agony oozing from him as he said goodbye to her.

"And how does she feel about him?"

My lips part to respond, but I quickly find that I have no words.

Helpfully, though, Calli seems to answer that question for me when her arms tighten around me and a soft, "Nikolas," falls from her lips.

"Well, shit, man. You're one lucky motherfucker, you know that? She's one in a million."

I nod, a lump too large to speak around suddenly jumping into my throat.

"I-I th-th-think I—"

"I know, Bro. I can see it. I've always seen it. And despite all this shit and what's going to happen when you get her home, I'm so fucking happy for you."

A smile curls at my lips, because damn it, I'm happy for me too.

"I n-never th-thought I'd get a ch-chance."

"You underestimate yourself, while everyone around her underestimates her. I'm not surprised. I think you're pretty perfect together, to be honest."

"Yeah?" I ask hopefully. It's pointless, but it's there anyway.

"Yeah." He drains the rest of his bottle before sitting forward and resting his elbows on his knees. "And I'll do whatever it takes for it to continue when you get home. She's right, Bro. You deserve this. This and so much more. We'll figure a way to make it all happen."

"Maybe I should just marry her," I say in jest. "Worked for Theo and Emmie."

"Very different situation. I can't see Dad signing off on that anytime soon."

"Only for a few more weeks. Then we'll officially be fully grown adults and we can do what the fuck we want."

"I'd better go choose a suit. You want your best man looking sharp, after all," he teases.

"Who the fuck said you'd be my best man?" I bite back.

"Well, who else is it gonna be? Nico?"

"I'm pretty sure Calli wouldn't want bloodstains on her dress, so probably not."

He smiles at me, his eyes shining with happiness for me and confidence in me to do the right thing. It's wholly overwhelming, but I silently vow to do everything in my power to make it happen.

"Come on, get your girl to bed."

"She would still be in it if some stupid motherfucker didn't decide to break in in the middle of the night."

He holds his hands up. "I can't help it if I missed my little bro."

"Fuck you, man. Fuck you."

I stand with Calli still tucked into my chest, and he watches with amused eyes.

"She looks good on you, Bro."

An image of her writhing beneath me, her back arching as I fill her body up, pushing her right to the edge fills my mind, and my lips twitch into a cocky-arse smirk as my cock swells.

"You've no fucking idea, man."

"Maybe not, you dirty motherfucker, but I know how much she enjoys it."

"Can't believe you fucking knew and said nothing," I grunt, following him out of the living room.

"You'd have freaked and run off, much like you did anyway. But I didn't want to be the cause. You need her, man. Just as much as I think she needs you, so you're gonna need to stash all this 'I'm not worthy' bullshit and come up with a way to make it happen." He comes to a stop at our old bedroom and pushes the door open. "Sleep tight, lover boy." He winks before closing the door on us.

"You're a pain in my arse, Alexander."

"Same to you, Nikolas," he quips back, and I walk into our bedroom with a wide fucking smile on my face and what I really pray isn't fruitless hope in my heart.

14

CALLI

Once again, when I wake, I'm alone.

But this time, there's no panic or fear.

Just happiness and contentment.

Alex knowing and accepting what's between Daemon and me is a massive weight off my shoulders, one I didn't even realise was pressing down on me until it lifted.

I roll onto Daemon's side, drowning in his scent as I drift in and out of sleep and memories of the night before.

But just like when I fell asleep, there's one part my mind keeps getting stuck on.

Daemon's words about this not being able to continue once real life returns rips me in two.

There's no way I'm letting him go when we get back. I refuse to allow my parents, my brother, to control my life anymore.

It was fine—to a point—when I didn't know what I

wanted. But all of that is different now. I know what I want. And it's him.

Somehow, we need to find a way to show them that we want this, that we're serious, and that it's right. Because it is. I feel it in my heart and right down to my soul.

They might have an image of how they want my life to look, what my husband should be like, but fuck that. It's not their life. It's mine. And I'll fight for what I want, what I need.

There has to be a way. There just does.

My need to go and find my devil boy quickly gets the better of me, and I swing my legs out of bed and pad toward the bathroom to get ready for the day.

Dressed in a vest and shorts, and my face free of make-up, I head out on my search.

The sun is already burning bright, the warmth of it seeping through the huge windows that lead toward the beach.

I spot movement beyond the glass, but I refuse to let myself look until I've made myself a coffee. Then, I head out.

My smile widens as the view becomes clear and I silently walk across the decking and sit on the stairs, just like I did last night.

Grunts and groans of pain mix with the crash of the waves and the squawking from the gulls overhead as they do synchronised burpees on the sand.

I lower to my arse, my eyes darting between the two of them. They're both shirtless—something that makes me smile because it shows just how comfortable Daemon is right now—and shorts that hang low on their waist. Their muscles ripple and flex as they move.

Placing my mug down beside me, I focus on Daemon, watching every movement of his body as he pushes it to the max.

I've watched him work out every morning since we've been here. Hell, I've been standing next to him for most of it as he's pushed me right alongside him. But seeing him competing with Alex just brings a whole new level of hotness to the situation.

The sun quickly begins to burn my skin as I sit here unnoticed, but I don't do anything about it. I'm enjoying myself too much, keeping count with them as they continue.

Their stamina astounds me, but I guess it shouldn't really. They've probably been training like this together for as long as they remember. And I know for a fact that Daemon won't stop trying to come out on top until he passes out. His desire to banish the image that he's the weak one is something I'm not sure he's ever going to be able to shake.

Eventually, and unsurprisingly, it's Alex whose body caves first. His arms give out on a push up and he quickly finds himself eating sand while Daemon continues to make a show of beating him.

Smug fucker.

"You're a fucking pussy, Bro. You been skiving off training?"

With a loud groan, Alex flips onto his back, throwing his arm over his face.

"Fuck you, Iron Man. We can't all be numb to pain."

"Trust me, that ain't fucking true."

Daemon drops to the sand beside Alex, his back still to me.

Part of me wants to make my presence known, but there's a bigger part, the wanton whore inside me who's more than happy to just lust over the pair of them.

He straightens his legs out before him and curls over them, stretching his muscles out.

I'm damn near drooling as his back and shoulder muscles twist and pull. My head is full of images of how he must look from behind as he brings me to ruin with his powerful body.

Eventually, Alex must catch his breath, because he sits up on his elbows, his eyes immediately finding mine. He sucks in a sharp breath, but other than that, he doesn't let on that he's seen me.

And I quickly discover that was intentional when a smirk curls at his lips and a wicked glint flashes in his eyes.

"You managed to sink that boner for your girl yet?" he asks, way louder than necessary.

"Fuck you, man. You try lying next to her, watching her for hours and not react," Daemon grunts.

"Oh, I have. Difference is, if I was you, I'd have done something about it."

"What the fuck are you trying to say?"

"Just that she was right there for the taking." Alex winks at me, and I wish my cheeks didn't heat, or that I was able to put an end to this. But damn him, he's pulled me right into this little game. "All you had to do was hook her underwear to the side and you could have sunk right into her—"

"Don't talk about Calli's pussy," Daemon barks, the promise of even more pain clear in his voice.

"Is it as good as I've imagined?"

A silent laugh of disbelief falls from my lips at his audacity and clear attempt to bait Daemon into a fight.

"Dude. You need to get any thoughts of my girl outta your head right the fuck now."

"She's hot," Alex says with a shrug.

"She's fucking everything," Daemon replies, all the fight disappearing from his tone.

"I fucking love this, man. Seeing you whipped is one of the best things I've ever witnessed."

"She can whip me anytime she fucking likes," Daemon confesses. He stops his stretching and rests back on his palms, tilting his face to the sun.

Curiosity swirls through me, the bizarre image of me standing with a whip in my hand popping into my mind. Something Alex can clearly read in my eyes.

"Bet she would if you ask her."

Daemon barks a laugh, the sound washing through me and filling me with joy.

"You're a fucking idiot, man."

"Just saying. I bet she's well kinky under that smothered princess exterior."

Daemon shakes his head. For a few seconds I don't think he's going to answer, but then he surprises me.

"You have no idea. She brings me to my knees every time. She just... she's not scared of me. In fact, she just pushes me harder and dives into the darkness with me."

"So..." Alex starts, and my hackles rise, knowing that he's going in for the kill before we're both discovered. "If she's that kinky, do you reckon she'd be up for a little twin action?"

Silence falls between them for a beat and my breath gets stuck in my throat. Because I'm not interested in the image he paints. Obviously. Yeah, that's why.

"You're funny," Daemon scoffs, pushing the comment aside as if he knows Alex is taunting him.

"Nah, I'm serious, man. I've held off for you, but damn, I could really use a taste of her p—"

Crack.

Faster than I thought was possible, Daemon lunges at Alex, his fist colliding with his jaw.

A scream rips from my lips as I jump to my feet and surge forward, ready to get in the middle of them —and not in the way Alex was just suggesting.

I'm almost in front of them when Alex throws his

head back and barks out a laugh.

"Bro, you're so fucking easy," he forces out through his amusement as Daemon jumps to his feet.

"You listen to all that?" he growls, closing the space between us with a dangerous expression on his face.

I swallow nervously, although excitement licks at my insides. I can't help but get turned on when he's in this mood, something I fear Alex might have just tapped into.

"M-maybe."

"And what? You think my cock's not good enough now you've got the option of two?"

My words get stuck in my throat as he prowls closer, my heart pounding like a bass drum in my chest.

"Answer me, Angel."

"N-no."

"No what?"

"No, I don't want both of you." Because I don't. The fantasy is one thing, but I know that all I want, all I need is Daemon. Alex knows it too, which is why he's using it to tease him.

"So what do you want?"

Dropping my eyes from him, I take in every sandy, sweaty inch of his chest before I find his waistband and then the bulge hiding behind the fabric.

Finding his dark, stormy eyes once more, I run my tongue along my bottom lip.

"Your cock," I breathe.

"We've been working out for almost two hours, baby C. I wouldn't go down there if I were you," Alex helpfully offers.

"I love him something fierce, but he's not getting a taste of you, Angel. I've shared almost everything with him all my life. But you're mine. And only mine," Daemon growls low enough so that only I can hear him.

"I'm yours, Nikolas. And only yours."

His chest heaves as he looms over me, his scent filling my nose and the heat of his skin warming mine.

"Fuck. I-I— Fuck."

Forgetting whatever he was going to say, his arm shoots out, his fingers wrapping around my throat as he claims my lips in a wet and filthy kiss that's entirely too dirty to happen in company. But I guess to Daemon, Alex doesn't count.

He hikes my leg around his hip, allowing me to feel everything I do to him.

"Take her. I promise I won't watch," Alex teases, I assume from his seat in the sand.

"If he thinks watching will stop me, then he really doesn't know me as well as I thought he did," Daemon murmurs against my lips.

His arm bands around my waist just as my body sags at his words.

I don't want him to fuck me while his brother looks on... do I?

I think back to the tipi and how hot it was knowing that we shouldn't have been doing it right there. Okay, yeah. So maybe I do have a teeny-weeny thing for a bit of exhibitionism.

Daemon rips his lips from mine, kissing along my jaw as his hips continue to thrust, ensuring his cock grinds against me in the most delicious way.

"Nikolas." His name falls from my lips in a plea as heat surges through me. My knees buckle as I dance on the edge of pleasure.

"Are you going to be a good girl and come for me, Angel?"

"Oh God," I whimper.

His hand drops from my throat in favour of my arse and he drags me closer. The sensation of his cock against my clit through the fabric of our clothes intensifies to the point that I have no control over diving head first off that cliff and throwing my inhibitions away as I go.

"Nikolas." His name floats away in the silence of the little piece of heaven as I come back to Earth.

"Jesus," Alex grunts somewhere behind us. And when I find the confidence to peek over Daemon's shoulder, I find him dropping his shorts, thankfully leaving his boxers in place, as he runs for the sea.

Daemon looks around to see what's captured my attention.

"He's going to cool off. Probably a good idea. Arms up, beautiful."

Even if I wanted to argue, I don't have a chance as he peels the fabric of my top up my arms, revealing the pink bikini I'm wearing beneath.

"It's a really good fucking job I love him," he mutters lightly.

"He's seen it all before."

His movements stop dead, his eyes boring into mine.

"Is that meant to make me feel better?" he growls.

"Put your possessive and jealous bullshit away, devil boy. He loves you just as much as you do him, so he can look all he likes, but he'd never fuck you over. And," I say, nudging the end of his nose with mine, "nor would I."

He shakes his head at me, and for a second, I think it's because he doesn't believe me. But then he steals my breath once more by growling. "You fucking slay me, Angel. I've always known my heart only beats for you, but I never knew it would be like this."

"Like what?" I whisper.

"Th-th-this..." He squeezes his eyes closed. "This all-consuming thing that I just can't get enough of. I don't care about having anything else good in my life as long as I've got you."

"Bro, if you're not gonna stick your cock in her, come play with me," Alex shouts, shattering the moment.

"I should have hit him harder," Daemon mutters, ripping the button of my shorts open and helping me shimmy them over my hips.

He doesn't bother shedding his shorts. Instead, he just sweeps me off my feet and throws me over his shoulder before turning and running for the sea.

"Daemon," I squeal, desperately trying to hold on and keep my tits inside my admittedly too small bikini top.

Water splashes around us as he wades into the ocean to join Alex. If he notices the temperature, then he doesn't react, and the second he's waist deep, he flips me upright once more and launches me deeper into the ice bath that is the sea.

I scream, but it's quickly cut off as I go under. I sink with such speed that I lose the fight with my bikini, and I'm still fumbling to right it when I finally surface once more.

"Oh, you should have said you wanted a re-do of our skinny dipping," Alex says with a smirk when he catches a glimpse. "I was trying to be polite keeping my boxers on but—"

"Don't even think about it," Daemon growls, coming to stand in front of me so I can fix myself without giving Alex an eyeful.

"Jeez, you're no fun, Bro."

"I think Calli would disagree, right, Angel?"

"Total hoot," I deadpan before a huge wave of water hits me as Alex launches at Daemon and the pair of them start acting like the kids I'm not really sure they ever got to be and begin wrestling and splashing each other in the water.

I forget about everything surrounding us, all the bullshit that is our reality, and just throw my head back and laugh at them as they enjoy themselves.

15

CALLI

Alex stayed with us for another two days after our day chilling on the beach and acting like kids in the sea before he headed back to real life in London.

I loved seeing the two of them together without the weight or pressure of real life pressing down on their shoulders.

Their bond is stronger than I ever realised, and seeing them working together blows my mind. Last night, they cooked together, and I swear, I spent the whole time sitting at the table in the middle of the room with my jaw on the floor as they moved together seamlessly. It was almost as if they were one person.

I wished we could have had more time, or more so that they could have more time together. Both of them look so much happier since having some quality time together.

"What are you smiling about?" Daemon asks as he

climbs back onto the outside lounger with fresh drinks and a bowl of crisps for me, since I was complaining that I was hungry again.

"When all this is done, I think we should go on holiday. A real holiday."

A wicked grin pulls at his lips as he drops beside me and stuffs a handful of crisps into his mouth.

"Hell, yeah. Private pool. Private beach. We can spend the whole time naked."

My thighs rub together at the image he paints despite the fact that he had me screaming his name in the shower not so long ago after we went for a moonlight swim.

"As amazing as that sounds. I was more thinking about all of us."

"All of us? Like... including your brother and cousin?" he asks sceptically.

"Yeah," I agree, but my stomach knots despite how much confidence I force into my voice.

"Calli," he warns, but I slap a hand over his mouth before he has a chance to say what I already know is going to fall from his lips.

"We're going to find a way. We have to. This," I say, twisting onto my side and slipping my other hand around the back of his neck, "is too important to let go of because others don't like it. I don't give a shit about their opinions, or their expectations of me. I want this. I want you."

"Calli," he breathes when I let my hand drop. "I

want this too. More than anything. But I just don't think it's going to be possible."

"It will. It has to be."

"But your dad—"

"Fuck my dad. Surely, they want me to be happy over wanting their ideal partner for me?" The sad, sympathetic face that stares back at me doesn't seem to support that statement and my heart sinks.

"He's been searching for and planning your future husband for years. Every guy has been unknowingly vetted for suitability. I'm pretty sure every one has failed, mind you. His standards are seriously fucking high."

"So are mine."

A bitter laugh falls from his lips. "Hardly."

"You're wrong," I say, abandoning my drink and pushing the bowl of crisps away, no longer hungry for anything but the man before me. Vulnerability bleeds from him and I desperately want to banish it. To somehow convince him of just how incredible he is.

Throwing my leg over his waist, I settle myself over him and drop my hands on either side of his head.

"I want my man to be strong." I brush my lips over his. "Independent." Drop a kiss on his jaw. "Powerful." I lick a line up his throat, the vibration of his growl of approval making a smile twitch at the corners of my mouth. "Dangerous." My hands slip under the fabric of his shirt, making his abs tense as I push higher. "Deadly," I whisper as he helps me out by sitting up so I can pull his t-shirt from his body. "Yet vulnerable." My lips find the top of his longest scar. "Brave." My lips brush down the length of it as his fingers thread through my hair. "Yet scared."

My eyes hold his as he swallows roughly, his lips slightly parted and a small frown marring his brow.

"Intelligent." He scoffs at that one, but his argument is cut off when my tongue finds the top of his V line. "Determined." I work my way lower, making him growl once more before my fingers find the tie on his sweats. "Passionate."

I drag the fabric down, and he helps me by lifting his arse from the lounger.

"Sexy. Dark. A little bit broken, but a lot perfect."

"Calli," he gasps as I lick up his hard length.

Wrapping my hand around the base of his shaft, I swirl my tongue around the head, loving the deep groan that rips from his lips and the way his hips jump from the lounger.

"Fuck, Angel," he barks when I finally take him in my mouth. "Argh fuuuuuck," he groans, his fingers twisting in my hair, sending a bolt of pain down my spine. "Your mouth. Fuck. I'll never get enough of this."

"Good. Because you're not going to get the chance," I confess before sinking back down on him again.

I might be inexperienced with this, but I've learned quickly what he likes. Where to lick, just how hard to suck, and in no time at all, his length is swelling between my lips, getting ready to blow.

"Fuck, you suck me so good, beautiful. Your mouth is sinful."

Just before he falls, there's a bang that sounds like it comes from inside the house. But not wanting it to end here despite the way his eyes widen as they hold mine, I don't let up.

I take him deeper, suck him harder, and not a second later, his low groan of pleasure rumbles around us as he comes down my throat.

Sitting up, I wipe my mouth with the back of my hand, his taste filling my mouth as I swallow him down.

"Fuck yeah," he pants, dragging me forward by my hair and crashing my lips to his.

His tongue barely touches mine before there's another bang and a shout.

"Fuck."

Before I know what's happening, I'm thrown down on the lounger with such force, I damn near bounce off the other side.

By the time I look up, Daemon is already hiding around the side of the sliding door and peering inside the dark house.

He looks like freaking James Bond, standing there. If James Bond was almost eighteen and incredibly freaking hot, that is.

"What is it?" I whisper.

He waves his hand at me to shut up before slipping into the house.

My heart jumps into my throat as he's engulfed by the darkness, and my panic ratchets up a notch.

"Oh shit," I breathe quietly as I sneak toward the doors, desperately trying to hear anything that might be happening inside.

Low voices filter down to me, but I have no chance of hearing what they're actually saying. My heart is beating so hard it drowns out everything else going on.

My hands tremble at the thought of the Italians finding us. Of them coming here to get me.

My stomach churns as I think of Daemon being caught, of them taking him too. Of them hurting him because of me.

My legs move without instruction to my brain, and I quickly find myself skirting around the edge of the living room toward the unit where Daemon stashed both his and Alex's guns after we did some target training on the beach yesterday.

I cringe when the drawer squeaks, but a second later, a loud pained cry fills the house and I move faster.

Daemon.

Holding the gun at my waist, I move toward the hallway. A loud bang and the shattering of some furniture make me jump, but I force myself to stay calm.

Daemon is lethal. The best soldier Dad and Uncle Damien have ever had.

If anyone can handle whatever is happening in the kitchen right now and keep me safe, then it's him.

But I refuse to cower like a weak little lady. Because I'm not. Cirillo blood runs through my veins, and I'm determined to prove myself. To not just be an heir-bearing airhead who can't protect herself and those she loves.

My steps falter at that realisation, but I don't have time to dwell on the weight of it right now. Especially as another loud bang and wail hits my ears.

Rushing forward, I pull back the safety on the gun just like Daemon showed me and step into the doorway.

My eyes widen at the state of it as three guys, a similar age to us, go up against Daemon, who's yielding a knife and looking much better off than each of them is.

Daemon's foot smashes into one of their stomachs, sending him flying back toward me. I jump to the side, still unseen as I hide around the corner.

"Motherfucker," Daemon grunts, and I look up to find the other two on him, the knife in his hand clattering to the floor.

"You said this place would be an easy hit," one of the guys complains, but no one responds.

The guy on the floor not too far from me begins to get to his feet, and I spot my moment.

The second he's halfway up, I wrap my arm around his throat in a chokehold—again, just like

Daemon has shown me—and press the butt of my gun against his temple.

"Let him go, or this one doesn't walk out of here with you." My cold, hard voice cuts through the air and all eyes turn on me.

Daemon's eyes widen in shock, but I'm pretty sure I also don't miss them darken in desire.

The two guys who were beginning to overpower him do as they're told and back away.

One of them reaches for his side, and I quickly realise that he's got blood pouring from him. One look at the knife that went skidding across the floor tells me exactly what happened there.

"We didn't come here for trouble," the guy beneath my gun cries, his voice cracking with fear. "We thought it was empty."

"So you were going to rob the place?"

"We're sorry, okay?" the guy without the stab wound says, attempting to back toward the door that's swinging open.

"We can't just let you walk out of here now. What if you call the cops on us?"

"We won't, man. We swear."

With his eyes locked on the two who were attacking him, Daemon moves closer before dropping to his haunches and studying the guy in my hold.

I have no idea what he sees, but it seems to captivate him.

"Which one of you has the stash?" he asks, standing back up again and wiping his hands down his sweats like this is just an everyday occurrence for him, while I fight not to allow my hands to tremble. "WELL?" he booms when no one answers.

"I-I-I do," the guy with the stab wound says.

"Show me."

Slowly, he shoves his hand into his pocket and pulls out a foil package.

"Drop it on the floor."

His lips part to argue, but he must see the promise of death lingering in Daemon's eyes and decides against defying him.

The small parcel lands right in the middle of one of the tiles.

"Did anyone send you here?"

"N-no. We've been watching the house on and off for months. It's always empty."

"Well, you certainly picked the wrong fucking day for it, huh?" Daemon mutters, his voice full of mirth.

A whimper rips through the room, and when I look at stabby, I find his face getting paler by the second as blood pours through his fingers, soaking into his already dirty jeans.

Reaching for a tea towel, Daemon marches toward me.

"I want your phones in the middle, too."

Hesitantly, the two opposite me comply, but the guy in my grasp doesn't move.

"That applies to you too, arsehole," I grunt, pressing the gun harder into his head.

"If you knew who she was, you wouldn't be hesitating right now," Daemon warns.

My eyes catch his and a million and one dirty promises fill his eyes right alongside the blood lust, which tells me he'd love to watch me shoot this motherfucker.

That thought alone is almost enough to make me do it.

Finally, he pulls his phone from his pocket and it crashes to the floor with the others.

"Let him go, beautiful." I do as he says, but I don't move the gun. "Go stand with your dumb-arse friends over there."

Daemon steps up to me and shocks the living shit out of me when his hand grips the back of my neck harshly and he licks up the side of my face.

"You make me so fucking horny, Angel. You holding that gun. Fuck," he grunts in my ear. "One day, I'm gonna watch you blow some motherfucker's brains out before I make you scream right there and then."

I manage to catch the whimper of desire that rumbles up my throat before it's set free.

The three boys standing on the other side of the kitchen stare at us as if we can't possibly be real, and my chest puffs out with the power we hold over the three of them.

"I want your IDs down there with your phones."

This time, they don't hesitate.

"Fuck it. Just throw everything down. Me and my

girl will enjoy having a little bonfire with all your shit once you've fucked off."

They do as they're told a second before a suspicious-looking wet patch appears on the jeans of the guy I was holding.

"Looking like a big man right now, huh?" I mutter. "I bet all the girls just love your piss-scented cock."

Daemon smothers a laugh at my words as he wipes down the gun he'd taken from my hand.

"Pass this around, make sure you all touch it good."

Again, they do as they're told and Daemon takes it back again, using the tea towel now it's covered in their prints.

"Okay, so I'm gonna just go ahead and assume that you're nothing but a few pussy, try-your-luck druggies who are shit scared of what will happen to your tight arses if we were to call the cops and let them have that," Daemon says, gesturing to the small pile of evidence he's had them collect for us. "And I'm also going to assume that you're going to walk out of here and forget any of this ever happened."

He reaches for me and tugs me into his body, wrapping his arms around my waist and breathing me in.

"I suggest you take him to A&E and say you all had an accident while you were high—and fucking stupid—and get him patched up before he bleeds to death. And all being well, we'll never have anything to do with each other again. That good with you?"

They all nod. I only just manage to smother the smile that wants to spill across my face at how quickly they turned from dangerous wannabes to scared little pussies because of the two of us. Okay, because of Daemon, but I'll happily take a little of that credit because I was the one with the gun after all.

"Good. Now fuck off before I'm forced to kill you all and dump your arses out in the ocean for the fish to feast on."

They scramble so fast it's pitiful really, and they even close the door behind them, which of course no longer actually shuts properly thanks to their bad attempt at breaking and entering.

"Now," Daemon growls, gripping the back of my neck and forcing me forward through the carnage that is the kitchen.

"What are you—" My words are cut off when he bends me over, his other hand dragging my arse back exactly where he wants it.

"Hold the counter. Lock your elbows. This isn't going to be gentle."

Oh fuck.

Heat pools between my thighs at the filthy promises of what's to come.

His fingers grip the waistband of my leggings before he roughly drags them down my thighs and abandons them just above my knees once he's revealed what he wants.

Crack.

"Holy shit," I gasp as the sting from his palm blooms on my arse.

"You have no fucking idea, do you, Angel?"

"I-I… uh…"

"Watching you with that gun. Watching you threaten that motherfucker's life. I've never been so fucking hard in all my life. You're fucking fierce, beautiful, and it's a fucking mind-blowing thing to watch."

"Yes," I cry when he spanks me again.

"I need to fuck you."

"Oh God."

"It's not going to be soft or gentle or loving in any way. It's going to be hard, brutal, and it's probably going to hurt," he warns as if I'm going to back down and run from him now.

"Yes. All of it, yes."

"Fuck, you're perfect," he groans before rubbing the head of his cock through my pussy. "And you're so fucking wet for me. Violence make you as hot as it does me?"

"Seems that way," I mutter, arching my back in the hope that he'll give me more than just teasing my clit with his dick. "Nikolas."

"Desperate little whore, aren't you, Angel? Tell me how badly you need me filling you up right now."

"So bad. Please, Nikolas. I need your co— yes," I cry as he finally thrusts forward, filling me to the hilt and almost sending me crashing into the counter I'm meant to be holding.

"Lock your arms," he grunts before pulling almost all the way out. He doesn't give me a second to catch my breath, he just slams right back in, fucking me until we're both sweaty, panting messes who can barely hold themselves up.

16

DAEMON

Calli is still sleeping as I put the rest of the kitchen back together. I secured the door before I carried her to the shower and tried to fuck the image of her holding a gun to that motherfucker's head out of my system. It was wishful thinking. Turns out, every fucking time I think about it, I'm hard as a nail all over again.

Dragging my arse out of bed to come and sort this mess out instead of waking my girl and taking her all over again was hard. Pun intended.

But despite my endless need for her, I left her to rest.

I was rough with her last night. Too rough. If she can walk properly today, I'll be amazed.

Guilt washes through me as I remember how tightly my fingers dug into her hips, how hard I took her. I know she's not made of glass, and I'll do anything I can to prove to her that I don't see her as some innocent, useless little princess like the others do. But even still. I took it too far.

I'm walking back into the house after tossing the unsalvageable dining table and chairs into the front garden when my phone starts ringing. My heart sinks just like it always does, and it only gets worse when I pull it from my pocket and find Evan's name staring back at me.

Walking through the house, I quickly slip through the sliding door and don't stop until I'm inches from where the water laps at the shore.

"Boss," I growl the second it touches my ear.

I send up a silent prayer that today isn't the day that this all comes to an end. But I already know it's pointless. There's a heavy ball of dread sitting deep in my belly. My subconscious already knows what's about to fall from Evan's lips. The unspoken words drip through my veins like poison, chilling me from the inside out.

"It's time to bring my girl home, Daemon."

Despite not wanting to react to his statement, all the air rushes from my lungs as disappointment hits me with the force of a jumbo fucking jet.

"Everything is sorted?" I ask, forcing a lightness into my tone that I certainly don't feel.

"Yes. We've come to an agreement which will keep her out of it."

"And that is?" I prompt, needing to ensure I agree that I'm not about to walk my girl directly into a war zone.

"You're off the clock, Daemon. The details don't matter. It's safe for her to come home."

"Don't you think that—"

"It's Cassandra's birthday this weekend. She wants her daughter here to celebrate with her."

I just about manage to bite back what I really think about that. You can always rely on Cassandra to attempt to cover up the ugliness that is this life, plaster on a face full of make-up and party like all is well with the world.

"Right," I mutter, my insides twisting up painfully.

"Security has been tightened. She will have eyes on her at all times."

Fucking great.

My legs give out and I fall to my arse.

"Everything okay, son?"

"Yeah. Looking forward to getting back."

"How's the revising been going?"

My mind flicks back to yesterday's naked study session. "Uh..." I shove my hand through my hair, pulling until the pain is stronger than my desire as I think about her sitting astride my lap, her tits right in my face as she quizzed me. "Yeah. Good."

"My Calli is an angel. I have every confidence in her."

I don't have anything to say to that. My heart is too busy shattering into a million tiny pieces.

"Let me know when to expect you home."

"Will do. If anything changes, let me know," I say,

hoping and praying that something kicks off in the next couple of hours, stopping us from going back.

We've still got another week before school starts. We could easily stay here longer. Well, we could if it weren't for Queen Cassandra's bloody birthday.

"See you soon," he says, his tone telling me that there is no room for movement here.

He hangs up before I get to say anything more. The second the silence falls, my arm drops, my heart plummeting right along with it.

"Fuck," I breathe, staring out across the sea, the early morning sun making the waves glitter with the promise of a new day. All the while darkness claws at my insides as my world begins to crumble around me.

Driving back into London is effectively signing a death certificate on everything we've built here. There's going to be no more late-night naked swims with my girl. No more dirty showers or lazy mornings. There's going to be no more... her.

Dropping my head into my hands, I squeeze my eyes closed as I fight to keep hold of everything I've learned about myself here. The strength Calli has given me to face a few of my demons and accept her help.

How am I meant to go back to my flat without that? Without her soft smile, her gentle touch, her desperate cries for more.

I have no idea how long I sit there, drowning in my own sorrow and self-pity. But the sun is much higher in the sky, and it started to burn my skin a while ago.

I half expected her to wake and come find me, but there's been no sign of her.

Aware that Evan wants her home sooner rather than later, I eventually push to my feet and head for the house. Each step is painful, my heart emptier and my soul darker with every step I force myself to take.

By the time I slip into the living room, I've built my walls back up so high I swear nothing can touch me.

I become the vacant, empty version of myself that I've been for so long I'd forgotten the boy I once was even existed.

My steps falter as I cross the threshold into the bedroom and find Calli still fast asleep, hugging the covers to her front, exposing the entire length of her body to me.

My mouth waters as I run my eyes over the dip in her waist and down to her round, delectable arse.

My cock stirs in anticipation, but I already know we're not going there.

After last night, this has come at the perfect time.

Our last time together is going to leave her with the memory of what a brutal, selfish, destructive cunt I really am.

It's how she should remember me. It's how she needs to. Because if she doesn't hate me, if she tries to fight for me and allows me to even believe for a second that we could be something outside of our little slice of paradise here, then I'll break and do something stupid like go to Evan, begging to let me have his daughter.

Doing so would be akin to writing my own death warrant.

Fuck.

How am I meant to just walk away from her?

I've trained my entire life to be strong and powerful. To always come out of any situation as the winner. And I have. Up until this point in my life, nothing has beaten me.

But then there's her.

My angel.

My solace.

My everything.

Now, I'm just going to have to figure out a way to carve out a future without her in it.

For her.

Because despite what she tries to make me believe...

She deserves better than me.

Locking the last bit of Nikolas away, I drag on my mask and set about doing what I need to do.

My priority has always been her. Keeping her safe and protected. And this right now is no different.

"I'm sorry, Angel."

17

_____

CALLI

Sunlight floods the room, burning my eyes through my closed lids as Daemon rips the curtains open, immediately waking me up.

He's obviously got plans this morning, but I could think of more than a few other ways he could have woken me.

My muscles ache and pull as I twist toward the light, reminding me of everything that happened the night before.

A sense of power washes through me once more as I think of holding the gun to that prick's head. I thought I understood the guys' addiction to this life. To the dangers, the violence, the darkness, but last night, I got it. I had a taste of that bloodlust I've seen shining so brightly in the guys'—hell even the girls'— eyes. And I can't deny that I want to taste it again.

It's not until darkness falls over me that I finally look up.

My heart jumps and my stomach knots in excitement as I find Daemon looming over me. But everything changes the second I look into his eyes, because I don't find the lightness that has been there for the past week, the unfiltered desire that oozes from him at all times. Instead, I find the closed-off darkness that I almost forgot existed.

My heart plummets as panic grips me.

Words fail me as I fight to drag in the air I need.

I know what that look means. It's one I've been dreading would follow any phone call he's received since the day I woke here.

I want to beg, plead, anything that will stop it from happening.

But I know it's impossible.

"No," is the only word I manage to force past my lips in the end as Daemon continues to stare at me blankly.

My Nikolas is long gone. In his place is Daemon, the soldier that everyone else sees.

Tears burn the backs of my eyes as a lump crawls up my throat.

"Get up and pack your shit," he demands coldly.

"Daemon, no. Please," I beg, swinging my legs over the edge of the bed and getting to my feet.

The morning chill in the air causes goosebumps to spread across my naked skin and my nipples pucker.

But he doesn't look.

His cold, detached eyes don't leave mine, and it fucking shreds me.

"Don't do this," I plead, lifting my hand to reach for him. But he sees it coming and takes a step back, ensuring my fingertips don't connect with him.

"I'm not doing anything, Calli."

Calli. Not angel, not beautiful.

Just Calli.

It breaks my heart faster and harder than I thought possible.

Tears balance on my eyelashes, and I fight to keep them in, not to shatter this fast in front of him.

"I don't want to go. I don't want this. I-I d-don't—"

"Pack your shit or I'll do it for you. We're leaving in thirty minutes."

He turns away from me, severing any connection that was still crackling between us, and marches toward the door.

"Daemon," I cry, pain ripping through my chest at this new reality I've woken to.

He pauses in the doorway, and just a little hope trickles through my veins that I might be able to scale the walls he's built back up since he learned what we had to do today.

His shoulders tense a beat before he looks back at me.

My hope withers and dies the second our eyes meet.

He's not going to be swayed.

He's been given his orders, and being the good little soldier he is, he'll follow, pushing aside everything he feels, everything he truly wants.

It's a harsh realisation that no matter what he's said to me during our time here, he'll always put the Family before anything else.

A sob rips from my throat as I silently beg him not to do this. Not to lock himself down and forget everything we found here.

All my hopes and dreams about this being something, any possibility that we could continue this at home, that we could fight for it together crash at my feet.

He blinks, and he might as well have just ripped my heart right out of my chest and stomped on it before he walks out without another word.

I stand there in the middle of the room, totally naked, with my entire world crumbled at my feet.

My stomach knots as my heart bleeds out, and before I know what's happening, I'm running to the bathroom. My knees hit the tiled floor the second I'm in front of the toilet, but I don't feel anything as my stomach convulses and forces me to throw up what's left of the vodka and crisps Daemon and I snacked on during our wild sex fest in the destroyed kitchen.

I heave until there's nothing left before resting my arm on the seat and resting my head on it.

Tears stain my cheeks from throwing up, but I refuse to cry. I refuse to let him see just how easy it was to break me.

Just one look.

One cold, detached look, and everything I've unlocked within him in the past week has been securely shoved back inside the impenetrable box it used to be hidden within. And something tells me that opening it up a second time is going to be even harder.

With a heavy sigh, I push to my feet and move to stand in front of the basin.

The emptiness in my eyes makes me gasp. They burn with the need to expel this desperate yet hopeless feeling that's swirling around inside me like a storm. But I won't cry. Not until I'm alone.

Suck it up, Callista, I tell myself as I stare dead into my cold eyes.

I stand taller and throw my shoulders back, doing my best to pull on my own mask.

"You're a Cirillo, and you are stronger than the devil."

With a newfound strength, albeit forced, I reach for my toothbrush to wash away my moment of weakness.

I work on autopilot, pulling on a pair of leggings and a hoodie in the hope I can hide inside them. If I had more time, my outfit choice might be different. I might put in more effort and attempt to show him the mistake he's making by shutting me out once more. But right now, my head is spinning and my stomach is still aching from its purge.

I give the room one final look, ensuring I've got everything before throwing my bag over my shoulder and heading out.

I keep my eyes on my feet as I walk toward the kitchen. My heart can't take the images of us over the past few days hanging out, laughing and enjoying each other.

Now I know this is happening, I just need to get home. I need it done, so I can figure out a way to deal with it without eyes on me.

Daemon is standing at the window, staring outside. He's pulled on a hoodie that's covering his head but doing an awful job of hiding the tension in his body.

The aura coming off him is dark. Danger ripples around the room. And I'm sure it would scare most people off. I guess it's just a shame for him that I'm not most people.

My muscles ache to walk over and run my hand down his back, whispering soft support in his ear that things are going to be okay. But I already know it's pointless.

He's shut down and any words I say now, any argument, no matter how convincing it might be, is going to fall on deaf ears.

Not waiting for him to acknowledge me, I walk toward the door and pull it open.

"You're a fucking coward, Nikolas Deimos," I shoot over my shoulder before fleeing the house.

He's not going to be far behind me, but having the final word like that does make me feel just a tiny bit better.

It's not until I come to a stop at the end of an empty driveway that I start to question everything.

They brought me here in a van, a van that

Daemon has since told me was driven back to the city by Ant when he left.

Thoughts of the boy who set this whole thing in motion don't make me feel any better.

I haven't had any contact with him since he walked out of here the day after they abducted me.

I know it's safer that way, and I know everything is well and truly over between us, but it still hurts. Not knowing if he's okay or if someone found out what he did hasn't been far from my mind since he left.

All I can do is hope. No one found us here, so that's got to be a good sign that he just returned to the city and got on with his life. Right?

"How are we getting back?" I ask when Daemon finally locks up the house behind us and joins me.

His eyes find mine for a beat before he looks away again, as if whatever he sees in my blue depths is too painful to look at.

Good. Right now, I really hope I cause him a whole world of pain, because that's sure what he's doing to me.

Without saying a word, he stalks toward the garage and throws the door open, revealing a—

"Oh, no. There's no way in hell I'm getting on the back of that," I state.

"What's wrong, Princess. Scared?" he taunts, his voice as cold as ice.

Throwing my shoulders back and pulling up my big girl pants, I take a step forward.

"You're not insured to drive that. You're not old

enough." I'm taking a risk, seeing as my knowledge of motorbikes is about as pathetic as that of guns. But it looks like a big and fast motherfucker to me.

"I'm more than capable of handling it. Now, are you coming, or do I have to figure out a way to tell your father that I left his defiant, pain-in-the-arse daughter here to walk home?"

He wouldn't. Even the devil himself wouldn't be stupid enough to go up against my father's requests like that. But even knowing that, it's not enough to douse the fire that's burning in the pit of my stomach.

"I think I'd rather take my chances on foot. Thanks though."

Hiking my bag up higher on my shoulder, I turn my back on him before he has a chance to say any more and take off toward the deserted street beyond the house.

I almost make it to the path which will lead me fuck knows where before his fingers wrap around my upper arm and I'm hauled back into his solid body. I might know whereabouts we are in the country, but anything past that is a mystery to me right now.

His hot breath dances over my ear, and my traitorous body shudders in response to his proximity.

"Now is not the time to test me, Calli." His voice is deep and laced with the threat of violence.

"What are you going to do? Drug me again and throw me on the back of it regardless?"

"If I have to," he mutters, dragging me back toward

the garage and out of sight of anyone who might drive down this sleepy road.

"I've been given an order, and I'm expected to comply no matter what."

"Pfft," I hiss as he drags my bag from my shoulder and stuffs it into a compartment on the bike. "Don't give me that shit. You've been put on ice. You're not a Cirillo soldier right now, so you can tell my dad to suck it."

A deep growl rumbles in the back of his throat before he stalks toward me, his hand shooting out to collar my throat.

"Careful, soldier. My daddy will shoot you dead in a heartbeat for putting your hands on me," I hiss, more than willing to play this bullshit game if he is.

His nostrils flare and his breaths rush past his parted lips.

For the briefest of seconds, I swear I've broken him. The darkness in his eyes cracks, and my breath catches in my throat.

But then, as fast as it appeared, it's gone again, shattering my hopes into even tinier pieces than they already are.

"I'll take my chances, if it's all the same to you, Princess."

I bare my teeth at him in irritation, but all he does is smirk.

Yeah, I didn't think for a second that made it at all intimidating.

"I'm gonna get on the bike, and you're going to

follow. Daddy wants his princess locked back up in her castle, and that's how this is going to go."

"Maybe I was wrong," I mutter when he's finally released me and taken a step toward me. "Maybe everyone hasn't been underestimating you. Maybe you are just a cold, heartless wanker."

He sucks in a sharp breath at my words, but that's the only reaction he gifts me with before he kicks the bike from its stand and pushes it out of the garage, closing and locking the door behind him.

Throwing his leg over the beast of a machine, he glances over at me, a barely veiled threat of what he might do should I refuse his instruction shining bright in his eyes.

"Hide as much as you like, devil boy. I see you. I see your mask, your act. Your lies."

"Get on the motherfucking bike," he hisses.

With little other option, I finally do as I'm told.

Putting my foot on the little handle thing, I throw my leg over and settle myself behind him, wishing like hell there could be some kind of barrier between us right now.

His arse nestles perfectly between my thighs, and I silently curse him out.

"Put this on," he demands, passing me a helmet. "And do it up tight."

"Yes, boss."

I do as I'm told, and by the time the thing is secured on my head, the engine is rumbling beneath me and Daemon is impatiently waiting to take off.

"Hold on."

"I am," I say sweetly, my fingers wrapping around the handles on either side of my hips.

"Not what I meant," he growls, reaching back and wrapping his fingers around my wrists.

My hands are tugged from the bike, and in a heartbeat, my arms are wrapping around his waist, my palms pressed to his tense abs.

"No, I—" I try to pull my arms free, but he holds me in position too tightly.

"Do as you're told, Callista."

"I hate you," I seethe. "I really fucking hate you." Those words are so far from the truth it's laughable, but right now, they're exactly what I want him to believe.

"Good. You should."

Before I get to even think about a response to that, he guns the engine and I have no choice but to hold on for dear life as he takes the sleepy street at a dangerous speed.

If I didn't know any better, I'd say he was trying to outrun his demons. But we all know the truth. He's driving straight toward them.

18

DAEMON

I've experienced some hellish situations in my almost eighteen years. But sitting on my bike with the girl I crave more than anything wrapped around me and holding on for dear life is one of the most torturous situations I've ever endured.

I should have left her holding the handles. But my need for her touch, even now, is too much to deny.

By the time we pull up at Evan's house, my jaw is aching from gritting my teeth the whole journey back to the city.

My need to turn around and take her away again burns through me. But as much as I might want that, I know I can't. I knew all this time that Calli wasn't, and never could be, mine. I knew this day was coming, I just tried my best to push it to the periphery of my mind and pretend it didn't exist.

Her hold on me loosens as I slow the bike and pull

toward the tall gates that guard this part of the Cirillo estate.

Soldiers in head-to-toe black appear the second they open, evidence that Evan's words about extra security are true.

Flipping up my visor, I let them see my face before they lift the guns that are more than obviously tucked inside their jackets.

"Daemon," the older of the two greets.

In no mood for a catch up, I nod my head and pull forward.

The short drive up to the house is the most agonising of my life. Pain slices through me as I picture her walking through the front door in only a few seconds and not even bothering to look back.

It's how it should be. But that doesn't matter, because it's going to rip me to shreds.

The moment I pull to a stop, the front door opens and both Evan and Nico step out, their eyes locked on us as they stalk down the steps toward us.

"I said bring her back safely," Evan scoffs, eyeing the bike I obviously shouldn't be riding beneath us.

"We're here in one piece, aren't we?" I snap, making his brows shoot up at my backchat.

I'm not usually one to say anything, especially to do with a job. But it seems that Calli has changed me in more ways than I thought, because right now, I'd take my chances and pull my gun on my underboss if it meant I could keep her.

"Careful, soldier," Evan warns, concern flashing through his eyes.

I kill the engine, and Calli's arms finally drop from my body.

Grief washes through me, the promise of the darkness right on the horizon threatening to swallow me whole.

I need to get home before that happens. I refuse to allow anyone else to see just how walking away from her, pretending she's nothing, pretending that the past week hasn't meant anything to me slays me.

"Daddy," Calli sings in a sweet-as-fuck voice before jumping into his arms.

I can't help but do a double take at her actions. They're so... fake.

But then I guess mine are too right now as I keep my steel mask locked in place.

"I assume you didn't cause Daemon too many problems," Evan says, amusement filling his tone.

"If you mean, was I nice to the guy holding me captive for a week, then no, not overly."

"Well, you're safe. That is all that matters."

She makes some disgruntled agreement to that statement before turning back to me.

The second her eyes collide with mine, everything I've ever wished for over the past ten years is shredded. I'd hoped to see hate in her eyes, anger, frustration. But what stares back at me is just... nothing. And it hits me harder than I ever thought it would.

I'm frozen, locked in her cold, hard stare.

If I were in a better place, I might recognise it as the same one I've spent years perfecting. But as it is, all I can focus on is agony as another part of my heart is ripped away.

Why did you let her in? You knew this was going to happen.

Her eyes widen in expectation as her hand lands on her waist, her hip popping out with an attitude I'm not used to seeing from her.

"I need my bag," she seethes.

"You go inside. I'll get your stuff," Nico offers. "I need to have a chat with Daemon anyway."

Panic grips my chest, making it hard to drag in the air I need for a few seconds as I finally rip my eyes from Calli in favour of her brother.

He's staring at me as if he doesn't know me. And I swear to fuck, as his fist clenches at his side, I see my death waiting for me at the end of whatever it is he wants to talk about.

"And life returns to normal once more," Calli mutters under her breath before turning away from me.

Evan catches her before she hits the stairs that lead to the front door.

"It's good to have you back. We missed you."

"Missed you too, Dad," she says before marching forward.

And just as I predicted, she never once looks back at me.

It fucking guts me.

The darkness of Nico's shadow finally makes me look back at him.

Not willing to see the questions and need for death in his eyes, I turn away and grab Calli's bag. The second it's free, I shove it into Nico's chest.

"My job is done. Your little princess is safe," I grunt.

By some fucking miracle, his entire demeanour changes as he finds the straps of her bag and drops it to his side.

"Thanks, man. We really appreciate you putting up with her while we sorted this shit out."

"Didn't really have much choice, did I?"

"You know they're just trying to push you to be your best," he says, telling me without so many words that he's now aware of the situation too.

"Because a certificate with a couple of grades on it makes me a better soldier," I scoff.

"I get it, man. I really fucking do."

"Right. Well, I'm gonna—" I thumb over my shoulder and back toward my bike.

"Yeah. I'm gonna take this down to the angry girl in the basement. I thought she was gonna be pissed, but I wasn't expecting that."

"She's had to put up with me for company for a week. What did you expect?"

"You're a good person, D. Don't let what's going on right now make you think otherwise."

"Sure," I agree, throwing my leg over my bike, more than ready to make my escape.

Movement in the kitchen window catches my attention, and my heart jumps into my throat that she might be standing there watching me, but then Evan reappears from the front door and I realise my hope was pointless.

"Thank you, Daemon. I'm grateful for everything you've done to keep her safe."

You wouldn't be saying that if you knew the truth.

"I've had worse jobs," I mutter, throwing my leg over my bike, more than ready to get the hell out of here now my cargo has been delivered.

"Go and enjoy some peace," he says with a laugh. "I can't imagine you got a lot of that in the past week with that with my girl talking your ear off."

"She's not been that bad. She was mostly angry and screaming at me."

"Well, yes. I can picture that too."

Can you?

With my face still set in its stone mask, I nod at the two of them and slam the visor of my helmet down, leaving the spare one that Calli wore on the gravel beneath Evan and Nico's feet. It might be wishful thinking, but maybe, just maybe, I'll find an excuse to have her on the back of mine again one day.

Without another word, I gun the engine, sending a spray of stones across the driveway as I take off toward the gates. I barely pause long enough to thank the soldiers who allow me to escape as I set my sights on home.

On the quiet solitude of my flat.

I've loved that place since before I moved in. The second Dad mentioned Damien and Evan's plans for the buildings, I was all in.

I'd had every intention of leaving home at the first possible opportunity. I just assumed I would have to finish Knight's Ridge first. So when the opportunity arose to have my own place sooner, I jumped on it. I'd have moved in with it half-finished if I had to. Anything to get out of Dad's house and away from the memories—nightmares—I have from that house. The only worse place in the world is my grandparents' old house. Or more so, our grandfather's shed.

A shudder runs up my spine just thinking about that place.

Gran was kind enough, but I got the sense, even as a kid, that she'd been jaded by the mafia life. She and Grandad had been together since they were kids, and he was as brutal as they came, so I can't imagine she had the easiest of lives. She put up with it though. I just have no idea if that was through fear or love. Something tells me it was probably the former.

A pained sigh rips through the enclosed space of my helmet as I turn off the road and into the outside car park for our building. The last time I was here was the beginning of the best week of my life.

I told myself time and time again while we were there that I needed to take every second as if it were going to be our last together.

And I thought I had.

Until it was over.

Now I know I never appreciated her smiles enough, savoured her touch, memorised the sound of her laughter, her moans.

The roller door to the underground car park opens for me as I drive toward it, and I quickly allow myself to be swallowed up by the building.

If I get my way, it'll be where I stay until I have little choice but to leave for school.

I can't lie, after revising with Calli and letting her explain things to me in her own way, things do seem a little more possible. But I fear that the second I get those books back out and am forced to try and figure it all out alone again, all the good she achieved will be smashed to jagged, useless pieces that, just like my heart, will never fit back together properly again.

My car is parked exactly where I left it when I dumped it before riding my bike into the back of the van we used for our kidnap mission. The bag of stuff I took in case I did stay in those tipis with the others still sitting on the back seat.

Grabbing it, I walk past Alex's empty space and head up, more than ready to lock myself in my flat and drown my sorrows in as much alcohol as I can find and stomach.

19

CALLI

"Callista," Mum breathes, an almost-real smile pulling at her lips as she pushes from the stool in the kitchen.

That fake happiness falls almost instantly when she takes in my outfit, her lip peeling back in disgust.

"I rode on the back of Daemon's bike, Mum. What did you expect me to be wearing? A summer dress and heels?"

"I thought a week away would have allowed you to relax. You look stressed."

"Right, well, being banished from town and forced to live with a psycho for a week isn't actually all that fun, just so you know." I cringe at my own bitter words, but I can't stop them from falling from my lips

"Did you at least get some studying done?" Mum asks hopefully.

"Yes," I hiss, marching toward the fridge and pulling a can of Coke out, much to Mum's horror.

"You shouldn't be drinking that," she chastises.

"I don't think one can of Coke will frazzle my brain cells," I mutter.

"Callista, I'm not sure I like this attitude on you," she calls after me as I turn my back on her and hightail it out of the room.

"Yeah, well, that's just tough," I murmur under my breath as I head for my basement.

I should feel some kind of contentment being back in the only home I've ever known, I'm sure. But I don't. I feel out of place, like a piece of furniture that doesn't match the rest of the insanely expensive shit Mum likes to fill the house with.

It makes me realise that I've always felt this way to a point. I just never had somewhere else I felt more at home before. But being in that beach house with Daemon... it was just so... right. So easy and relaxed. I've never had that here. I'm always on edge, wondering if Mum or Dad are going to appear at some point and tell me that I'm not quite fitting their incredibly high and unachievable expectations.

I make my way down to my basement in the hope that my own space will make me feel better. But as I descend the stairs and push through the door, my scent might be right, but the place has been tidied within an inch of its life. It will have been Jocelyn, not Mum, and that makes me feel a little better, but still, there's a huge part of me that just wanted to fall into the chaos of my life instead of this perfect, fake version.

With a sigh, I push forward, cracking open the can in my hand and walking toward the floor-to-ceiling windows.

My eyes scan the tree line that runs down the side of the house, searching for a branch that Daemon might use to look in on me.

He wasn't lying about that being where he hides when he watches me. I saw the raw honesty in his eyes as he confessed, so I know his perch is out there somewhere.

Movement makes my heart jump into my throat, but then one of Dad's soldiers emerges from behind the trees, scanning the area as if he's in a freaking war zone.

"No," I breathe, already knowing what the sight of him means.

I reach forward and grip the door handle. It's pointless, but I still do it, even when Dad's voice rings through the space. "They're locked."

I tug harder, my heart racing as adrenaline spikes through me.

"No," I spit, wheeling around to face him. "You can't do this to me."

"Until I know it's completely safe."

"Then why am I here?" I ask, already beginning to sound like a mad woman.

"Because we missed you." A bitter laugh falls from my lips before the truth finally emerges. "And your mum desperately wanted you here for her party."

"Ah, of course. Now it all makes sense," I mutter,

walking to the corner of the room where the blind controls are and quickly lowering them, blocking out both the sun and Dad's men who are patrolling the estate. The guards at the gates should have been a clue to how serious this all is.

"You should have just left me there. At least I wasn't locked in a cage."

"Callista, it's not like that. It's just—"

"Just what, Dad?" I ask, my hands landing on my hips as I glare at him.

Guilt flashes through his eyes. The sight of it makes my heart sink. Dad never shows his vulnerability, just like someone else I used to know, so it's really saying something that he's letting it show so obviously.

"I let you walk out of his house, Calli."

"Because you were being an overbearing—" I swallow down the next word as Dad's brow lifts.

"Yeah," he concedes. "I was. I should have explained properly."

"You should have done that many, many times in my life. But just like those, you chose to cover it up, to try and pretend everything was okay. If you'd have just been honest, I might not have left like I did." Honestly, I'm not sure how that is. But I'd like to think that if Dad had said 'stop, the Italians are out for blood and it might end up being yours,' it might have made me question my choices that day.

"I know I should," he confesses, for the first time in

my life genuinely looking regretful for something he's done.

"I refuse to live down here like a prisoner."

"It's not safe."

"I thought everything was sorted. Hence why I'm here right now."

He hesitates. "Yes and no."

"What is that even meant to mean?"

"They're no longer after you specifically. But the threat against all of us is still there. War is still imminent. I refuse to put your life at risk more than it already is."

"Great," I mutter, longing for the freedom I had for the past week. We may not have actually left the house, but at least I could walk down onto the beach. Apparently, even the garden is a risk here right now.

"If you need to leave, you'll take your brother or one of the boys with you for protection."

"You know, I could protect myself. All you have to do is teach me." It's a lie. Daemon, and Alex while he was with us, did a damn good job of teaching me. I'm feeling more confident than I ever have about being able to do what might be necessary if something were to happen again.

He nods in agreement and my chin almost hits the floor. "I will. I won't allow you to be helpless again."

"Uh..." I stutter, shocked to my core. If I'd have known that all it would have taken was to be abducted to make him see sense, then I'd have done it years ago... maybe.

"I've got to go out and sort a few things. But I'm going to take you out to the range. And I've spoken to Nico and Stella about giving you some self-defence lessons."

"You have?" I breathe, not believing what I'm hearing.

"I'm man enough to admit that I was wrong, Calli. Your mother, she never wanted to be involved in any of that, and she convinced me that you wouldn't be either. But I'm seeing that you're more your father's daughter than your mother's."

"You're only just noticing that now?" I ask.

"This life... it's—"

"Dangerous, scary, brutal. I know, Dad. I know all those things. But it's my life too. I don't want to hide. I don't want to be weak and vulnerable. I don't want to be this useless member of the family that you all feel you need to protect. I'm not that girl, Dad."

"I know, and I'm sorry I assumed you'd be happy to be."

I stare at him, my mouth agape.

"It's so good to have you back, kiddo."

I smile at him, unable to keep the same level of irritation with him as when he first walked down here.

"Thank you," I breathe, falling forward into his chest.

His arms wrap around my small frame, and I instantly feel like a little girl again.

"Please, Calli. Be sensible. We need you to be safe.

If you need to go anywhere, call me. Call one of the boys."

"I will," I promise. I'm not really in the mood for being kidnapped for real, after all.

"Your mother's party is Saturday night." Brilliant. "But we're having a meal with friends tomorrow that she expects you to attend."

"I'm sure it would be better to just—"

"Please, Calli. Just do this one thing for me." Just like every time he uses that tone, I find myself instantly crumbling.

"Okay, fine," I agree through gritted teeth. "I'll be there, and I promise to call the guys if I want to go anywhere, but you need to keep your end of the deal."

"Thank you," he breathes, pulling me close once more and dropping a kiss on my head.

The second he turns and leaves me to unpack the bag he brought down with him, the silence and solitude of my basement swamps me.

I haven't been alone for a week. Whenever I needed something, someone to talk to, a shoulder to cry on, he was there. And now... he's just gone.

Gone, as if what we had meant nothing.

I'm busy putting everything where I want it once more when the window in the single door that leads outside catches my eye.

Something tells me that he's not going to be out there, but there's a little bit of doubt that flickers through me that forces me into action.

As I cut a piece of card to size, I tell myself that it's

to keep the guard dogs that Dad has out there from peeping in on me, but I know I'm only lying to myself. None of those men would risk my father's wrath by taking advantage of the security job they've been given.

I breathe a sigh of relief when I cover it up.

Surely, he wouldn't risk getting caught by coming to watch me. He's done everything he can to this point to keep me his dirty little secret.

A sob rips up my chest at that thought, because that's all I was to him.

A dirty little secret. Some twisted holiday romance. A little bit of fun while he was forced to babysit me like a good little soldier.

"Oh God," I gasp, barely holding myself together.

All of this... it was just a job.

I was just a job.

I stumble back until my legs hit the bed, and then I fall down onto it.

Grief, pain, and regrets all collide and send me deeper into the pits of despair.

I allowed myself to think it was real. To believe everything he said to me.

Was it all lies, bullshit, and manipulation?

Their voices hit my ears the second they descend the stairs, and I smile for the first time since being rudely awoken this morning.

"Come out, come out, wherever you are," Stella sings as I finish washing my hands.

After my epic meltdown earlier, I gave myself a good talking to and put myself in the shower in the hope of washing away both the evidence of the tears that stained my cheeks and the devastation that seemed to ooze out of every pore.

I pulled on some of the sexiest underwear in my drawer, not because I had plans for anyone to see it, just because I needed something, anything to make me feel less like I was dying inside. I found my favourite dress and teamed it with a pair of leggings, and styled my hair and applied my make-up as if I was hitting the town.

Both Stella and Emmie are standing in the middle of my basement as I emerge from the bathroom with concerned frowns on their brows.

"Hey, what's wrong?"

"Calli," they both gasp, rushing over and pulling me into a three-woman hug.

"Uh... have I missed something?" I mumble, crushed between the two of them.

We've chatted most days while I've been away, and they've been normal. But this... this is not normal.

"We've been worried about you," Stella confesses.

"W-why?" I ask once they finally release me.

"We didn't know where you were, and shit's been tense around here. The boys are keeping schtum about everything no matter how many times we blow them and—"

"Whoa. I missed you both too, but any chance we can hold off on the blow job chat for at least thirty minutes?"

"Fine," Emmie says with an animated sigh. "But you know how much we love talking about them."

"Don't I just," I mutter, walking over to the fridge. "Do you want a drink? I've got... fuck," I sigh as reality hits me in the face like a wet fish. "Water or..." I turn the carton around, my nose wrinkling as I read the label. "Coconut water."

"Wow, you really love us, huh?" Stella muttered. "Lucky for you, we predicted this and brought supplies." She lifts a bag before dumping it on the counter and dragging out the contents. "And we've already ordered Chinese. We sweet-talked one of the guys at the gate. He's going to text me when it arrives so we can sneak out and get it. Your mum will never know you ate sugar."

"Fuck my mother," I scoff, reaching for one of the bottles of cider she placed on the counter. The second I've found my bottle opener, I knock the top off it and lift it to my lips, swallowing down mouthful after mouthful while my friends' concerned stares burn into me.

"Do you want to talk about it?" Emmie asks.

"What? How I was forced out of town for... 'my own good'," I say mocking my mum's voice. "Protected like a useless little girl because I clearly can't handle the hard shit?"

"Calli, I don't—" I glare at Stella.

"But you seemed so happy when you were away," Emmie says, her brows pinched tight in confusion.

"I was by the sea; the sun was shining. Everything always looks better that way. Now, I'm stuck down here and only allowed to go out if I have a fucking chaperone. Which I'm assuming you didn't have to get here."

"Uh... no. I've got this, though," Stella says with a wince, pulling a gun from the back of her jeans.

"Of course you do. I'm not allowed one of those either. I swear to God my parents think I'm eight. I mean, just look at this..."

Slamming my almost-empty bottle down on the counter, I storm toward my wardrobe and the other delight I found waiting for me when I unpacked earlier.

"What the hell are they?" Emmie asks, disgust dripping from each word.

"Pretty sure they're someone's grandma's clothes," Stella quips.

"I know you spent a week in some sleepy seaside place, but was shopping in their charity shops really necessary?"

"Ha ha ha," I say bitterly. "You're funny. I did not choose these."

"They've got Cassandra written all over them. They're basically imitations of the shit we threw out when you moved down here."

"They're hideous," Emmie says, pinching the fabric of one of the dresses between her thumb and forefinger.

"They're designer," I say, forcing myself to sound serious.

"Designer shit. Seriously, there is only one place for them." Emmie snatches both of the dresses and the hangers they're on and throws them into the corner of the room with a flourish.

"Pretty sure she wants me to wear them for the next two nights of hell."

"Her birthday party?" Stella confirms.

"Yep, and some bullshit meal tomorrow night."

"Well, at least we'll all be there for the party. And we've got time to get you replacement dresses, because you are not wearing those." Stella shoots a look at the heap of floral fabric. I'm surprised it doesn't go up in flames from the pure hatred in her eyes.

"Mum will kill me if I don't—"

"What did you say about your mom only minutes ago?" Stella asks, staring at me with encouraging eyes.

"Yeah, yeah. Okay. Give me more cider and let's order replacements. If she's going to lose her shit at me, I might as well look hot as fuck doing it."

"Amen to that." Stella raises her bottle of cider in salute before downing half of it in the most unladylike way I think I've ever seen.

A massive smile spreads across my face as I watch her.

Being ripped away from Daemon and our little sanctuary might still be eating at me, but being here with my girls helps soften the blow that he's left without even a word or a message about our time together.

"Grab your iPad, Cal. Let's get shopping," she demands, falling down onto my sofa.

"Why are all the blinds shut?" Emmie asks. "It's like... a perfect spring day outside."

"Huh," Stella mutters. "I'm surprised the princess of darkness even noticed the sun rose this morning."

"Fuck you. I saw it. It was shining off Theo's abs as he walked past the window in our bedroom naked, teasing me with my favourite plaything."

"Em—" I start to warn, but she quickly cuts me off.

"What? You said thirty minutes. It's been—" She glances at her phone.

"Exactly. As much as I appreciate the company, I don't need... that."

"You need to get laid," Emmie sings behind her bottle. "Who's coming to this dull-as-fuck party Saturday night? Any potential suitors for our Cirillo princess?"

Images of Daemon from our week away flicker through my mind. Watching him emerge from the sea with water running over his muscles, him smiling down at me, the way he held me as he taught me how to aim my gun.

Shit.

"In your minds or my parents'?"

"Ours, obviously. No parent would be planning the sort of thing we want for you."

"Then none, because any boys that bad would be too terrified of the wrath of my father and brother."

"Still think it should be Alex," Stella mutters. "He'd show you a—"

"Does he know I'm back?"

"No idea. He hasn't really been about. Think he's been at Stefanos's place."

"Seriously, what is the deal with that?" Emmie asks. "He's got his own flat, his own freedom, yet he keeps running home to daddy. Why?"

"Does it matter?" I ask, in the hope of steering the conversation away from either of the Deimos twins.

The second Alex learns that the two of us are home, I have no doubt that he'll turn up for a visit, and quite frankly, that's something I'm happy to put off for as long as possible.

They both stare at me, their eyes narrowing.

"What's wrong?" Stella asks, obviously reading something in my expression that I wasn't willing to talk about.

"N-nothing."

"Has something happened with Alex?"

"What? No, of course not."

They both stare at me as if they don't believe me.

"Seriously, nothing has happened with Alex. He was nothing but a gentleman in the tipi." While he listened to his twin brother be the total opposite.

Heat blooms on my cheeks and I inwardly groan.

I'm never going to keep this under wraps if I can't even keep my cool when their names are mentioned.

What the hell is it going to be like the next time I'm forced to be in a room with them?

With him.

20

———

DAEMON

"**B**ro, unlock the fucking door," Alex booms, but I don't move from my position on the sofa where I fell after reluctantly showering her scent off me.

The memories in my head are bad enough. But being able to smell her, too?

Fucking torture.

"Go away," I call back, not even bothering to move my arm from covering my eyes.

It's still light out. Despite the fact that I've closed my curtains to allow me to drown in my own dark regrets and misery, I know the sun is going to be sneaking in through the cracks the second I open my eyes. And if I let him in, it'll only make it worse.

Alex has always been the light to my dark. The humour to my misery.

I don't fucking need that right now.

I just need the rest of the bottle of vodka sitting on

my coffee table and the sleeping pills that are in my bathroom. Only then will the pain ripping through my chest lessen.

"DAEMON," Alex barks. "I'm not fucking about. Open this door or I'll fucking smash it in."

I don't react. Why would I? There is no fucking chance of him smashing it down. It's locked up tighter than a duck's arsehole with the deadbolts on.

The only way to get inside is to override the security system.

"Shit," I hiss, knowing full well that Alex would stoop that low in order to get to me if he had to. "What do you want?" I shout back.

"To see you. Is that too much to fucking ask?"

Yes.

"I'll see you tomorrow, yeah? Just..." *Fuck off and let me drown alone.*

"Nah, man. It's not happening. We need to talk after everything that happened with—"

"Don't," I bark. "Don't fucking say it."

"Yeah, see? You fucking need to let me in."

"Jesus fucking Christ," I mutter quietly to myself as I swing my legs from the sofa.

"I swear to God, Daemon. I'll— finally," he hisses when I disengage the first lock.

"What?" I bark the second I pull the door open and just glare at him through the two-inch crack.

"Jesus. You look like shit," he says, his brows pinching in concern.

"Great. You've seen me. Can you fuck off now?"

He glares at me, silently informing me that there is exactly zero chance of that happening.

"Dude, what the fuck happened? You were so... happy."

At that enlightening comment, I release the door and storm back to the living room for my vodka.

Inviting himself in, as expected, his footsteps grow closer as his concerned stare burns into my back.

"What happened?"

"Nothing. I brought her home as requested. Life may now continue as normal," I state, the bitterness in my tone making me wince.

"Normal as in you walk around miserable as fuck, trying to forget that you're madly fucking in love with her?"

I spin around so fast that the room blurs around me, making me wonder if I'm about to hit the deck.

Reaching out, I press my palm to the cold wall and close my eyes for a few seconds.

"Yeah, I think you've had enough of that, don't you?" Alex says, attempting to tug the bottle from my grasp.

"Fuck you," I snarl. "You don't have the slightest fucking clue of what I need right now."

His brows lift, but he doesn't back down. He doesn't so much as flinch.

"Nah, you're not really my type. Too much cock and all that."

I bare my teeth at him, my free hand curling into a

fist, more than ready to wipe the smirk right off his face.

"What happened with Calli, Daemon? What have you done?"

"My fucking job, arsehole."

I'm too lost in my own head, the moment she turned her back and walked into the house as if I wasn't even standing there playing on repeat over and over, ripping my heart out again and again.

"You've hurt her, haven't you?"

"I wouldn't lay a fucking hand on her and you know it," I snarl, getting right in his face.

"I didn't mean physically," he grunts, his forehead bumping against mine as he stands toe to toe with me. "Tell me what you did."

"Why? So you can go and dry her fucking tears and prove to her that she's been fucking the wrong twin all this time?"

An angry growl rumbles deep in his throat.

"That's what all this is about, isn't it? You want her. You want her and you can't stand that for once I've won. That I beat you."

Crack.

His knuckles hit my jaw with a brain-rattling punch.

Pain shoots down my neck, the right side of my face burning from the collision. And I fucking relish in it.

I need this.

I need to feel pain from somewhere other than the

black, gaping hole in my chest where my heart should be.

Alex might think I love her.

But I can't.

How can I?

I was born with a fucked-up heart and I'm pretty sure the inability to love anyone. What I feel for her… it's an obsession. An unhealthy obsession that she would be better away from.

"More," I growl when he doesn't immediately hit me again.

"I'm not feeding your fucked-up need for pain, Daemon. I came to help, to talk."

"I'm not interested in that. Just make me pay for fucking her over. Make me hurt, make me bleed, and then walk out of here and go to her. We both know she'd be better off with you anyway."

"Yeah," he says with a sad laugh. "She probably would be, looking at the state of you, but I think it's a bit fucking late for that, don't you? She's just as fucking gone for you as you are her. Don't you see the way she looks at you?"

"With pity and confusion like everyone else?" Lifting the bottle to my lips, I down a few more shots before slamming it on the coffee table.

"You're a fucking idiot. Open your fucking eyes and see what's right in front of you."

"A girl who's too good for me. A girl I never should have touched. A girl who has the world at her feet and doesn't need to be dragged down by the likes of me."

He stares at me, his chest heaving as if he's just run a fucking marathon, but he doesn't give me what I need. What I crave.

Instead, he just continues to rip shreds off me just like she's unknowingly done all day.

"A girl who fucking loves you, man. A girl who would do fucking anything for you, even if it meant hurting herself in the process. She's the best thing that's ever happened to you. And if you think I'm going to watch you rip both of your hearts out because of your insecurities, then you really need to fucking think again."

It's me who makes the first move this time, my fist colliding with Alex's face with a sickening crunch before blood begins pouring from his nose.

An animalistic growl rips through the air a beat before he flies at me, finally caving to his dark need to hurt me over what I've done. All the air rushes from my lungs as his fist lands in my stomach, forcing me to bend over, but I manage to recover before his second hit comes.

Reality finally vanishes and I fully let myself drown in the dark abyss I'm so used to living in.

***

The first thing I feel when I wake is agony. But I'm not sure what hurts worse—my face or the empty void in my chest.

"Fuck," I groan, flipping onto my back, every inch

of me aching with a delicious, addictive kind of pain that I know I'll never get enough of.

It's almost enough to override that in my chest. Almost.

Another loud groan rips through the air before something warm touches my hand.

"What the—" I sit up, immediately reaching for the knife that lives under my pillow.

Although I quickly release it again when I discover who's decided to make use of the other side of my bed.

"I've got a fucking spare room, prick," I mutter, my tongue thick from the lingering effects of vodka and whatever else I might have found last night, and my voice rough as fuck from sleep.

"Thought you might wake up crying and need me."

"Un-fucking-likely," I grunt.

Pushing onto my elbows, I attempt to sit up. I soon discover it's a fucking stupid thing to do when my head swims and my stomach lurches.

"Do not fucking chuck up on me," Alex warns as I crash back to the pillows and throw my arm over my eyes.

"Fuck off," I grunt, not interested in an audience while I drown in my hangover and misery.

"I told you not to drink so much."

"Well, I'm so fucking sorry for disappointing you," I deadpan. "Although you should be used to it by now."

"Bro," he breathes.

"No," I snap, lifting my arm and glaring at him. "No. You don't get to lie there and tell me all the things I should and shouldn't have done. You have no idea what I've been through. What Calli and I had. So I do not need your advice on the situation. She is where she belongs, and she is safe. That's what's important right now."

"But—"

"No, Alex," I bark, swallowing down the bile that rushes up my throat when I force my body to stand upright. "I don't need your advice right now. I just need you to leave."

I storm toward my en suite, swinging the door closed behind me, wincing the second the bang hits my ears.

Fuck. I really am fucking hanging.

I turn the shower on, twisting the dial to cold before taking a piss and brushing my teeth, all the while fighting the need to barf.

My body trembles the second I step under the stream of ice-cold water, but I don't cower away from it. I force myself to stand there and endure the pain. It's what I deserve for the way I ended things yesterday.

I startle when Alex slams his fist down on the door. He twists the handle, but he doesn't get very far because I engaged the lock the second I pushed away from it.

"Fuck off, A."

"Yeah, yeah. I'm fucking going. I just wanted to say one more thing."

"Great," I mutter to myself, knowing that whatever nugget is about to fall from his lips is going to be the hardest blow to take.

"I just want you to know that I think you're a fucking coward. All my life, I've been in awe of you. Of your strength, your ability to let all the bullshit roll off your back. To focus on what you really want and ensure you get it. But you fucked up with this, Bro. And not only have you disappointed me, but you've fucking let her down, and she's the best fucking thing that ever happened to you."

My palm collides with the tiles with a painful slap as my heart races so hard it makes my head spin.

"Think about that, yeah? And when you've grown a pair of balls, go talk to her. In the meantime, I'll be there for her, because she deserves a friend if nothing else."

Nothing but the sound of my heaving breaths follows that statement.

Slamming my palm down one more time, I step forward, pressing my brow to the wall and closing my eyes tight as I run through all the things I should have done differently in the past few weeks, well... months really, because all this started with my fucking pathetic self-control on Halloween.

"Who the fuck pissed on your kitten?" Isla says after inviting herself into my flat later that afternoon.

I grunt in response as I stare down at the textbook before me, trying to figure out why none of this shit makes sense now I don't have a hot girl in a bikini sitting on my lap at the same time. Doesn't exactly bode well for the real exams, because I'm pretty sure a lap dance would be frowned upon.

Ripping my eyes from the bullshit book, I find her staring down at me with her hands on her hips.

"Don't think I've ever seen you studying before, D. Something is definitely up."

I glare at her, my eyebrow quirking.

"Are you really going to stand there, pretending to be innocent?" I ask. There's no way her turning up this afternoon is a coincidence. Alex has called in backup. I knew it was coming—it's why I didn't reengage the locks when I finally emerged from the bathroom. Honestly, I was expecting it to be Mum. I'm not sure if I'm disappointed or relieved that I've actually got my straight-talking, gives-zero-shits-about-anything best friend.

"Still being a little bitch then, I see," she mutters, kicking off her Vans and falling down on my opposite sofa like she owns the fucking place.

"Make yourself at home," I mutter when she rests her ankles on the armrest and her head on one of my cushions.

"When don't I? What are you doing?"

I glower at her. Most people would probably cower, but Isla isn't most people.

"Revising. What the fuck does it look like?"

"Honestly? Torture. That frown on your brow is so deep, you'll probably never get rid of it."

My glare only gets more deadly, but she's not having any of it.

Lifting her hand, she points at my face. "You can turn that shit on someone else. Hell will freeze over the day you scare me, D."

"More's the pity. Maybe I'd get some peace if you had a soul like normal people," I scoff.

"Ouch, my blackened heart bleeds," she gasps, pressing her hand to her chest as if she's in pain.

"You're a dick."

"And you're a pussy by all accounts, so what gives?"

"I'm gonna kick his arse for dragging you here."

"Feel free. Can I watch? There's nothing I like more than watching soldiers bleed."

"There is something wrong with you," I mutter.

"Takes one to know one. So, what's got you resorting to the distraction of school work? And the real answer this time. I've had my fill of bullshit this week."

My lips part to comment on that, but she's quicker than me.

"We're not talking about my shit, we're talking

about yours." She pins me with a look that stops me from arguing.

"Dad's taking me off shift unless I pass this shit," I say, knocking the book that's hanging over the edge of the coffee table and flipping it over. I figure it's the easiest of my issues to deal with right now. And if I'm lucky, she won't see through my bullshit to know it's the least of my problems after letting Calli believe I wasn't interested in trying to fight for us.

"That explains a lot."

"Yeah, because I'll never fucking pass."

"Shut the fuck up, D. You're more capable than you give yourself credit for."

Fuck my life, I'm fed up of people saying that.

"I guess we'll find out how true that is when the results come out."

"So you're off the clock until the exams or until the results?"

"Fuck knows," I say, falling back against the sofa and lifting my feet to the coffee table.

"You know what you need?"

"Nope, but something tells me that you're going to point it out."

"A night out." She beams at me like it's the best idea in the world.

"Seriously?"

"Hell yeah. All work and no play makes the devil a boring motherfucker. Plus, get a few drinks in you and you might actually man up and tell me the fucking truth about what's really going on with you."

"I'm not going out."

"Okay, so just tell me then." She grins annoyingly and just waits.

"You're a pain in my arse, Isla Kallis."

"But you love me anyway. Go get dressed. I've got a friend who's playing an open mic night at Rick's. It'll be chill."

"A night out with you is never chill, I."

"And we're never usually out trying to distract you from a broken heart, so apparently it's the day for change."

"I haven't got a bro—"

"Lie to me again, D. I fucking dare you."

21

CALLI

Despite the ear defenders that Dad insisted I wear, the gunshots from either side of me still reverberate through my body as Nico and Dad fire shot after shot at the targets they set out.

I hold my gun up, exactly as I'd been taught.

They went right back to basics, and I let them. I mean, I could hardly tell them that Daemon had spent a good chunk of our time together doing the exact same thing. He was meant to be protecting me and nothing else.

I allowed them to think that everything I'd learned was because of them. And I was glad I did when both their chests puffed out with pride when I hit the target the first time.

It felt good, proving them wrong after all these years of being smothered by them, but mostly, it just hurt. Like everything seems to right now.

The girls helped yesterday. They stayed with me

until late, finding any way they could to make me laugh despite not knowing I was dying inside.

Guilt ate at me for not telling them. But I figured, what was the point?

Daemon made his choice. He chose the Family, something that shouldn't have really been a shock to me. The Family was Daemon's entire life. It was foolish of me to think for even a second that I might have seriously rivalled that in any way.

Silence falls around us, and eyes turn my way.

'What's wrong?' Dad asks, although I'm forced to lip-read it as his voice barely even rumbles through the ear defenders.

"Nothing," I say, forcing my pain and regrets deep inside the box they should be locked up in and focusing on the task at hand.

Aiming, I wrap my finger around the trigger. My entire body jolts with the force of the shot when I finally fire.

The power, the control, the danger... fuck it's a heady feeling. One I already know I could get very used to.

The first time when Stella snuck me out here while all the guys were on a job, I was hesitant. There was still a lingering part of the good, smothered little princess within me that wanted to follow the rules and expectations that had been demanded of me.

But the moment I wrapped my hand around the weapon and felt its weight, something just felt right.

Just like it does now, as I hit the target again and again until my clip runs empty.

"Holy shit, baby C. That was epic," a familiar, impressed voice says from behind me the second I pull my ear defenders off.

I know exactly who that voice belongs to. But I can't help the hope its recognition drags up in my body.

"Fuck, man. Did I miss a fight night or something?" Nico asks, making my heart jump into my throat.

If Alex is wearing the war wounds from a fight, then surely there's only one person he's got into it with.

Sucking in a deep breath and swallowing a little strength down with it, I spin around.

My chin damn near hits the floor as I take in his face. Guilt swirls around in my gut, achingly aware that I'm the reason for his pain.

"Alex," I breathe, my gun falling limply at my side as I take a step toward him.

"I'm good, Cal. Wipe that concern off your face."

"I bet the other guy looks worse, right, man?" Nico says lightly, reloading his gun, ready for another round.

"Obviously," Alex scoffs, but he winces as his eyes hold mine, an apology washing through them.

Without any warning, the bang of Nico's gun rips through me, forcing a little squeal of shock from my lips, and I curse myself for acting in the exact way they've seen me for the past seventeen years.

"You'll need to swallow those noises if you want us to take you seriously, Sis."

I grit my teeth and purse my lips as I bite back my response that will only result in us bickering. I don't have the strength for that right now.

"I think I'm gonna call it a day. My shoulder's aching," I lie, dropping my ear defenders and gun to the cabinet.

"No worries, kiddo. You've had a hard morning. Go chill out before tonight. Apparently, there's something to wear in your wardrobe."

A bitter laugh falls from my lips. "Oh yeah, I found it."

"That good?" Nico asks, having paused his latest round to eavesdrop on me and Dad.

He's more than aware of the monstrosities that our mother has dressed me in over the years.

I glare at him in response, letting him know silently that it is just *that* bad.

"Well. I can't wait to see it," he teases.

I suck in a breath, ready to shoot back a cutting remark, but I quickly release it again.

"I'm gonna go shower," I say, grabbing the hoodie that I abandoned on the chair and hanging it over my arm.

Now I've stopped, every inch of me is starting to ache.

I was woken at the arse crack of dawn this

morning when my brother bravely ripped my sheets from me and demanded I get my fat, untrained arse—his words, not mine—up and ready.

When Dad told me that Nico had agreed to train me, I didn't think that he would take it quite so seriously.

But there he was, staring down at me with determination filling his dark eyes.

He might never admit it, but deep down, I think he's actually excited about turning me into a bad-arse. I'm sure there are selfish reasons in there somewhere, but right now, I'm just glad that both he and Dad are on board with this.

I'm yet to discover what Mum thinks about the whole thing. But honestly, I really don't give a fuck.

"You need to be ready by seven," Dad calls as I walk away, quickly eating up the space Alex had put between us.

"Yeah, I'll be ready," I say, although my words are missing any kind of enthusiasm.

My eyes hold Alex's as I get closer. "I'm fine," I assure him. "Play with the boys, yeah?"

I take a step, ready to keep going, but he reaches out, catching my arm.

"Don't lie to me, Cal. I can see it in your eyes."

"It's done. Over. Time to move on."

"That's bullshit and you know it."

"Is it?"

Ripping my arm from his grip, I focus on the house in the distance and take off.

"Bro, I need some fucking competition here. The old man has lost his touch."

"Watch your mouth, kid, and remember who trained you in the first place."

"I do. Uncle Damien."

Shaking my head at their banter, I force myself to keep moving. Dark figures move in the tree line, their eyes burning into me, the reminder I really don't need that I'm being constantly watched and protected.

I get it. The Italians are a threat. But are they really stupid enough to take a hit at us on our own property? Probably not.

I grab a bottle of water, seeing as that's all the options I have in the main kitchen as well, and then head down to hide in my basement, hoping that Nico keeps Alex entertained for long enough that he won't feel the need to come down here and drag up everything I'm desperately trying to ignore.

I wanted to tell the girls everything last night. The truth burned through me to be honest about everything I've kept hidden from them all this time. But every time a silence came and the opportunity presented itself, the words just got stuck on my tongue.

So I kept my story straight, pretending that I'd been alone for the past week, all the while letting the lies poison my veins and fill me with even more bitterness and regret.

I downed half the bottle before I've even hit the basement, but instead of marching straight to my bathroom to wash off my epic workout with Nico, I head straight toward my bed and fall head first onto it.

I figure a little rest before getting ready for what is sure to be one of the most painful nights of my life is due.

I must have almost immediately passed out. It's not hard to imagine why, seeing as I spent most of the night before sobbing into my pillow in the hope of expelling all the pain and heartache so that it would be non-existent by sunrise.

It was wishful thinking.

A groan falls from my lips as I roll over and every single one of my muscles pulls and aches.

I was already feeling it from a week of working out with Daemon. I thought he'd gone hard on me, but turns out it was child's play compared to my brother's brutal punishment. It seems he took Dad's words seriously about my self-defence classes, and he went hard.

Reaching for my phone, I find that I've been out for almost five fucking hours.

"Jesus," I mutter, rubbing the sleep from my eyes and blinking around my room.

Thankfully, Alex isn't watching me like a creeper, and there's no sign that Daemon's been here.

I reply to the couple of messages waiting for me from Stella and Emmie, pull up my favourite playlist in the hope that some music flooding through my surround sound speakers will help pull me out of my melancholy, and I finally head for the bathroom.

I have the water just hot enough to burn, and I stand under the spray for way longer than necessary, hoping that all my pain will just wash down the drain with the bubbles.

Dread seeps through my veins for what tonight is going to hold. It's going to be a fancy dinner party for Mum to show off to her friends. Why the hell she wants me there, I have no idea. She probably just wants to parade me around, trying to show off how pretty I look in my granny dress. It's something most of the others can't do, because unlike me, they all grew a backbone a while ago and have shed their overprotective shell and embarked on their own lives.

Images of Isla flicker through my mind and jealousy twists up my insides.

I remember her as a little girl. She'd turn up here with her mum, dressed in pretty floral dresses with bows in her hair, and not two seconds after she was released would she mess it up.

She used to make a beeline for Nico and he'd be forced into playing with her like she was one of the boys. They'd chase each other through the trees, get muddy, rip their clothes and always emerge laughing while both our mothers lost their shit and I just sat there, torn between wanting to do the right thing and having fun.

Growing up as a good girl in a man's world has been hard.

Maybe if I had Isla's balls or tenacity, it would have been easier to force my parents' hands.

Maybe if they didn't look at Nico every single day like he was the golden child who could do no wrong and occasionally shoot that pride my way, I wouldn't have craved pleasing them so badly.

All the ifs, buts and maybes pointlessly float around my head. It's too late now.

I can push back all I want. But I'm not sure I'll ever be able to shed that need to please them.

I'm almost eighteen, coming to the end of sixth form, and here I am, still following the route they want for me. I've applied to the universities they deem appropriate and selected the courses they think will benefit me. All the while, I'm hiding everything that makes me happy because I'm scared of their reaction, of their disappointment.

Needing something, anything to help me get through the night I have ahead of me, I wrap a towel around my body and twist another around my hair, and I rip my door open in the hope of finding some alcohol. I'm sure I saw Stella stash the remaining ciders at the back of my wardrobe last night. I was pretty wasted, though. It could have been a dream.

"Holy shit," I squeal, my hands flying to the top of my towel to make sure it doesn't magically drop when his eyes land on it. "Jesus," I pant as my heart fights its way out of my chest at the sight of Alex sitting on the end of my bed as if he belongs here.

A weird sense of déjà vu washes over me as I rip my eyes from his concerned ones and march toward my wardrobe.

"Here," he says, obviously sensing what I need as he lifts a bottle of pink glittery liquid from his side.

"What the hell is— is it alcoholic?" I ask, forgetting about the finer details. I couldn't give two shits about the colour, glitter, or taste, as long as it's strongish.

"Sure is. Thought you might need it for a number of reasons."

"You're the best," I say, walking over and snatching it from his hand.

His eyes flash with pain at my words, and I regret them instantly.

"I'm sorry," I whisper, my heart cracking open once more.

If it could have been him instead, then everything would have been so different right now.

He shakes it off, and his usual boyish charm returns to his eyes.

"So what's the deal with your dad and Nico? Bit of a one-eighty."

"Apparently having a hit out on me made them reconsider allowing me to be so completely incapable of protecting myself. They were impressed by my shot for a virgin." I wink.

"Virgin my arse," he scoffs, making my cheeks burn.

Focusing on the bottle of glitter, I twist the top and go in search of a glass.

"You want some?"

"Of that?" he asks, his eyes dropping to the bottle in disgust. "Nah."

"It won't make your dick shrivel up and turn into a vagina, I promise," I tease.

"I'm not so sure about that," he quips as I pour myself a drink and down half of it, wincing at just how sweet it is. "That good, huh?"

"You really should try some," I say, running my tongue over my teeth, half expecting to find grains of sugar clinging to them.

"I'm good, thank you." His eyes track me as I move toward my drawers to dig out some underwear. "Want me to help pick?" he offers.

"There's something wrong with you," I mutter through a smile.

"Maybe. I've cheered you up though, right."

"I'm fine," I argue.

"Sure. Just like he is."

My breath catches in my throat at the thought of him going back to his life as if nothing ever happened. As if me and the time we spent together meant nothing. Less than nothing.

"He's a mess, Cal."

My fingers tighten on the pair of knickers I'd pulled from my drawer.

"Is that meant to make me feel better or something?" I hiss.

"No. It's meant to make you realise that walking away from you wasn't what he really wanted. That the things I can only assume he said to you yesterday weren't true."

"Well, he sure sounded convincing," I mutter.

"Calli," Alex sighs. "He's so gone for you, but he's terrified."

"He's not the only one." The words come out so quietly, there's no way he hears them. "If he's not brave enough to be honest, to try and fight for this, then I'm not interested."

I shove the drawer closed with more force than necessary, making the bottle and trinkets on the top rattle.

Alex is silent as I rip open my wardrobe and pull out one of the dresses I had delivered this morning that Jocelyn brought down for me. Neither of them are something that Mum would ever choose for me, but this one is a little bit more demure than the one I'm saving for tomorrow night. I figure we should build up to that. Plus, there's every chance that Daemon is going to be there, and I feel like I really need to pull out the big guns if I'm going to have to face him and pretend nothing has happened.

"Your mum chose that?" Alex asks, his eyes on the dress.

"This? No. Stella and Emmie chose it about ten minutes after putting the ones Mum left for me in the bin. If the doors were unlocked, then I wouldn't have put it past them taking them out on the patio and burning them."

"The doors are locked?" he asks, his brow knitting together.

"Yeah. I'm not sure if it's to keep me in or the Italians out, to be honest."

"To keep them out," he assures me.

"I've come back and been basically locked in a cage. I may as well have just stayed there because this is..." I throw my hands out to the sides, regretting it instantly when my towel loosens.

I just manage to catch it before I flash him.

"Go get dressed, baby C."

With a huff, I do as he suggests, because yeah, I'm standing here naked with just a towel covering me.

I make quick work of pulling the dress on, and I can't help but smile to myself as I stand in front of my full-length mirror, because it fits perfectly.

I'm not usually a fan of going braless and showing quite so much boob, but fuck it. I'm also not really feeling like myself right now, so Mum is going to have to like it or lump it.

I pause as I move toward the door, wondering if actually I am feeling myself and the timid girl of my past was never the real me.

Ruffling my hand through my damp, dark hair, I roll my shoulders back.

"Holy shit, Cal. You probably should have stayed in the towel," Alex blurts, his chin damn near hitting the floor when he gets a look at me.

The dress is a full-length maxi dress with a very low-cut front. The fabric plunges almost all the way to my belly button—something that is going to make steam billow from my mother's ears. I can't wait.

"No, Alex. Don't do that," I argue when he pulls his phone out.

"What? The miserable prick is at home moping. He needs to see this."

Rushing over, I wrap my fingers around his phone and attempt to rip it from his grasp.

"Too late," he says with a less-than-innocent smile.

"You're a menace. I was feeling bad about the arse-kicking he clearly gave you."

He scoffs. "I think you'll find that I was the one kicking arse, baby C."

"Yeah, it looks like it."

"He fucked up. He fucked up bad, letting you think he doesn't want you."

Walking over to my dressing table, I drop my arse to the stool and strap some armour around my heart. "Are we still really talking about this?"

My eyes meet his in the mirror. Anger heats my insides when I find pity staring back at me.

"It's over, Alex. We're done. So if you still want a chance, now is probably a good time to make a play for it. I hear rebound sex is fantastic."

His jaw tics and his lips purse as he stares back at me, his head shaking slowly.

"If I thought for even a second it would do any

good, I'd be right there, Cal. But I have zero intentions of hurting either of you."

He falls back on my bed as if everything is cool and I didn't just offer to fuck him in the hope of getting his twin out of my system.

Jesus. What the fuck is wrong with me?

22

DAEMON

"Huh, it's like everyone is scared of us," Isla mutters loud enough for me to hear over the music as she lowers two bottles of beer to our table and looks at the empty ones surrounding us. It does look suspiciously like everyone has given us—me—a seriously wide berth. "I wonder why that is?"

"Fuck off," I snap, reaching for my drink. "You knew I'd be no fun when you dragged me out of my flat. Suck it up."

"Pfft." She falls into her seat dramatically. "Just a couple of cuts and bruises and everyone thinks you're a thug. He's had his heart broken. Give him some sympathy," she announces loud enough to make me wince but not loud enough to carry to the other tables. Especially while the band up on stage murder some cover of an old Led Zeppelin song.

"Jesus, I. Fancy shutting your big fucking mouth?"

"So I am right, then? Someone has broken your black, little heart."

I glare at her, hoping—predictably pointlessly—that she might drop it.

"Who?" she demands.

"It doesn't matter. It's over and forgotten about."

"You wanna tell your face that? Fuck's sake, D. It's hardly like I'm going to go and—"

"It was Calli," I blurt without meaning to.

Shock renders her useless for a beat as if she can't physically process that bit of information.

But then her chin drops and her eyes widen, and I know she heard it loud and clear.

"Calli?" she echoes. "Calli Cirillo? Daddy's perfect little princess who never puts a step out of line?"

"I," I growl, not liking the judgemental tone of her voice.

"What? It's true."

My lips part to argue, but I struggle to find any words as I think about the version of Calli that everyone but me sees.

"There's a whole other side to her."

Isla leans closer, intrigue filling her eyes.

"Well, there must be, because not everyone willingly dances with the devil, or even gets close to breaking his heart."

"It was... nothing. The whole thing was a mistake. I never should have—"

"Stop," Isla says, holding her hand up between us

to cut me off. "Can you just stop with the bullshit? I know I'm not Alex," I shake my head when she says his name with nothing but disdain, "but I see you, D. I see what the others don't. And I might joke about your black heart, but I see it. I see it all the fucking time. So don't bullshit me with mistakes and it not meaning anything or any of that shit.

"You're a mess. So it wasn't nothing, and it probably wasn't a mistake." My lips part to argue, but I don't get a chance to say anything because she keeps going. "Calli doesn't seem like the kind of girl to do something impulsive, or irrational. If she was with you, then she wanted to be."

I shake my head. "I'm not that guy for her, I. I was just a bit of fun. A fuck you to her parents."

"I fucking hate that you can't see what I see when I look at you," she complains.

"You see what you want to see."

Her expression hardens as she glares at me. "I'm going to ignore the insult in that statement for now and just focus on the facts. I think I might see exactly the same as Calli sees. Everything you try and hide from everyone else on the planet."

"I don't need this, I," I mutter, draining my beer in a few large swallows.

"So ignoring it and getting fucked up is a better option than hearing my advice?"

"Not sure you've given any advice."

"That's because I've spent all this time trying to drag the truth out of you."

I scoff, ripping my eyes from hers to the commotion on the stage as a new band gets ready to play. Hopefully something better than the last shitty one.

"Do you know what she's doing tonight?" Isla asks, capturing my attention once more.

"No," I grunt.

"She's being forced to attend her mother's poncey birthday meal at the house."

"Right?"

"Jerome is going to keep her entertained."

"Jerome?" I hiss, my fists curling in my lap as I think about another guy getting close to her. Even if it is a pussy like Jerome. He's gotta grow some balls at some point, right?

"Yeah, from what I heard, he's got a bit of a thing for your girl. Maybe Cassandra and Iris are trying to play matchmaker."

The thought of that alone makes my blood boil. Isla damn well knows it too, which is why she continues to push.

"He'd be a solid choice for her. Loyal, genuine, nice, reliable."

"Jesus, you make him sound like a fucking dog, I."

"He's got pure Greek DNA. And he's pretty hot. If you like that pretty, I-rub-one-out-over-computer-coding kinda vibe." My brows lift as I stare at her. She nods, agreeing with her own thoughts. "They'd be a good couple." A growl rumbles deep in my throat. "Don't you think?"

Fury begins to boil over in my stomach as jealousy slowly drips like poison through my veins.

"Yeah," I grit out, the word like acid on my tongue. But I'm unable to argue her point. After all, he is the exact kind of guy I'm sure Evan and Nico have always pictured for their little princess.

Thankfully, my phone buzzes in my pocket, giving me a good excuse not to say any more on that subject.

I pull it out anxiously. I've already got multiple messages and at least one photo from Alex that I've been ignoring. Chances are each message just contains more evidence that I'm a dickhead. Something I really don't need to read right now. Especially while I've got Isla telling me to my face.

But when the screen lights up and I find a message from an unknown number staring back at me, excitement stirs deep within me.

If this is what I think it is, then I am so fucking in.

Mickey has been desperate to run a night for weeks now. He's been losing money since the Italians fucked up our chances of sneaking under the radar with our underground fights, so I've been expecting something to pop up. And this couldn't have come at a better time.

I've barely got the message open to see the location when my phone starts ringing and Alex's face appears before me.

Prior to that message, I wouldn't have answered. But now, I swipe the screen and put my phone to my ear.

"You get it?"

"Yeah, man," I shout over the music.

"You coming?"

I glance at Isla, who's watching me curiously.

"We just got a message for a fight," I tell her.

"Go," she encourages. "I know you need blood more than you do music and listening to advice from me."

"Yeah," I bark. "I'm coming."

"Stay there, we'll pick you up in twenty." He hangs up before I get to say another word. Of course the motherfucker has tracked me to find out where I am.

"Another for the road?" Isla asks once I've lowered my phone once more.

I stare at the little red dot that tells me I've got unread messages.

My thumb hovers over it, part of me dying to see what he's sent, another part not wanting to know.

"Yeah, make it something stronger than beer though," I say, not lifting my eyes from the screen.

"You got it, boss."

She disappears into the crowd, but I barely glance up to see her go.

Without another thought, I allow my thumb to hit the message icon and I open our chat.

I ignore the messages in favour of the bottom of the image I can see in the thread.

Opening it up, my heart drops into the pit of my stomach.

Calli stands, looking totally relaxed and happy in a sinful dress which shows off way more skin than I'm sure either of her parents will approve of. But she looks stunning. And she's going to be spending the night with someone who isn't me.

That dress is wasted on someone like Jerome. There is no way he has the skills it would require to peel it from her body later, to leave it pooled on her bedroom floor as he discovers what she's hiding beneath it.

Jealousy bubbles up within me faster than I can control as a red haze of fury descends around me.

She's okay. She's not even spared me another minute since I allowed her to believe we were over. No, worse than that. That we never even existed.

Closing it, I scroll up higher, finding another picture. This one is of her back. She's got her gun raised and looks everything like the mafia princess she craves to be. My cock swells as I vividly remember how she looked with my gun in her hands.

Once I've had my fill, but before my need for her completely makes me lose control, I read through his messages.

Alex: Calli is a bad-arse with a gun. Gets me all kinds of hard...

Alex: You're only punishing yourself, Bro.

And as if that's not bad enough, the one that accompanies the dress picture almost pushes me over the edge.

Alex: Shame you won't be here to keep her company tonight. I might just wait in her room for her to be done later. You know that dress will look better on the floor…

My grip on my phone tightens. I know he's baiting me. I know he wouldn't do anything with her. If he had any intention, then he'd have done it by now. Doesn't stop his words from hitting the exact spot he wants them to, though.

The second a shot of something appears before me, I throw it back without any hesitation.

It burns all the fucking way down, but I crave it and then some.

"More," I demand, and thankfully, my best friend knew exactly what I needed, because she lifts two more off the tray in her hand and lines them up before me.

"Fuck," I bark after throwing back the third one. Warmth floods my belly as bloodlust and the need for pain collide.

Standing tall, I snatch the tray from her hands, throw it down on the table and wrap my arms around her.

"You're the fucking best, I."

"Yeah, I know," she mumbles against my chest.

"You sure you don't wanna come?"

"Not tonight. I'm meeting friends here. Just promise me something?" she asks as I release her.

"Sure."

"Do not get in the ring tonight. You're not in the right place for it."

"I know," I whisper. I might have got into it with Alex, but I'm fully aware that my focus is shot right now. "Thanks for this afternoon."

My phone buzzes in my pocket, letting me know that they're outside, and I take a step back from the table.

"Be good," Isla warns with a naughty glint in her eyes.

"Always."

"I'll call you tomorrow," she calls before I get swallowed up in the crowd who've congregated in front of the stage. Apparently, the next band isn't going to suck. It's almost a shame I'm going to miss it.

The second I step outside, my eyes land on Alex's Audi. It's exactly the same as mine, other than he's got a white interior and mine is all black.

Spotting the passenger seat is empty, I rip it open and drop into the seat. Before anyone who might be inside gets a chance to say anything, I lean over pinning my brother to his seat by his throat.

His eyes widen in shock, but he quickly recovers and amusement covers his face. He knows exactly what he's done. Cunt.

"You're a fucking dick."

Laughter erupts from the back seat, and when I look up, I find Nico and Toby watching us with smirks on their faces.

"I left, didn't I?" Alex growls low enough so that only I can hear him.

"Yeah, because you're too much of a pussy to do anything else."

"Glad to see Isla helped you come to your senses."

"Fuck you," I grunt, releasing him and falling back into my seat. "Let's go. I need this."

23

CALLI

"Sweetheart, are you ready? Your mum's about to blow a— whoa, girl," Jocelyn gasps when I appear at the foot of the stairs she's walking down to find me.

As usual, her appearance is flawless. The perfect showpiece for Mum to flaunt around her friends tonight.

"You like?" I ask, a wicked smile pulling at my lips.

I knew the dress was going to be perfect the second we saw it online. But seeing Alex's reaction really nailed that home.

Mum is going to lose her shit, and for the first time in my life, I'm ready for it.

"I love, but what happened to the dresses I put in your wardrobe for tonight?"

"Oh, those... I couldn't possibly tell you." I wink cheekily, and Jocelyn laughs.

"I like this fire in you, Calli. I don't know who's put it there but you need to keep them around." Her eyes flash with something, and my brow wrinkles before my heart plummets as I think about the reason for my new, gives-no-shits attitude.

"I just figured it was time to stand up for myself a little."

"I'm here for it, sweet girl," Jocelyn says with a smile, her excitement glittering in her eyes.

"Just be ready with the mop for when her head explodes."

"I've got your back, Calli," she jokes.

I follow her up the stairs and through the house. My heels clack against the spotless marble floors as I take in the sheer perfection of the house. There is not a thing out of place.

"You've had a hard day, huh?" I whisper over my shoulder, sensing Jocelyn is still there.

"I like to be busy."

My response falters as we step into the hallway and both Mum and Dad turn our way.

Just for a few seconds, I swear time actually stops as they both stare at me with their mouths agape and their eyes wide.

Smugness washes through me as I stand there confidently, owning my dress choice.

It takes longer than I expected, but finally Mum seems to come back to her senses.

"Callista, where is the dress I provided you?"

"I didn't like it," I say nonchalantly with a small shrug, "so I chose this instead."

My heart pounds, trying to beat its way out of my chest, but I refuse to give in to the fear that edges its way in as I stand in front of both of my disappointed parents.

Swallowing it down, I force my body to spin.

"What do you think?"

Jocelyn just about manages to smother her amused laugh when I catch her eyes.

My mother's gasp rips through the air as she discovers the open back that damn near goes right down to my arse crack and just a couple of ties holding the fabric together.

"Callista," she warns. Her tone sends a shiver down my spine, but I refuse to cower like a naughty little kid. "You need to go and—"

The doorbell rips through the air, and faster than I thought she could move, Jocelyn rushes to the door to greet our guests.

Iris and her husband, Christos, stand on the other side and she quickly ushers them in, offering both of them a glass of champagne waiting on the unit that almost runs the length of the hallway.

"Thank you," Iris says before meeting Mum's eyes and moving toward her. "Happy birthday, Cass—" But she doesn't get to finish that sentiment because her eyes land on me. "Wow, Calli. You look incredible. That dress is stunning."

A wide smug smile appears on my lips as her eyes run the length of me.

"You look so grown up. It amazes me every time I look at Jerome to think how quick the years have sped by."

"And where is he?" Mum asks in a clipped, clearly pissed-off tone.

My breath catches at what she's alluding to.

"Jerome is coming?" I ask, my brow pinching.

"Yes, sweetheart. He's just grabbing your mum's gift from the car."

Why? Why the hell would he agree to this hell?

The word 'setup' screams loud in my head, but I don't want to believe it.

All four of them smile at me, although it's only Iris and Chris whose are full of happiness. Mum looks about ready to kill someone, her eyes dropping down to my pretty exposed chest every few seconds. All the while, Dad looks half amused, and half mortified. He wants to stand with Mum. The past seventeen years have been evidence of that enough. But with him caving to finally train me up, I'm starting to wonder if I'm not the only one who's rebelling.

"Oh, I think Clio and Michail have just arrived," Jocelyn says, mentioning Isla's parents. I bet there's a very, very slim chance of them dragging one of their kids with them.

Footsteps head this way and we all look to the door as Jerome appears, carrying the biggest bouquet of weird and colourful flowers I've ever seen, and he has a blue Tiffany's bag swinging from his wrist.

"Happy birthday, Cassandra," he says politely, passing her the humongous arrangement which she quickly shoves at Jocelyn, who can barely lift the thing, before taking the bag.

"Thank you so much, Jerome. You're such a good boy. And you're looking so smart tonight. Don't you think, Calli?"

At her mention of me, Jerome's eyes lift and he immediately finds me. Much like everyone else, his eyes widen in surprise, but there is no anger in them. If anything, I'd say there is some desire. And I'm not entirely sure how I feel about that.

Jerome and I have been friends for years. But I have never, ever felt any kind of flutters of excitement or desire when it comes to him.

Something I've always wondered if Mum is disappointed by.

"Whoa, Calli. You look..."

I drop my eyes down his standard Cirillo black suit, but still there's nothing. He just doesn't wear it quite right. He doesn't have the swagger that gets my heart racing and my belly knotting with desire.

I swallow down my disappointment. I'm sure it would be a hell of a lot easier if I did react that way to him.

Mum and Dad would surely be more than pleased, and there would need to be no sneaking around, stealing forbidden moments in the dark if my heart wanted Jerome.

Sadly for everyone in this room, I couldn't be less interested if I tried.

"You too," I breathe. It's not a lie, he's clearly put some effort in for tonight. The reason behind that makes my stomach knot uncomfortably.

"Why don't you two go and get a drink," Dad encourages as more voices hit my ears.

"Sure." I can only hope my options are a little more varied than water tonight.

I turn to escape, more than ready to go and hide somewhere away from Mum's judgemental looks. But before I get to move, her hand wraps around my upper arm.

"I don't appreciate your defiance, Callista."

"I thought you'd be pleased," I hiss. "Jerome seems to love it."

Her grip on my arm tightens, but she quickly releases me with a little shove in his direction. "Then you'd better go and remind him how incredible the girl falling out of it is as well then."

My teeth grind at her words. I'm hardly falling out of this dress. If she truly believes I am, then she really needs to attend a Knight's Ridge party and see the kind of outfits Teagan and her posse turn up in.

Jerome's hand lands on my lower back, his skin brushing against mine. But still. Zero tingles.

Pain slices through me once more. I hate that even

now, I can't shed the memory of Daemon's touch from my body.

"She looks happy," Jerome whispers in my ear once we're out of earshot.

I can't help but bark out a laugh, and it feels good to be able to banish just a little bit of the tension that's pulling my shoulders tight as I do so.

"I'm not living up to her standards tonight."

"Why the hell not? You look..." he trails off, and when I glance over, I find his cheeks are blazing red.

"Thank you, Jerome. I appreciate it."

"What are we drinking then, kids?" Jocelyn asks, thankfully smashing through the tension that has momentarily descended.

"You mean, I have options?" I ask hopefully.

Jocelyn smirks at me. "And here I was thinking you weren't playing by the rules tonight, Miss Cirillo."

"You got me there. Vodka and anything you've got to water it down a bit then, please."

"Jerome?"

"I'll... uh..."

"Beer?"

"Sure, that sounds great. Thank you."

We take our drinks and head through to the den while the adults have pre-dinner drinks in our formal dining room.

"So what's the deal then, Jerome? How did your parents sell this to you?" I ask, curious as hell about what he's agreed to.

He shrugs, sitting on the other side of the sofa to me.

He shrugs. "Mum just said that you might need someone to keep you company, seeing as Nico wasn't going to be here."

My grip on my glass tightens at the mention of my brother slipping out of something else that will be dull enough to send me to sleep.

"I appreciate that. I really do. But surely you have something else to be doing that's way more exciting on a Friday night? Isn't there a party or something you could go to?"

"It's totally cool. You know I'm not really in for all that."

"There is though, isn't there?"

"Yeah." He hesitates. "Teagan is having a house party."

"You should go," I encourage. "I'll tell our parents you were sick or something."

"Spending the evening with you is no hardship," he says with a genuine smile.

"Well then, maybe we should both make a run for it and party the night away instead."

He stares at me as if he can't decide if I'm joking or not.

I am, obviously.

I might be feeling rebellious, but I'm not going to go running out of the house again when I know how real the threat is out there.

I flinch when his hand lands on mine. He notices

and quickly pulls it back, regret flooding his face. "I'm good here, Calli. The night is what we make it, right?"

I smile at him and relax a little more. There's no pretence when I spend time with Jerome. He doesn't take anything too seriously, and he doesn't put too much pressure on himself—school work aside. He's never going to be a soldier like the guys, but he's okay with that. He doesn't have that burning need to be one of them despite the fact that we've all gone through school together, and he doesn't want to compete. It's refreshing.

"So, how have you been getting on with your revision? Mum said you'd gone out of town for a week so you could really focus. Sounds like heaven, if you ask me."

"It was... it was something," I mutter, my chest aching as if he just reached in and gave my heart a real good squeeze. Lifting my glass to my lips, I swallow down a less-than-ladylike gulp, more than a little relieved that Jocelyn wasn't shy with the vodka. "Can't say I feel all that well prepared, though."

Because I spent most of the week with a soldier between my thighs.

I lock those thoughts down. They're not helpful in getting me through this night.

"Same. I actually feel less confident as the days go on, despite doing nothing but work."

"If you want to study together now I'm back, all you've got to do is say the word. I've been locked up in this house like a damsel in distress so I'll always welcome the company."

"This life is hard at times, huh?"

I study him as he rubs his hand down his face, and I catch a flash of something that wasn't there before. A darkness I don't like seeing in him.

"What's wrong? Has something happened?"

He shakes his head. "No. Not really. Dad's just expecting more of me than I'm willing to give."

"Oh?" I ask, happy to dive into his problems over mine.

"It's nothing you want to hear about. Just Family bullshit." I smile sadly at him. "I wasn't made for fighting and shooting people."

"You don't have to want to do that to be a valuable member of this Family, Jerome."

"I know. Dad just wants me to be more... well-rounded or some bullshit."

I smile sadly at him, understanding completely how he's feeling right now.

Maybe I was wrong earlier. He is no different from the rest of us, failing to meet all those impossible expectations that were placed on us even before we were born.

"We'll figure it out, J. We'll find our places."

He downs his beer before leaning forward and placing it on the coffee table.

"I'm glad I came tonight."

"I'm glad you did too." *You might just make an unbearable evening bearable.*

24

DAEMON

The blood and brutality does help to settle me as I stand at the edge of the ring in the venue Mickey managed to score for the night.

We're right on the edge of our territory. Just about as far from the Italians as we can get.

It's still a risk. But it seems that there are plenty of us willing to put that aside for a night of pain.

Almost all of the younger Cirillo Family members are here, along with a few of the elders. Although it seems that all the capos are missing. It makes me wonder if Damien has stopped them from coming. Or, if they're all outside keeping watch. Probably more likely.

The Italians are nowhere to be seen. After they fucking destroyed our last fight venue, they've been blacklisted.

These nights are meant to be a neutral event we can

all enjoy. Some bloody, yet good-natured fun. But they fucked up when they followed Jonas's fucking orders and torched the place in the hope of hurting Stella.

So while they're banished, the invitation has been opened up to the Wolves instead. With Luis no longer at the helm and Archer now leading his men, it seemed right to have them here.

"How're things in Lovell?" I ask Archer and his two boys, Dax and Jace, when the two guys in the ring have been dragged off. It's been a few weeks since we helped them take back control of their territory, and as far as we've heard, all is good.

"Yeah, man. Things are quiet, and business is good. Shit is looking up."

"Glad to hear it. And Jesse?" I ask. "Sara?"

The reality is, I know the truth. Emmie and Stella kept Calli up to date with everything that was going on back here while we were away, so I know that she's still in the coma in the hospital.

"He's a mess," Archer says, rubbing at his chin anxiously. "He's barely left her side. Fucking breaks my heart to see him in such pain."

"Sorry to hear that, man."

Archer blows out a pained breath as he thinks of his brother.

"What about you? Shit's been getting serious, from what we've heard."

"It's nothing more than we can handle."

The roar of the crowd stops me from saying

anything else, and when I look back toward the ring, I find Xander, one of the Royal Reapers' best fighters, shirtless and ready for his opponent.

Movement behind Archer catches my eye, and when I focus, I find Jace pulling his hoodie off.

"Is he going up against Xander?"

"Sure is. And he's gonna kill it. Ain't that right, bro?" Archer says, clapping Jace on the shoulder.

"Hell yeah."

"He's good," I warn.

"Well, good thing I'm better then, huh?"

I nod, impressed with his confidence and hoping that he's as good as he believes he is.

"Jace is unbeaten in Lovell. He needs this challenge."

Archer turns toward the ring, our shoulders brushing as Alex appears with beers.

I take a pull, keeping my eyes on the ring as the crowd goes wild. Mickey steps up and introduces Jace and the cheering gets louder. Apparently, he's got quite the fan club in Lovell.

And it turns out it's for a good reason, because Jace is something fucking else. We probably should have been including them in these Circuit fights before, because Xander hasn't seen an opponent like this in a while.

But as good as it might be, watching their fists fly and blood coat almost every inch of them, it doesn't stop my phone burning a hole in my pocket, or the ache in my chest that seems to have taken up permanent residence.

When my phone buzzes, my fickle heart shatters my restraint and I rip my eyes from the fight and pull it from my pocket.

All the air rushes from my lungs when I don't find the name I was hoping for.

Isla: How's the bloodbath? You feeling any better yet?

Daemon: It's good. And I'm fine.

Isla: Suuure. You should go and see her.

Daemon: She's not interested.

Isla: Fine, let her fall asleep thinking about a boring, uneventful life with Jerome then. *shrugging emoji*

Daemon: You're not funny.

Isla: Nor are you. *winky tongue out emoji*

Tapping out of her conversation, I find the photo that Alex sent me earlier, something the guy in question doesn't miss.

"Just go see her. Tell her the truth."

"Fucking hell, are you two ganging up on me or something?"

"Me and Isla? Un-fucking-likely. We just both happen to agree on this one thing."

"Oh?"

"That you're a fucking idiot, Bro."

I blow out a breath, telling myself all the reasons I did what I did yesterday.

"Fuck, yeah. Take him down, X," Alex screams in my ear, losing himself in the excitement of the fight once more.

With him distracted, I slip away, leaving the roar of the battle behind me.

It takes me a good few minutes to fight my way from our front row position, but when I finally break free, I don't head for the bar like I told myself I was going to do. Instead, I turn toward the exit.

The temperature plummets long before I get to exit, and I find out why when the two soldiers guarding the door push it open for me and the rain sprays in.

"Everything okay, Daemon?" Jon, one of our older guys asks.

"Yeah, man. I'm just not feeling it."

"Fair enough. Word has it there's quite the fight going on down there." Disappointment laces his tone as longing fills his eyes.

"Yeah, Xander has found a worthy opponent. I

don't think this will be their last fight though, so you should catch them next time."

"Here's hoping," he says, nodding at me as I prepare to step out into the downpour.

In only seconds, my hair is soaked through and my shirt is practically glued to my body, but at no point do I stop to call an Uber or duck down into the tube stations I pass.

In all honesty, I don't even feel it. I'm in too much of a mess over the one person I never should have got close enough to turn my life upside down.

I knew this would be the result if I were to cave to her. There was never a doubt in my mind that I'd be able to truly give her up if I had a taste.

My hands curl as rainwater drips from my fists, my feet squelching in my shoes.

I have no idea how far or how long I've walked for, but when I finally lift my head from the pavement, it becomes obvious instantly that I have no fucking clue where I am.

Spotting another tube station, I head in that direction, finally giving into the elements.

A laugh rumbles deep in my throat when I realise that I've stumbled onto a line that takes me right to the end of the street the Cirillo estate sits on.

Fate?

Bullshit. I don't believe in any of that crap.

Although, I find it hard to ignore as I wait on the platform for the next train to appear.

Thankfully, the carriage is almost empty, so I don't

have a whole host of curious eyes on my battered face as I fall down into a seat, quickly creating a puddle at my feet.

Leaning forward, I rest my elbows on my knees and squeeze my eyes closed. Going to her is the wrong thing to do.

I walked away from her for a reason.

I need to remember all the ways I'm wrong for her, all the reasons why we can't work.

But that does little to squash the need that's only growing within me.

I've gone from watching her from a distance, to being able to spend a week pretending that she's mine.

Having that ripped away, even if it was my own fault, hurts more than I ever could have imagined.

My legs move on their own accord as the train pulls into their station, and without second-guessing my actions, I head for the stairs. In only a couple of minutes, I emerge in the rain once more.

The walk down to Evan's is quick, and with only a few words to the soldiers guarding the place, they allow me inside believing that I'm here on official business. Idiots.

I seriously hope they're a little more protective if a stranger—an Italian—should appear before them in the dead of night.

Lights shine brightly from the fancy living room that Cassandra has never let us inside, and as I skirt around the perimeter of the grounds, remaining hidden in the shadows, I find both Evan and Cassandra, and Jerome and Isla's parents, are all still in there, drinking and laughing. Although, they don't exactly appear to be having all that much fun. Their postures are stiff and their smiles fake.

That all changes when I continue around the building and find myself staring into the den.

My breath catches in my throat, pain lashing at my insides as I watch my girl laughing and enjoying herself with another man.

The two of them are in the middle of the room, dancing and laughing, and generally looking like they're having the time of their lives.

I stare at Jerome for a few minutes as he spins her around the room, wondering if I'm looking at the same guy who always seems so dull and uptight.

It doesn't take long to realise what it is.

It's her.

It's always her.

The only one who has ever peeled back my layers and wriggled her way inside my heart without even doing anything.

It seems she has a similar effect on our quiet soldier.

I lean against the tree and just watch the two of them.

It becomes obvious fast that both of them are drunk. Their dance moves are sloppy and their legs unsteady. But even with her losing control, Jerome never steps out of line. He never once touches her inappropriately or tries to take things to the next level. He just seems content to be spending time with her.

Jealousy eats me. It's poison dripping through me until I'm sure it's going to consume me whole.

The only bonus is that the rain has almost stopped, the air warming around me despite the fact that I'm sopping wet and shivering with every inch of my clothes soaked through.

I watch them for the longest time, and eventually, Jerome is called away to leave by his parents, and he abandons my girl in the middle of the room.

She stands there looking lost. For the first time since I made my way back here to watch her, she looks utterly defeated by the world. Her shoulders drop as if that sexy dress is too heavy to hold up.

Her eyes remain on the door, as if she's waiting for someone—her parents maybe, because there is no way she can be expecting me to walk into the house and pull her into my arms, whispering that everything will be okay.

It might be what I ache to do. But I know I can't.

When the door on the other side of the room never opens, Calli throws her hands up, walks over to the side, swipes a bottle of vodka and lifts it to her lips.

The sight of her clearly drowning wrecks me. But what can I do about it?

Everyone else's voices finally disappear, before the rumble of engines fills the air as they pass through the gates before it turns deadly silent once more.

Lights go off around the house, but still, Calli

stands alone in the middle of the room, dancing with her vodka.

Her body sways and her hips roll as she moves to the beat only she can hear. I can't take my eyes off her. She utterly enthrals me.

The time ticks by. I'm sure song after song plays out in that room, but she doesn't stop until her legs give up.

I gasp as she suddenly plummets, disappearing from sight.

"Fuck," I gasp, darting from the trees and running toward the window.

It's not until I've got there that I realise how fucking stupid that was. Evan has guys patrolling the entire estate. One wrong move and I could be gunned down as if I'm a ballsy Italian.

Forgetting all that, I press my face to the window and breathe a sigh of relief when I find her asleep on the sofa, the bottle of vodka still hanging from her fingers.

"Angel," I breathe, my heart shattering at the sight of her.

My pulse races as my hand lifts to the glass, as if I'll be able to touch her through it. A violent shiver rips down my spine as the coldness seeps into my bones once more.

"Shit," I hiss, knowing that I can't just walk away now. I should—it's exactly what I should do. But I can't.

As I slip around the side of the building, a light I

was hoping for shines from one of the biggest rooms in the house. I've just got to hope that Evan and Cassandra aren't in there having a nightcap.

But the risk isn't enough to stop me.

The second I find the room exactly as I was expecting, I allow myself to be seen, coming to stand right in front of the floor-to-ceiling windows.

It takes a couple of seconds, but Jocelyn soon feels the weight of my stare as she works her way through what seems like an endless pile of washing up.

I don't hear anything, but there's no way a shriek of horror doesn't leave her parted lips as her eyes widen in fear.

I hold my hands up in defence and force a soft smile onto my face.

Shaking her head at me, she walks over and unlocks the door.

"What the hell are you doing..."

"Daemon," I offer when she looks at me closely, trying to figure out which twin I am.

"You could have been shot, running around in the dark out there."

"Nah, I'm not that lucky," I deadpan as I slip inside the warm kitchen.

"What on earth is going on?" she asks, her eyes tracking down my still wet clothes. At least I'm no longer leaving puddles everywhere I go.

"You never saw me, okay?" I say with a wink as I move through the room, the scent of the meal she prepared for the party tonight hitting my nose and making my stomach growl.

"You're playing with fire."

"I'm more than aware."

As I rush toward the hallway, I sense that she's hot on my heels. I don't question her. She'll probably be as concerned as I am about the state of Calli right now.

This isn't the first time I've had to make use of the Cirillos' discreet housekeeper, and something tells me that it might not be the last.

She steps into the den behind me, a soft gasp leaving her lips as we both stare at the passed-out girl on the sofa.

"Did they leave her here?"

I don't respond. It's not necessary.

Walking over, I take the bottle from her fingers before swallowing down a hit and placing it down.

Dropping to my haunches, I brush my fingers over her cheeks, my eyes taking in every inch of her face. Her make-up is flawless still. She looks beautiful, peaceful, and nothing like the defeated and beaten-down girl she did when I was watching her in here alone.

"I'm sorry," I whisper, needing to say the words, to acknowledge that all of this is my fault.

I should never have touched her. Should never have let myself have something so good in my life.

I hang my head for a beat, my self-hatred getting the better of me before I do what I came here to do.

Sliding my arms between her and the sofa, I lift her into my chest.

"Nikolas," she whispers.

My heart fractures as that one word hits my ears, yet at the same time, something else feels like it slots back into place with her in my arms.

"I'm here, Angel."

Coming to a stop, I rip my eyes from my girl and look up at Jocelyn, who's standing in the doorway, watching us curiously.

Her eyes soften and a sad smile pulls at her lips.

She knows. She sees it. I'm pretty sure she always had, which is why she's turned the other way when she's caught me in Calli's room, or left a door unlocked for me in the past.

"You need to fight for her," she whispers.

"She's not mine. She never will be."

Jocelyn sucks in a breath.

"But she is. You just need to find a way to show the rest of the world."

My eyes lift to the ceiling, gesturing to where Calli's parents are sleeping somewhere above us.

"Excuse me," I murmur, not willing to have this conversation right now. Or ever, to be fair.

"Have you at least told her how you really feel?" Jocelyn asks as I walk down the hallway toward the basement door.

"It doesn't matter," I whisper to myself. She can't be mine.

"Life is too short to live with regrets and what-ifs."

Her words repeat over and over as I descend the stairs with Calli still peacefully sleeping in my eyes.

"This is going to hurt in the morning, Angel," I tell her as I lay her out on the bed, pressing my hands on either side of her head and staring down at her.

My heart races, my need to strip us both down to nothing and crawl into bed with her burning through me.

Something tells me that now Jocelyn knows I'm down here, she'd do anything to ensure we weren't interrupted. But I still can't risk it.

So in the end, I settle for just sorting her out.

I then drag the chair over from the corner and indulge myself in my favourite pastime of watching her sleep while she is blissfully unaware.

25

CALLI

My eyes track Daemon across my bedroom floor, and my brows pinch when I find him wearing a white t-shirt instead of his usual black.

But I don't question it. I'm too relieved that he's here to question anything right now.

Although, as I watch him for a few more seconds, I realise his intentions and my heart jumps into my throat.

"They're locked," I say, my voice barely above a whimper with how dry my throat is.

He stills, his entire body going rigid as if he's not expecting to hear my voice before he lowers his head.

"You're meant to be asleep."

"Come here," I demand. "Don't run from me. Not again."

The pain that's still lingering in my chest collides with hope from finding him here, and I reach for him, desperate to feel his touch, his warmth, to breathe in his scent.

"I can't," he says, his voice deep and haunting.

He cuts across the room toward the stairs.

"I shouldn't be here. I just..."

"Please, Nikolas. I need you. I—"

"I'm not what you need, Angel. I'm not worthy of you. I never have been, and I was foolish to believe that I could be even for a second. Spend more time with Jerome. He'd be good for you. He could be what you need."

I suck in a gasp as he disappears from my sight, and when my eyes fly open, I find I'm sitting in the middle of my room, looking toward where he was just standing. Or at least where I thought he was standing.

The reality is that he's not here. Nor has he been.

"Fuck," I breathe, falling back onto my bed as shame rolls through me.

Just for a minute, I really thought that—

Despite the pounding in my head and the rolling of my stomach, I sit back up and look down at myself.

I'm wearing a vest. A vest I don't remember putting on.

My eyes scan the room, searching for evidence that there was some reality to my dream, but I don't find anything. It looks exactly the same as I remember.

"Shit." It was just a dream.

But it felt so real.

Reaching over, I find my phone on the side,

exactly where I left it, and I wince when I light the screen up to find that it's almost lunchtime. I've got a whole stream of messages from Stella and Emmie asking how last night went, wanting to know if I gave Jerome my V-card, and at what point I'm going to wake the fuck up so we can go to our spa appointments for this evening's party.

The bright, colourful lights damn near burn holes in my eyes as I attempt to reply, but my brain and fingers don't seem to be on the same wavelength.

I send them something half legible before finding my conversation with Jerome.

Calli: What happened last night? The last thing I remember was dancing...

I hesitate to send it. What if something did happen? What if he was the one to change me and put me to bed? The last thing he would want to read this morning is evidence that I've forgotten all of it.

My message shows as read almost immediately and my stomach knots. I really don't want him to reply, reminding me about him putting me to bed and me doing something I'm going to regret.

Jerome: My head hurts too much to think. What did you give me, arsenic?

A small laugh tumbles from my lips.

Calli: Just your standard vodka…

Jerome: I don't remember anything after dancing with you.

"Yes," falls from my lips at his words. Even if it was him, which is unlikely, if he were that drunk, then at least he doesn't remember.

Someone got an eyeful of my boobs last night, and I'm relieved that it wasn't Jerome. It probably would have been his first time seeing some, and I'd really like that experience to be a better one for him.

Calli: Me neither. I've woken up in bed though… kinda confused.

Jerome: Lucky you. I was on my bedroom floor. No idea if that's where my parents dumped me or if I fell out of bed.

I can't help but burst out laughing, which in turn makes my head hurt and my stomach lurch.

"Oh shit," I gasp, throwing the covers off and running for the bathroom.

My skin is flushed with sweat, my body trembling, as I sit back against the wall and wipe my mouth.

Why the hell did I allow myself to drink so much?

I rest my head back against the tiles and tip my

head up, closing my eyes and sucking in a deep breath.

My stomach continues to churn, but thankfully it doesn't feel the need to make me barf again.

After long, uncomfortable minutes on the floor, I drag my aching body up and stand in front of the mirror.

I keep my eyes on the basin for a few seconds before I risk looking up. I'm going to look like a car crash, I just know it.

Reaching up, I wipe one of my eyes of the wetness still clinging to my lashes from throwing up, and I frown when my hand doesn't come back with black make-up smeared all over it.

My eyes find the mirror, and I gasp when I find my face clear of the dark make-up I spent so long perfecting last night that I knew would only add to my mother's irritation.

"What the hell?" I mutter, staring at my bare face.

Yeah, okay, my bags have bags, making my skin look pale and dull, and my eyes are bloodshot, but it's a hell of a lot better than I was expecting.

Confusion continues to war within me as I reach for my toothbrush and attempt to fix the state of my mouth. It works, it's just a shame it does little to help my head and stomach.

I shuffle back into my bedroom, in desperate need of some coffee but also aware that I don't have the energy to make myself one, even if Mum hadn't stolen my coffee machine in her quest for me to live a clean life, or whatever she's trying to achieve with the coconut water bullshit.

I fall back into my bed and curl up into a ball.

I get two minutes drowning in my poor decisions from the previous night before footsteps sound out around my room.

I suck in a breath, praying to whoever might listen that I'm not about to be forced to endure Mum's shrill voice as she rips me a new one over my defiant behaviour.

But when it doesn't come, and instead the scent of the liquid gold I'm so desperate for hits my nose, I crack an eye open, risking seeing who it is.

Jocelyn stands before me with a soft, understanding, yet concerned smile on her face.

"Thank you," I whisper as she places a huge mug on my bedside table.

I expect her to leave again, but to my shock, she lowers down and sits on the edge of my bed.

She reaches for my hand and squeezes gently.

"I think it's time we had a little chat, don't you?"

My lips part to respond, but I'm too confused to actually find any words.

"Uh... I know I drank too much. I'm sorry if I caused—"

"You don't owe me any kind of apology, sweetheart." She gives me a soft smile, one which I should probably receive a time or two from my mother. But I'm not sure she's capable of it.

"I've known for a while," she starts, not helping me

out with what we're actually talking about in any way. "I hoped that maybe you'd figure out that I knew and that you'd talk to me about it."

"I'm sorry, I have no idea what you're talking about."

"He really cares about you, Calli. And I must admit, I was concerned when Alex started hanging out down here with you, but it seems that nothing has changed. He was here when you needed him, just like he always seems to be."

My mouth opens and closes like a fish plucked right out of its tank.

"You know?" I whisper, barely able to process this with my veins still sixty percent vodka.

"Talk to me, Calli. I can see you're hurting and I hate it. I'm not your mother, I won't judge you or criticise your choices. You are a smart, thoughtful young woman, and I trust you know what's best for you."

Tears burn the backs of my eyes as I stare at her kind face.

A sob rips up my throat a second before I fall into her arms.

"It's such a mess, Jocelyn. I don't even..." I suck in a shaky breath.

She cups my face in her hands and stares into my eyes.

"He was here last night." It's meant to come out as a question, but it doesn't, because deep down, I already know. I might have woken up dreaming about him, but just like previous experiences, it was drawn from reality.

"I think he must have been outside watching. Silly, silly boy. If anyone had seen him, they'd have shot him dead, loitering in the shadows."

I suck in a breath, thinking of him risking his life like that.

"He's fine, sweetie. Well, aside from the broken heart he's suffering with."

Her words do little for my emotional state and silent tears continue to track down my cheeks, dripping down and soaking into my vest.

"He knew that you'd passed out on the sofa. He scared the living daylights out of me, turning up like a ghost in the dead of night, and then marched down to the den, scooped you up and carried you down here. "

"How long did he stay?"

She shakes her head. "I have no idea. I didn't intrude. When I checked in on you this morning, he was gone."

My heart gets heavier with every word she tells me.

"What happened last week, Calli?"

"Can I?" I ask, nodding toward the mug she brought, needing something, anything to get me through this.

Cupping the mug in my hands, I sip the hot coffee, allowing it to warm me from the inside out.

"It was everything," I confess. "He... he's incredible, Jocelyn. And no one really sees it. It's heartbreaking. I hate that he feels like he has to put this front on for everyone, like they'll only like him, include him if he's this ruthless, brutal soldier and not the person he hides beneath the mask."

She takes my hand again, encouraging me to keep talking.

And I do. I tell her everything. The relief of finally telling someone—other than Alex, who's lived through it with us—takes such a weight off my shoulders, I wonder why I haven't done it before.

"My parents will never accept it," I say finally. "That's why he's walked away."

"Calli," she warns, sadness and compassion in her voice. "Did the girl last night who wore that sexy, revealing dress care about what her parents thought?"

I think back to the moment I walked into the hallway last night and just how powerful my defiance made me feel and shake my head.

"I was so proud of you standing up for yourself like that. I've been waiting for it. I've watched you edging closer over the past few months as you finally had enough of their crap. You need to embrace that, Calli."

"It's not that easy," I murmur.

"Anything worthwhile never is, sweetie. That's what makes life so..."

"Hard."

"Challenging. Fulfilling," she corrects. "You need to talk to him. There's no way that boy believed a word of what he said to you before you left that house. He's just as scared about this as you are. Love is terrifying, Calli. Opening up his heart is by far the scariest thing he's ever done. And from the things I've overheard, he's done some alarming things in his short life."

I nod, aware of just a few of them.

"He's been through a lot."

"I don't doubt that in the slightest, sweetheart. And that is exactly why he needs you to fight for him."

I nod, unable to disagree with anything she's said.

"He's spent his life trying to fight his own battles, to not have to rely on anyone. He's expecting you to walk away because he doesn't believe he's worthy of something as beautiful and incredible as you."

"But he is," I argue.

"So prove it to him. Don't prove him right by listening to his fears and allowing him to walk away from something I think you both need."

My phone starts ringing on the bed between us, lighting up with Stella's smiling face.

"You're almost eighteen, Calli. You've got your whole life just waiting for you. You need to decide if you've got the backbone to make it what you want it to be, or if you're going to be pushed into the life your mother wants for you."

I nod, on the verge of losing my grip on my emotions once more as my phone continues ringing.

"I'll leave you to it. If you ever need me, I'm right here, okay, sweetie? Judgement-free zone. Always."

She leans forward and presses a kiss to my brow before getting up and walking toward the stairs.

Stella cuts the call before I get a chance to answer, but I ignore it for a few more seconds.

"Thank you. I really appreciate everything you do for me," I say, my voice cracking.

"I just want to see you happy, sweetheart. In whatever form that is."

She's gone before I get a chance to say another word, and I'm left wondering why I wasn't gifted a mother more like her. Understanding, compassionate, loves me for who I am, not the version of me she wants me to be.

My phone starts ringing again, and this time I swipe the screen and answer it.

"About time," Stella mutters. "We're ready to leave here, you good to go?"

I glance down at myself. "I'm gonna need like, thirty minutes. I'm hanging."

Laughter floats down the phone. "Who knew Jerome was a party animal. I hope he treated you good, baby C."

"It was nothing like that, so don't even think about suggesting it. We just talked and got wasted."

"Well, to be fair, I didn't know he had that in him, so colour me impressed."

I can't help but laugh.

"Okay, I'm going to shower. Just don't expect me to be looking my best."

"Pretty sure the point of the spa is to sort that out."

"Well, they've got their work cut out for them," I

say as I push from the bed and walk over to the windows to peek outside.

I've kept the blinds down since I got back, not wanting anyone looking in. But after talking to Jocelyn, I'm feeling a little lighter, freer, and suddenly, I want the sunshine back inside my little home.

I press the buttons to lift the blinds and slowly, the afternoon sun floods the room. Warmth hits my skin and I immediately feel a little better. A little stronger.

"Okay, just come down when you're here."

"Sure thing. See you soon."

I hang up and just stare out at the garden for a minute or two, glad that I don't see anyone lingering around.

With a sigh, I turn on my heels with the intention of heading for the bathroom, but a knock on my door stops me.

"Yeah," I call, hoping that it's Jocelyn coming back for another heart to heart.

But unfortunately, Mum's perfectly styled blonde hair comes into view and I swallow a groan.

"Shouldn't you already be at the spa? I thought your appointments were before ours."

"Yes, Stella is picking me up shortly," I force through gritted teeth.

"Right, well. I just wanted to give you these dates for your diary."

"Dates for what?" I ask with a wince. The last thing I need is more meals like last night, or the event I'm going to have to endure tonight.

"Just a few socials. And some babysitting for Aunt Selene."

"Oh, you're giving me notice this time?" I sass, earning myself a stern, unimpressed stare from the cold woman before me.

"Callista," she chastises as if I'm still a child. "Please just open your diary so I know you've written them in."

"Worried I might forget?" I ask, reaching for my iPad and opening my planner app.

I flip ahead a few pages seeing as it's still sitting on the last week of school. The sight of it makes me realise just how easy it was to forget real life while I was locked away with Daemon.

But before I get to this week, my eyes lock on something I missed last week.

My heart jumps into my throat, my stomach turning over in panic.

"What's wrong?" Mum asks as I stare down at the little red heart I'd drawn on last Saturday.

If I weren't so shocked, I might be impressed that she's noticed something's wrong.

"N-nothing. I just missed something last week. What do I need to write down?" I ask, my hands trembling and my head spinning as she slides a piece of paper across the counter.

I make quick work of noting them down. If she notices the state of my handwriting then she doesn't comment.

"Great. Now you need to hurry. We need you looking perfect tonight, which means the full works."

"Sure thing," I mutter as she spins on her heels and hightails it out of my basement as if the space offends her. I might be hurt about her full works comment any other day, but right now, my world is spinning out of control.

"Fuck," I breathe, reaching out to wrap my hand around the counter as the door at the top of the stairs slams closed. My body burns red-hot, panic starting to overwhelm me.

I'm a week late.

I'm never late.

With a trembling hand, I flick back a month and count, telling myself that I must have fucked something up.

I have to have done, because anything else just isn't an option.

Four weeks. Just like it should be.

I go back further. It's pointless, because I know I've tracked my cycle diligently.

When I first started my periods, they were erratic as fuck. But in the past year or so, they've settled down to the point I can pinpoint the exact day. Or I did until Daemon turned my world upside down.

I stumble back, my calves hitting the sofa, and I lower my arse down.

I'm numb. Utterly fucking numb.

26

DAEMON

"Is this party tonight a good idea?" I ask, looking around at everyone.

We're in Theo's flat. The girls have all gone to the spa, and Alex gave me little choice when he dragged my arse through my front door, demanding that I attempt to be normal for once after bailing on them all last night.

I didn't really have a leg to stand on, and I could hardly argue when he gave me his kicked-puppy face.

He's already spent long enough trying to get the truth out of me as to where I disappeared last night and is pissed off that I keep refusing to tell him. Although, really, he knows. He can see it in my eyes. But he hasn't ripped me a new one for it. He knows as well as I do how badly I need her.

To my surprise, he's kept off my case other than that. I'm not sure if he's changing tactics in the hope that he might get the answers he wants out of me by playing different cards. But so far, I'm just relieved he's shut the fuck up about it.

"It's all planned," Theo says confidently. "The decoy is in place and we all know the plan, right?" he asks, looking around at everyone.

"Care to fill me in?"

"If you'd have stuck around last night, you'd already know," Alex pipes up, earning himself a death glare from me.

"We're letting the Italians think we're holding the party at the hotel. It's the safest place, and after New Year, we've increased security. It makes sense that we'd all want to be there."

"This all seems like a lot of effort for a bloody birthday party."

"You know what my mum's like," Nico grunts. "What she wants, my dad makes sure she gets." He rolls his eyes.

"You'll be like that one day," Toby points out, "making sure your little woman has everything she needs to be happy."

He scoffs in disgust. "The only thing any woman is getting from me is my cock."

"Such an old romantic," Seb teases.

"Like you can talk," Nico mutters. "What the fuck have you done that's romantic?"

We all stare at Nico like he's lost his mind.

"Oh, I don't know. I chased Stella halfway across the world and told her how I felt about her. I've got a tattoo that I allowed to be put on me without seeing it, just blindly trusted her. Either of those any good?"

"You let her carve her initials into your thigh," Alex points out.

"That's romantic as fuck right there, Bro," I mutter.

He barks out a laugh. "You gonna try and tell me that you wouldn't want your girl's name permanently etched into your skin?" He lifts a brow at me.

"I don't ha—"

"Wait..." Theo barks happily. "Daemon has a girl?"

"No. He's lying. No girl would ever put up with me," I mutter, in the hope I can bat this fucking conversation away.

"Fuck that, you're a catch, man," Seb assures me. "Girls love all that dark and broody shit."

"Stella sure seems to love your psycho side," Toby says with a wince.

"The darker the better, my friend." Seb winks.

"Not quite a marriage though, is it?" Theo smirks.

"Oh yeah, because you got down on one knee and asked your girl." Alex rolls his eyes hard and Theo flips him off.

"So do you have a girl or not?" Nico asks, looking at me a little too hard.

"Of fucking course not. I ain't getting tied down anytime soon." But those words taste bitter as they roll off my tongue. "So where is the actual party if it's not at the hotel?" I ask, seeing as no one is very forthcoming with the details.

"That's for us to know and you to find out," Theo teases.

"Don't pull that shit with me, Cirillo," I warn darkly.

"You're off the clock, man." I damn near growl at Nico when he joins in.

I fucking knew coming up here was a bad idea.

"If that's the case, then I think I'll spend the night alone in my flat." I push to stand, but, faster than I anticipated, Alex wraps his fingers around my forearm and tugs me back down.

"You're working tonight. We need all the manpower we can get," he tells me.

I look around at all of them as they stare at me like I'm a piece that doesn't quite fit.

"For the record, I think this is a fucking stupid idea given the current circumstances."

"The boss has signed off on it. He's confident."

"Yeah, and I'm pretty sure he didn't expect the Reapers to storm New Year's either, but it sure as fuck happened, didn't it?"

They all remain mute.

"What? What aren't you telling me?"

Nico and Theo share a look that pisses me the fuck off, because if this were just a month ago, I'd be right in the thick of whatever this plan was. I fucking hate being left out of something that should be my life.

The Family is my life, and I've been forced to the outskirts, watching my brothers live my life from the sidelines.

"Fuck. It's a trap, isn't it? This whole thing is a setup?" I ask, realisation suddenly hitting me.

The slightest twitch of Theo's lips is all the answer I need.

"This is a fucking mistake," I bark, shooting out of my seat before Alex gets a chance to do anything about it this time.

"Everything is in place. Our snakes have dropped the intel to ensure the Italians are going to walk straight into our trap, and we've got enough soldiers and backup to take them down."

"And what if this goes wrong, huh? They've proved more than once that we're not the only ones with snakes behind enemy lines. What if they already know all of this and they're going to turn up at the actual location and take us all out?" My heart pounds erratically as I think about Calli finding herself in the middle of this shit once again.

"It won't happen. Damien and Evan have everything in place," Theo says confidently.

"I trust the boss, Theo, I do. I trust all of you. But those fucking Italians? Not a fucking chance. I'm telling you, this is going to blow up in all our faces. I don't care how well you think it's been planned. It's fucking suicide."

Theo pushes to his feet, ready to challenge me on

this. His eyes hold mine as he stands chest to chest with me.

"What exactly are you saying, soldier? That you're not with us?"

"Fuck that, Theo. You know I've got your backs no matter what. I just don't think you should be sending your girls into this tonight."

His jaw tics as he stares at me, but there's not even a flicker of hesitation in his eyes.

He believes that this is all going to be okay.

So what more can I really say?

I have to trust him. I have to trust the boss and follow the plans, just like I have done a thousand times.

It's just that this time is different.

Calli is going to be there, and I refuse to put her in any kind of danger. Ever.

"The cars will be here in thirty minutes," Nico points out.

"And what about the girls?" I already know that Isla is meeting me there along with her parents. But what about the others?

What about Calli?

"They're arriving separately. They're getting ready with Selene and Cassandra," Seb informs me.

"And what are we doing while they're left like sitting ducks?"

"You need to chill, man," Nico suggests, making my blood damn near boil over.

"Chill? Are you fucking shitting me, Cirillo?

You're about to send your mother, your sister, everyone else you fucking love into the middle of an Italian war," I boom.

"It's not going to come to that. What we're doing is getting them to safety."

"Then put them on a fucking airplane and get them the fuck out of here. Some secret location for a party isn't good enough."

"You need to get your head in the game, or you'll be the one who's not a part of this," Theo warns.

"I'll fucking be there. It's my job," I seethe.

Tension ripples around the room, the air turning toxic and dangerous as Theo and I continue to stare at each other, neither of us willing to back down.

A phone ringing finally cuts through the atmosphere before Theo pulls his phone from his pocket and lifts it to his ear.

"Yeah, Boss. We're ready."

Damien says something on the other end, but I can't make out his words.

"The girls?" Theo asks. "Good. Yeah. Okay." He glances at Nico. "Yeah, we've got it."

Without saying goodbye, Theo hangs up and drops his phone back into his pocket.

"Everything is good to go. We head to the hotel, we go inside to meet our girls, who have been seen going inside to get ready."

"Where are they now?" I ask, hating how panicked I sound.

Theo's eyes narrow on me, suspicion swimming in

their dark depths. But for the first time, I don't give a shit if he sees more than I want him to.

"Heading toward the venue. The hotel is having renovations done. There's a lot of coming and going from the underground car park."

Ripping his eyes from mine, he turns to Nico and begins a hushed conversation with him.

A hand lands on my shoulder, and I'm dragged back.

"Nico's right, you need to chill, Bro. You're beginning to look a little neurotic," Alex says quietly so his words don't carry.

"Do not tell me that you're okay with this," I beg.

"Bro, I—"

"No," I hiss. "Don't fucking 'Bro' me. We can't let her walk into the middle of this."

"Oh, so now you admit you care," he teases me.

"Of course I fucking care. I fucking lo—" I cut myself off before I spill words that have no right falling from my lips. "We need them all safe. We shouldn't be throwing them to the wolves."

"Did you shit out your faith along with your confidence?" Alex asks me. He's so serious that it makes my fist curl. "Damien, Evan, Charon, everyone has this planned to a tee. None of them would put any of us, let alone the girls, at risk. Get your head out of your heart and get in the game, yeah?"

I blow out a long breath, wishing I could soak up some strength from his confidence. But everything feels wrong. So fucking wrong. But if none of them feel it, then what the fuck am I meant to do about it?

"The cars are here," Nico announces.

Everyone stands, straightening their suits and checking their weapons.

Anticipation goes around the room as we each make eye contact with each other.

Despite the fact that none of them agreed with me when I stood up against Theo, I can see the unease in their eyes, and it does fuck all to make me feel better about all of this.

I just really fucking hope that I'm wrong.

27

CALLI

By some miracle, I'd managed to pull myself together enough by the time Stella appeared in my basement that she didn't immediately question me.

She just assumed I was pale as fuck because of my hangover, and for the first time since I woke to that shitshow, I was happy about it.

Happy, and tinged with a heap load of guilt and a fuck ton of fear.

My hands continue to tremble in my lap as the five of us sit around the pool at Mum's spa on the loungers.

Mum, Iris, and Clio are all having treatments—not that they've chosen to actually spend any time with us.

I got one hell of a death glare when I arrived—late —with Stella. Obviously, she's not over my dress of choice and lack of respect for her wishes last night yet. Something I am more than okay with.

I don't have the headspace or the energy to deal with her bullshit right now. I'm too busy silently freaking out while the girls talk to me about tonight's party.

It's nothing big, although not as small as last night's intimate dinner. It's just basically a way for Mum to swan around, showing off whatever ludicrously expensive jewellery my father will have bought her for her birthday while telling anyone who will listen who she is wearing and how rare the design is.

I've seen it time and time again, and it never gets any easier to swallow.

I have no idea how my dad puts up with it.

A groan rips through the air as I watch this evening play out so vividly in my mind, and I don't realise it came from me until the burning stare of everyone around me makes my skin prickle.

"Everything okay?" Emmie asks.

"Yeah." Somehow, my voice comes out steady, instead of the shaky, emotional mess I was expecting. "I'm just thinking about what tonight might hold."

"Sounds like it should be a fun night," Bri chips in. She's the only one here who's been lucky enough not to have an invite for tonight.

If only I could switch places with her.

"You should just come," Jodie says, and the way

Bri glares at her in return makes me think it's not the first time she's tried.

"Give it a rest, Jojo," Bri sighs. "I've already told you, I've got plans tonight. And I do not intend to let this fresh wax go to waste." She points at her crotch and Jodie groans.

"Your date is a lucky guy," Stella chips in. "Lexi is a miracle worker with a wax strip. He's gonna have the time of his life down there."

"A-fucking-men to that, sista," Bri cries, lifting her hand to high-five Stella.

"Any news on Sara today?" Emmie asks, changing the subject.

"She's had a good week. She's progressing again. They're hoping to try and wake her up next week if things stay the same."

"That's good, right?" Emmie asks when Jodie looks less than excited about the prospect.

"I hope so. I'm just scared of how she's going to adjust to her new reality."

"One step at a time," Stella says softly. "And she'll have you and Jesse there every step of the way. And who knows, it might end up being the making of her. Often people find the best of themselves in the shittiest situations."

Jodie sighs as my stomach knots once more, Stella's words hitting a little too close to home.

"Cal, you okay?" Emmie asks, her eyes narrowing in suspicion.

"Yeah," I say, swallowing down my unease.

"You really are suffering today, huh? Maybe you should take it slow tonight," Bri suggests like the mother hen of the group.

Trust me, I'll be taking it slower than slow.

My stomach turns over as my own possible new reality hits me and I push to my feet.

"Sorry, I just need a minute."

Suddenly, the scent of the pool, the humidity, everything is too much as I bolt for the bathroom, hoping like hell that they're not all about to follow me.

"Calli?" Stella calls.

I wave my hand behind me. "Vodka," I mumble, much to their amusement, and I just pray that it's enough to cover up the real reason why I'm losing my goddamn mind.

I need to know the truth.

I need to stare down at the evidence that I can't count to four correctly and know that this is a false alarm. Because it has to be, right?

I can't be...

I retch and lurch myself toward the basin, but nothing actually comes up. No surprise there, seeing as I puked up the coffee Jocelyn gave me and haven't had anything since.

"Fucking hell," I groan, resting my hands on the counter and bending over, hanging my head between my shoulders.

I suck in a deep breath, hoping that it might help calm the riot of emotions raging within me.

I need to not be here right now. I need to find a shop and I need to—

I heave again, the reality of what I need to do shaking me to my very core.

What the hell is my mother going to say about this—

"Calli?" The concerned voice from the other side of the room cuts off my thoughts and interrupts my panic.

I stand in a rush and have to reach for the basin once more when the room spins around me.

"I'm fine. That vodka last night really wiped me out."

"Yeah," Bri agrees suspiciously. "It really has."

She walks toward me with her brows pulled together and concern oozing from her.

"Are you sure that's all this is?"

"That and the dread for what tonight is going to hold," I say weakly. "Why?" I mentally kick myself for asking when I should be doing anything to get the heat off me right now.

"You just seem... different."

"There's a lot of shit going on and I j-just—" My voice cracks, and I swallow down the rest of that statement.

"Calli," Bri whispers, stepping closer and taking my hand in hers. "Whatever it is, you can talk to me. You can trust me, you know that. Has something hap—"

"I'm late," I blurt, my eyes widening in shock at my outburst.

"Oh, um... I don't think your next appointment is for a bit yet. I think they're bringing us food fir—"

"I don't mean my appointment. I mean... I'm late. Like... late." My eyes beg for her to hear my unspoken words.

There's no way I can admit the truth out loud. That is not going to help me in any way. But fuck, I need someone to know. I need someone to tell me that this is going to be okay. I need her to tell me that I'm overreacting and that this kind of thing happens all the time and that it'll be nothing.

It takes a couple of seconds, but eventually her jaw drops and her eyes widen.

"Oh, that kind of late," she murmurs. "How much?"

"A week," I confess.

"And is this normal or..."

"No. Not normal. Bri, tell me that I'm not... Tell me that he hasn't..."

"It's more than likely a false alarm. You took precautions, right?"

"Y-yeah, I'm on the pill, but we never used... oh fuck. Everyone is literally going to kill me. He's going to hate me, and I'm going to be alone and..." My breathing increases to the point that I have no control over it and my vision blurs as I lose grip on reality.

Hands grip my upper arms, and I know she's talking to me but I don't hear any of it. There's nothing but the deafening sound of white noise racing past my ears.

"Calli. Calli. CALLI." The volume of Bri's voice and the gentle shake of my shoulders finally drags me out of my panic.

"I'm going to make an excuse and go and get you a test, okay? You need an answer."

"No, you can't just walk out of here. They'll ask questions and I haven't even told them that—"

"Shhh," she soothes, taking my face in her hands just like Jocelyn did earlier.

My eyes flood with tears as I stare into her kind, supportive eyes.

"Trust me, yeah? I'll get what you need, then you can figure out what's next once you have the facts. Deep breath."

I do as I'm told and eventually, everything returns to normal.

"Now, unless you want them all knowing, you need to pull up your big girl bikini bottoms and get it together fast."

I nod, because as much as I hate lying to them, I also know that I can't handle them all knowing about this. Not yet, anyway.

One step at a time. They need to know I've been screwing the devil first.

"I've got your back, okay?"

Bri pulls me in for a hug.

"And so will they, when you're ready to tell them

what's been going on," she whispers encouragingly in my ear.

———

I was expecting Bri to find a way to sneak off straight away and was a nervous wreck when I finally returned to the loungers, giving the girls only a half-lie about the two of us getting lost in conversation in the toilets. But in reality, it was a couple of hours before she announced that she'd just received a booty call from her regular hook-up and was in desperate need of a screaming orgasm. And the second she started giving us all a detailed description of exactly what he can do with his tongue, we all ushered her out of the room so she could go and bang him in the back seat of his car.

The others fell for it hook, line and sinker. I wasn't sure if I was impressed or mortified by Bri's reputation. Her best friend didn't bat an eyelid about her slutty ways, so I can only assume this kind of activity is more than normal for her.

As grateful as I am for her right now, I can't deny that it leaves a bitter taste in my mouth where Nico is concerned.

I know they both claim that there is nothing there. And there may well not be. But I swear there is something different about my brother whenever she's in the room. He might be a dickhead and a player of epic proportions, but at the end of the day, he's my big brother and all I want for him is to be happy.

The rest of our time at the spa is a blur, and when we finally leave, my make-up is once again darker than I'd usually opt for, my hair has been styled perfectly, and I'm rocking my first ever set of black nails.

I want to say that I didn't do it for him, but I would be lying.

When Jocelyn walked out of my room earlier, I had every intention of calling him, of trying to talk to him. Even if it was just to thank him for last night. But then reality came knocking and shot all my plans to shit, and here I am, standing in the middle of the bathroom in one of the platinum suites at The Prestige, holding a pregnancy test that I'm meant to pee on to discover my fate.

I was expecting the party to be at The Empire, and that was where our car went initially. But then we were ushered out, made to sit in different cars and took off again.

All our parties are at The Empire, and being somewhere else right now doesn't help with the anxiety flowing through my veins.

Having this party at all seems beyond insane right now.

I was literally banished from town for a week because of the threat from the Italians. And here we are, all the main players of the Cirillo Family congregating under one roof for my mother's goddamn birthday? It seems utterly ludicrous.

But who am I to question the great Damien and Evan Cirillo?

They've proved time and time again that they know what's best for all of us. So I just have to put my trust in them, and push at least that issue aside.

I've got a more pressing one that I need to deal with.

Tearing open the packet, I pull the stick from inside and stare down at it, my heart like a runaway train in my chest.

I've always hoped that I'd do this one day. I just never imagined that I'd be seventeen, single—I think—and standing alone in a hotel bathroom.

If I thought my life was pathetic before Stella and Emmie entered it, then I should probably reconsider that right this second, because this is most definitely a low, even for me.

I've read the instructions over and over, but that doesn't stop me from doing it again before I pull the lid off and make my way over to the toilet.

My hand shakes as I hold it in what I hope is going to be the right place. I can't say I've ever paid much attention to the direction of my flow.

Fuck my life.

I do my thing, put the cap back on and rest the test upside down on the side of the basin as I wash my hands, trying to think about anything but what I just did.

I stand there, counting the seconds, and when I get

down to twenty left, my name is called through the door and the handle rattles.

"Cal, what the fuck is taking you so long?"

I swear to all that's holy that I locked the door the second I stepped inside, but to my horror, not a second after Emmie pushes the handle down does the door fly open.

Faster than I thought possible, I stuff the test back into the packet and shove it to the bottom of my clutch. Bri already took care of the box before she gave it to me in the hope that it would be a little more discreet.

"What the hell are you doing? Snorting coke off the basin or something?"

"What?" I gasp, although saying yes to that accusation would probably be better than reality. "No, of course not. I was... uh... just on the phone."

The instructions I dropped beside the toilet catches my eye, and my heart jumps into my throat.

"To..."

"A-Alex," I stutter.

"Oh yeah. He want to see you in this sexy dress before everyone else, huh?"

My cheeks blaze as I fight to keep my eyes on hers and not alert her to what's hanging around on the floor.

"Something like that," I mutter, letting her imagination run wild with that thought.

"So anyway," she starts, accepting my lie easily,

"apparently we're not actually staying here for the party."

"What?" I ask, my brow wrinkling as I take that information on. "Where the hell is it then?"

"I have no idea. Selene just knocked and said the cars will be two minutes and that we need to be ready."

I stare at her in disbelief.

"I know as much as you. But between you and me, this has setup written all over it."

"Please," I beg. "Please don't say that."

"You said it yourself earlier. Throwing this party is beyond insane with everything that's going on. The boys are up to something."

"Jesus," I mutter, lifting my hand to rub my face but thinking better of it with the amount of make-up that's covering it.

"I brought you a gift. You know... just in case." Emmie opens her bag and passes me a gun. "I hear you're a shit-hot shot these days, so it might come in useful."

"Where the hell am I meant to stash this?" I ask, looking down at my slim, tight-fitting black dress.

"Ah... are you ready to blow Alex's, or Jerome's, mind?"

"Uh..." Not really, no, but I doubt I have a choice in this right now.

Emmie drops to the floor in front of me, and I make the most of the opportunity to shuffle around a little so there's no chance of her seeing the paper sitting on the floor behind her as she pulls something else out of her bag.

"What is that?" I ask, although really, it's damn obvious.

"A holster, obviously. We just strap it here." She opens the high split in my floor-length dress and wraps the black fabric around my thigh, securing it and then shoving the gun into the straps. "And now, you look fucking hot. The guys are going to shit a brick when they see you."

"Emmie," I hiss. "I can't walk around with a gun strapped to my thigh."

"Says who?" she asks, pushing to stand once more and lifting her own dress up to show me her concealed weapon. "Stella is packing too."

"Jesus."

"Just in case. If this is some plan to lure the Italians out and wipe them from the face of the Earth, then we want to be ready to help our boys, right?"

"Sure," I whisper, feeling very, very uncomfortable about all of this.

I wonder if they'd let me go home if I were to tell them the truth. Surely, they wouldn't want me anywhere near this shitshow if I'm...

My stomach lurches before I even think the word.

"Emmie, Calli," Stella calls. "We need to go."

"Come on," Emmie says, reaching for my hand and dragging me from the bathroom and away from the evidence I left on the floor.

I want to breathe a sigh of relief, but the unknown

of what the rest of the night holds stops that from being possible.

We're all loaded into blacked-out SUVs in the hotel's underground car park before we head out.

"Anyone would think we're the freaking prime minister," Jodie breathes as a few cars go ahead of us as others fall in behind.

"Safe to assume the party is at an undisclosed location then," Stella announces as we leave the hotel and watch as the cars take different exits.

"Isn't this all a bit much for your mum's birthday? No offence," Jodie says with a concerned frown.

"Yeah, it's crazy. I want to say that I'm surprised she's letting it happen if it's all part of a job. But she's never one to turn down even a few minutes in the limelight."

Silence falls amongst the four of us as we're driven through the streets of London to God knows where.

As the minutes and the miles pass, it soon becomes obvious that we're heading out of the city, which is probably for the best. Although why we couldn't have done this earlier, before getting dressed, is beyond me. Surely it would have been safer?

It's well over an hour later when the car finally pulls to a stop outside a fancy country club I've never been to before.

Fairy lights are strung up everywhere, and there are two doormen waiting to greet us. It's fitting for their guest of honour tonight, that's for sure.

"Fancy," Jodie mutters.

"Did you expect anything less?" Emmie asks.

"I guess not."

The doors are opened and we all step out.

Unease rushes down my spine, my skin prickling with an awareness that only comes with being watched.

Suddenly, four suited boys appear at the main doors, and I relax a little as Alex's eyes lock on mine before dropping down my body.

Even from here, I see desire sweep through his features. It shouldn't affect me, but everything is such a mess right now that I don't even question the way my lower belly clenches.

Dressed up in his black suit, he looks so much like his twin that it's unnerving.

Theo, Seb, and Toby march forward and collect up their girls as Alex makes his way to me.

"Fuck, baby C. You look sensational," he breathes, his eyes taking in every inch of me.

"Thanks," I breathe, forcing a smile on my face. One that he doesn't fall for.

"What's wrong?"

My lips part to assure him that I'm fine, but when words roll off my tongue, they're very different.

"This isn't just a normal party is it?"

"What makes you say that?"

"Well, the incognito departure from both The Empire and The Prestige. The fact that I can feel a million sets of eyes on me right now. Need I go on?"

"There's nothing to worry about, okay? Damien and your dad have everything under control."

In the past, those words would have given me some comfort. But today, I'm struggling to find any.

I don't know what it is, but there's just this nagging deep in my gut that something is going to go very, very wrong tonight.

Leaning into Alex, I whisper, "Is he here?"

"Of course. He's inside. And he wants to talk to you."

Straightening my spine and pushing my fears aside, I thread my arm through Alex's. "Lead the way then, kind sir."

"It would be my pleasure."

28

CALLI

My body trembles from head to toe as Alex leads me through the foyer that's full of massive arrangements of my mum's favourite flowers. But I don't really see any of it.

My head spins and my blood rushes past my ears at such a rate, I can't help but wonder how I'm still standing.

"Are you okay?" Alex breathes in my ear, sending a shiver racing down my spine.

Plastering a fake-arse smile on my face, I turn to him. "Of course."

"Yeah, nice try, baby C. That shit might work on Nico, but you're not fooling anyone here."

"He came to me last night," I confess.

"Yeah, I figured. Although he never actually said the words."

"He looked after me when I passed out in the den. Carried me to bed. Tucked me in."

"Who knew the devil had such a sweet side," Alex teases.

"He was gone before I woke. I don't think he wanted me to know."

"So, how do you?"

"His little helper ratted him out," I say, a small smile pulling at my lips as I think about Jocelyn and her desperately needed advice this morning.

"Helper?"

"He's got Jocelyn wrapped around his little finger, it seems."

"Okay, wow," Alex breathes. "I guess that makes a lot of sense."

"Talking to her helped. It made me see things from a different angle."

"And?" Alex asks as we step into the grand room where the party is being held.

The ostentatious gold and purple decorations pass me by, as do all the people who are already in here, ready to celebrate another year of my mother trying to control my life.

Yet, the only thing I see is him.

I swear, my heart stops at the sight of him. My stomach knots, my hands shake, and my chest aches as if someone just slid a knife straight into it.

He's dressed like all the men here in his black Cirillo suit, and he looks just as hot as I knew he would.

"They're only friends," Alex whispers, as if the girl pressed right up against his side is the reason for me stopping the second my eyes landed on him.

"I-I know." Isla pressing her tits against his arm is literally the least of my worries right now.

But despite knowing it's the truth, it doesn't stop the green-eyed monster popping its ugly head up as I continue to watch them talking together.

They've always been close, but I've never seen it quite like I am right now.

"Cal," Alex warns, sensing my inner turmoil. "It's you. He doesn't see—"

"I know," I assure him, squeezing his arm. "It's just not that easy."

"But it can be. You two just need to talk, clear the air. He needs you, Cal. And I suspect you need him too."

Right now, like you wouldn't freaking believe.

My clutch burns red-hot under my arm. The answer to my fate sits inside, begging me to pull it out and confirm if my life is about to change forever.

"I just need to visit the ladi—"

"You're not running from this," Alex states, holding me tighter before he begins marching us closer to the bar.

We make it halfway across the vast room before we catch Isla's eye.

She studies us—or more so me—for a beat. My skin prickles with awareness as she clearly decides right then and there if I'm good enough for her best friend.

The two of us have always got on okay, but we've never been friends exactly. We've always been too different. Or maybe, with the way I've been breaking through the shackles that have been around me all my life, we're not so dissimilar after all. It just took me longer to find my inner strength and confidence.

After getting her fill, she finally nods her head, indicating for Daemon to turn around. My heart jumps in my throat as anticipation rushes through my veins.

The last time I looked into his eyes, he'd had his gives-no-shits mask on, and I'd been well and truly locked out. What side of this complicated man am I going to get today?

I swear time stops around us as he turns around.

I stop breathing, and everything around me ceases to exist as I just wait.

The second our eyes connect, it's like someone has literally ripped the world from beneath my feet.

My knees buckle, and if it weren't for Alex, then I'd have been in a heap in the middle of the room.

"Shit, Calli. You okay?" Alex asks as Daemon pushes away from the bar and strides over. His long legs eat up the space between us in only seconds.

"What's wrong?" he asks, clearly having seen the way my legs gave out. Concern oozes from his dark, stormy eyes as tears fill my own.

Shaking my head, I fight to keep my emotions in check.

Tonight already has the makings of a total disaster.

The last thing I need is to make a spectacle of myself and invite unwanted questions from my brother. Or anyone, really.

What I need to do is run away as fast as I can with Daemon right beside me. Fat chance of that.

"N-nothing. It's good to see you," I say politely, forcing a smile on my lips.

He frowns at me before his eyes flick to Alex in concern. He just shrugs as they embark on an irritating silent conversation that, obviously, I'm the centre of.

"How are you feeling?"

"Awful," I say honestly, right as a waiter appears beside us with a tray of champagne and whisky.

Everyone reaches for a glass, Daemon instantly throwing his back and placing it back down.

"Miss?" the waiter asks politely.

"No, thank you. Could I get a glass of water please?"

"Of course, I'll be right with you." I smile sweetly at him.

"Wow, you must have had a really good night if you haven't got back on the horse yet," Isla announces.

"Yeah, it was something. Excuse me, I—"

But before I get to turn around and escape, voices get louder behind me and I quickly find myself in the middle of our group.

"This is nice, the whole gang together. Plus that cling-on," Nico says, shooting Isla a teasing wink.

"Fuck you, Cirillo. I'm the best person in this huddle and you know it."

I look between the two of them and groan.

Please, for the love of God, don't tell me he's fucked her too.

"Water?" Jodie asks when the waiter returns with my drink and a refreshed tray for everyone else.

"I just can't face it. Not yet."

She studies me suspiciously, and my face heats. Surely Bri hasn't said anything. She promised me, and I trusted her.

"Been there more than once. There was this one time that Bri and I went to some holiday park for the weekend, and I swear I couldn't even stomach the scent of alcohol for at least a week after we returned. You'll soon be back in the saddle though, and nursing another hangover."

"Can I at least get over this one before we start talking about the next?"

She laughs before falling into conversation with Toby and Nico.

I glance around at my friends, happiness filling my heart, although it's laced with concern.

Everyone seems so carefree and happy, but I still can't shift the unease within me. Unease that has nothing to do with the test in my clutch.

Fuck.

Backing away from them once they're all distracted, I attempt to finally make my escape.

Finding out the answer in the middle of this party could be the worst decision I've ever made, or it could be the best and I might be able to face a glass or five of that champagne. Christ knows I could do with the distraction those bubbles would bring me right about now.

I've got my eyes fixed on the sign to the bathrooms, so I don't notice the guy I'm about to steamroll over until he speaks.

"Hey, how are you feeling?" a familiar voice says, interrupting my one-woman mission to lock myself in a cubicle.

Looking up, I find Jerome's kind yet tired eyes locked on mine.

A laugh tumbles from my throat as my emotions continue to get thrown around like they're on a freaking roller coaster.

"I've been better, can't lie. You?"

"Pretty sure I'm dead. What the hell was in that vodka?"

"Our painful deaths?" I deadpan.

"Hangovers aside, it was a good night. I just wanted to say thank you for listening to me. I really appreciate it."

"Jerome," I sigh.

"Don't," he warns. "I had my moment last night. I'm good."

I smile at him, seeing a strength in his features that wasn't there last night.

"I'll catch up with you later, yeah? I just need to..." I nod to the bathroom and he smiles at me, finally letting me go.

I breathe a sigh of relief as I take off.

"Callista."

"For the love of all that's holy, can I please just get to the freaking bathroom?" I mutter under my breath.

It's a good job I don't actually need a pee, or I'd be in serious trouble by now.

I spin around at the sound of my father's deep voice and allow him to look me over.

"When did my baby girl grow up?" he breathes, his eyes all soft as he forgets about being the Family's underboss for a few seconds and just becomes my father. "You look beautiful. But something tells me that your mother was about as impressed by that dress as the one you chose last night."

A smirk curls at my lips, and I'm sure I see pride flash through his eyes.

"You could say that. I guess it's really good that she hasn't seen this."

I press my leg forward, allowing the fabric to part across my thigh and flash my weapon.

"Jesus, Calli. I'm not sure that's necessary," he blurts in shock.

"Are you armed, Dad?" I ask innocently.

"Uh... of course I am."

"Then there's no reason why I shouldn't be too."

His mouth opens and closes, seemingly unable to find any words to respond.

Letting my dress fall back into place, I step forward, closing the space between us.

"What is really going on tonight, Dad? We don't go to parties undercover. We don't hide. Ever."

He swallows nervously, and it's all I need to know that my suspicions are correct.

"It's none of your concern what we have going on in the background, sweetheart."

"And that may well be true. But can you stand there and tell me without any doubt that none of the people I love are at risk tonight?"

When his response doesn't come immediately, a bitter laugh falls from my lips.

"I should take my friends and get the hell away from this place," I warn.

"We have everything covered, Calli. There is no reason why anything should happen."

"But it might?"

"There is always risk, sweetheart."

"But this one isn't big enough to send those you love into hiding like last week?" I ask with my brow quirked.

"That was directed at you. That was different."

"So if this place goes up later tonight and I don't see tomorrow, that's different, is it?"

"Calli," he warns, his soft, fatherly voice giving in to the brutal soldier that lingers beneath. The switch between the two is so familiar to me now with all the men in my life that it's almost normal.

"What? I'm just asking. I know you love Mum unconditionally and all that, but I just want it to be known that this is a really bad idea."

His dark eyes hold mine, and I swear I see a flicker of hesitation within them.

He knows. He feels it too.

"Evan, darling," Mum purrs from somewhere behind him, forcing us to end our silent battle of wills. Not that I ever stood a chance of winning against him. "We need to go and take our seats. They want to bring the starters out soon."

"Okay, we'll be right there. Right, Calli?" Dad says, turning Mum's eyes on me.

Her expression hardens, her eyes dropping to my dress.

"I can't wait," I force through clenched teeth. "I just need to use the bathroom first." I take a step back, ready to run this time.

"No time. Go later. Your daddy has a speech prepared. You can't miss it."

"But I just need—"

"Come on, Calli," Alex says, sweeping in behind me and wrapping his arm around my waist protectively. A move that my mother certainly doesn't miss.

"I thought Jerome was your date tonight?" she asks with a frown.

"She's with both of us, right, Cal? Things are always more... fun in threes."

A grunt falls from his lips when I shove my elbow into his ribs, but I don't really mean it, because I would have paid to see Mum's face turn the shade of purple it does at his comment.

"Lead the way then. I'm more than ready for all the fun," I tease.

With his hand pressed to the small of my back, he encourages me toward the large table where the rest of our group is already congregating.

"I legit thought your mum's eyes were about to pop out then," he jokes in my ear.

"Can you imagine if it were true and I came home to tell her I had two boyfriends? I think she might actually die."

He chuckles. "Maybe we should try it. Once everything settles, maybe Daemon and I could turn up to take you out on a date and watch the top of her head shoot off."

"You're wicked."

"Gotta get you out on a date somehow, baby C."

"You can take me out any time you want. Just don't expect any added benefits."

"Ugh, but they're the fun bits."

"You need a girl," I state. "Anyone around here catch your eye?"

"You mean there are girls here other than you?"

"You're cute, and you work wonders for my confidence. But I'm serious. You deserve a nice girl who will put up with your weirdness."

"I'd prefer a naughty one who will indulge my weirdness."

"And here I was thinking you were all sweet and innocent."

"Take off the rose-tinted glasses, baby C. There is no sweet and innocent around this table." He pulls my chair out for me just as Jerome steps up on my other side, finding his name on the setting beside mine. No huge shock there. "Oh, maybe there is," Alex jokes.

"Behave," I warn over my shoulder.

I shiver as he lets his fingers trail over my mostly bare shoulder, and I swear the air actually crackles as Daemon glares at his brother. I don't think I've ever witnessed such a promise of pain in all my life.

But being Alex, he doesn't seem to give a single fuck as he takes his seat and turns toward where my dad is clinking a knife to a glass to get everyone's attention.

29

DAEMON

Anger and need for my girl surge through me as I watch Alex brazenly touch her in front of me.

I know what he's doing. Isla too.

But it's not fucking necessary.

My heart is like a fucking bass drum pounding in my chest, my senses hyper-aware as I wait for something to happen.

No matter how many times everyone tries to convince me that we're all safe here, I refuse to believe it.

I'm all for baiting the Italians and throwing them for a loop by not being where they're expecting us to be. But the girls, Calli, should not be in the fucking middle of it.

There are so many other things we could have done to pull them out of their hiding places and cut them down.

My fists curl beneath the table, but Calli doesn't miss the way my shoulders tense, because lines form on her brow simultaneously.

The image of her damn near hitting the deck when our eyes first collided earlier is still playing out in my mind, and I'm still as confused about it as I was then.

I know things are intense between us, but that was...

Isla's warm, whisky-laced breath races down my neck.

"I'm not saying I didn't believe you or anything, but fuck, that girl is so far gone for you."

My heart jumps into my throat at her words, my eyes still locked on my girl as she talks to Jerome, although her attention wanders to me every few seconds as if she can't keep her eyes off me.

"Yeah?" I ask, hating that I sound like a hopeful pre-teen girl, but also not really giving a shit about it.

All I care about at this moment is her, and making sure that if the worst should happen tonight, I get her as far away from it as fast as possible.

"Yeah, and the sexual tension between the two of you is making even me horny. You think anyone would notice if I—"

"Please, don't finish that sentence. I really don't need to know how it ends."

She chuckles beside me as Evan continues to drawl on how wonderful his wife is.

No one at our table is listening, not even Nico or

Calli, so I don't bat an eye about letting it all pass me by. As far as I'm concerned, Cassandra is a control freak with a stick shoved so far up her arse that even the world's best doctor couldn't wiggle it free.

Finally, Evan encourages us to raise a toast once the waiters have handed out fresh glasses of champagne, and I happily oblige in the drinking part of his speech.

I throw the bubbly shit down with a wince as it seems to explode down my throat.

"Ugh," I complain.

"Here," Isla says, passing me a bottle of whisky that she had hiding... fuck knows where.

I stare at her in confusion.

"Knife one side, whisky the other," she says, tapping her thigh.

"I have no words," I say, taking the bottle and sinking a shot.

Calli still doesn't drink. Instead, she just places her glass back on the table after raising it with everyone else.

My brows pull together as I watch her.

Despite her make-up, her skin is pale. She looks exhausted, which I guess isn't all that unusual after a hangover from hell, but it sure doesn't help settle any of my concerns right now.

She gasps when she finds me staring at her once more, her head shaking slightly as if to tell me off before she gazes over my shoulder.

Looking back, I find her staring longingly at the bathroom.

Heat stirs within me as dirty, wicked thoughts I certainly should not be having during her mother's birthday party fill my mind.

But before she gets a chance to make a break for it, waiters appear and food lands in front of us.

The scent immediately makes my stomach growl, and my mouth waters as I stare down at the ravioli, mushrooms and truffles.

As uncouth as ever, both Nico and Alex dive straight in without waiting for everyone to have their plates. Not that anyone at our table gives a shit. I'm pretty sure Cassandra would have something to say about it, though, if her own table weren't too busy blowing smoke up her arse.

Silence begins to fall over the room as everyone eats, but my eyes still barely leave my girl as she pokes her own food around her plate.

Both Alex and Jerome notice and check in on her, and it fucking kills me that I can't do the same.

No sooner have the starters been cleared than the mains are landing in front of us, once again halting Calli's escape.

The food is mouth-watering. The venison is tender and perfect, but I don't enjoy it as much as I know I would if I were sitting next to her, finding out what was really causing those shadows in her eyes that she's playing off as her lingering hangover.

The more I watch her, the more I call bullshit on that story.

It's probably my presence that has her on edge, but fuck. I hate it.

Finally, she sits back after once again pushing her food around her plate, places her napkin on the table, and excuses herself.

I force my eyes to the table, not wanting anyone to catch me watching her walk away.

"What the fuck are you waiting for?" Isla whispers in my ear.

"I can't, I. What if Nico notices?"

"Seriously?" she asks, shooting a glance at him. I follow her line of sight to see him throw his head back on a booming laugh at something Toby and Jodie are telling him. "He won't bat an eyelid."

My phone buzzes in my pocket and I slide it out, finding a message from the arsehole on the other side of the table.

Alex: I've got your back. Just go and get your girl.

Fuck it.

I follow her move, push my chair back and head for the bathroom as if nothing unusual is happening.

Thankfully, no other women are heading in the same direction, and I just have to hope that none are already in the bathroom, because that could get awkward fast.

The door to the ladies' is just falling closed as I rush down the hallway and catch it, slipping inside and flipping the lock I thankfully find on the inside.

Calli is just about to slip into one of the cubicles before my voice rips through the air.

"Stop."

She immediately does as she's told, her spine straightening and her shoulders tensing, but she doesn't turn around. She doesn't do anything, and it makes a wave of fear wash through me.

"Calli, please. I just need—"

"You shouldn't be in here," she says in a weak, broken voice.

My feet carry me across the room without any instruction from my brain until I'm standing right behind her. Her scent fills my nose and my muscles ache with the need to wrap her in my arms and never let her go.

"I'm sorry," I blurt. "I'm sorry for everything I said from the moment I woke you up that morning. It was all bullshit. You were right. I was scared. I'm nothing but a coward and I don't deserve a second chance with you, but—"

She spins, her eyes finding mine as her tiny palms slam down on my chest, the shock of the move forcing me to take a step back.

"Shut up. Just shut up," she growls. "I'm sick of you telling me what I should do, what I should think.

When you pull this 'I don't deserve you' shit and pull away, you're no better than them out there trying to control my life.

"Don't you think I'm able to make my own fucking decisions? To come to my own conclusions about who is and isn't worthy of my time? Of my love?"

All the air rushes from my lungs as she says those final words.

"I'm in l-love with you, Calli," I blurt. "I-I have been f-for a long fucking t-time. Y-you're it f-for m-me. The only one I've ever s-seen. The only one I've e-ever wanted."

She melts before me. All her anger from before washes away the second my words hit her ears.

"So trust me to know what I want too," she whispers. "Stop putting up the walls, thinking you know better than me. Only I know what I want, what I feel."

I nod as she just continues to stare at me, my words still floating around us as I damn near bleed out all over the floor for her.

"S-s-so." I pause, trying to pull myself together. Her hands slide up my chest until she's cupping my jaw, giving me the strength I need. "What do you want?"

"You, Nikolas. I want you. I want the scary soldier and the vulnerable little boy who lives inside you and everything in between. I want your fear, your anxiety, and I want to shatter it with you and prove to you that it's all in your head, because you're fucking extraordinary."

Her breath comes out in a rush and her bag lands on the floor as I slam her back against the wall behind her and crash my lips to hers.

"Fuck, you're perfect," I growl into our kiss before plunging my tongue past her red lips to find hers.

A groan that's full of lust and primal need erupts from my throat as she eagerly falls into the kiss right alongside me.

Reaching down, I hook my hand under her knee and drag her leg up to wrap around my hip, but I still when my fingers brush something.

"What the—" I pull back from her addictive kiss and stare down at her thigh. "Fuck me. You just got even hotter."

"Nikolas," she moans, grinding herself against me.

"Fuck, Angel. I'm fucking aching for you. Spend the night with me. I want you in my flat again. I want you in my bed."

"Yes," she moans as I kiss down her neck. "Yes, I want it all."

"Good," I breathe, my lips hitting her pulse point and a smile curling up as I feel just how much I'm affecting her. "And then you can tell me what's really bothering you tonight."

She tenses, and instantly, it's like those few words from me sucked all the air out of the room.

"W-what do you mean?"

I pull back, take her face in my hands and stare deep into her eyes.

"I know you, Calli. I see you. And I know this hangover excuse is bullshit. Something else is bothering you."

Her lips part to respond, but a rattling at the bathroom door cuts through the room.

"Hello? Is anyone in there," someone calls.

"Shit," Calli hisses. "You can't be caught in here."

"It's okay," I assure her. "I'll hide in one of the cubicles. You do what you need to do, then walk out as if nothing happened."

"What do I say about the lock?"

"Accident? That you were on autopilot?" I shrug.

"And what about you?"

"Angel, you don't need to worry about me. I've got myself out of worse situations than this before."

The woman on the other side of the door knocks again.

"Tonight, yeah? Me and you."

"Yeah. I'll make it happen."

"I love you," I say in a rush again before dropping a kiss on the end of her nose and slipping into one of the toilet cubicles.

Calli blows out a long breath before her heels clack against the tiled floor and water runs.

The seconds feel like hours before she finally walks to the door and pulls it open.

"Oh my gosh, I'm so sorry. I have no idea what

happened," she says, sounding more than convincing. Little minx.

The woman who was waiting says something in response, but I'm too busy reliving our few moments in here together to focus.

It's just a shame that doesn't continue and I'm not able to block out the sound of her taking a piss in the cubicle beside me before she lets out the most unladylike fart I've ever heard in my life.

Who said life in the mafia was meant to be glamorous?

It seems to take forever for her to leave, and just when I think I'm free to bolt, two more women enter.

Fuck my life.

It's a good job Calli's worth every second of this.

Thankfully, when I do finally make it back to the table, the desserts are just being passed out and Nico and Theo are deep in conversation.

"Have fun?" Isla asks, looking stupidly smug despite the fact that she wasn't just the one hooking up in the toilets.

"Do you have to be enjoying this quite so much?" I ask, turning to look at her the second my arse hits the chair.

"Oh shit," she gasps, reaching out to rub at my lips. "It's not really your colour. You're more of a deep purple, I think."

"I'll remember that next time," I deadpan.

A cheesecake with some fancy sugar cage thing on

the top is placed in front of me, and after studying it for a second, I risk a glance up at Cal.

Her cheeks are pink and her lips are swollen from my kiss.

And I'm fucking hard again.

Alex smirks at me as I tug at my trousers, as if he can see exactly what I'm doing beneath the table.

Needing a distraction that's going to sink my boner, I look back at Nico and Theo.

"What's going on?" I ask, the seriousness of their conversation making the hairs on the back of my neck stand on end.

"The ants have found the honey," Nico replies cryptically, earning himself an eye-roll from Stella.

As far as I know, none of the girls are aware of what's actually happening, but none of them are stupid and they have to suspect something.

"All to plan?" I ask, my skin continuing to prickle.

"Yep. What else did you expect, man? You need to have some fucking faith. Bottoms up, boys," he calls, lifting his glass of whisky from the table. "It's a fucking good night to be Greek."

Calli's stare burns into the side of my face, and when I turn back, I find fear in her light blue eyes.

She knows.

And she feels it too.

30

———

CALLI

Whatever has happened outside of this party seems to lift the spirits of everyone around me, even those who are as clueless as me.

But I don't feel it.

My heart is so full after hearing those words from Daemon in the bathroom, but the guilt that goes along with them threatens to swallow me up and never let me go.

I should have told him how I really felt instead of stumbling over the words as our new reality loomed over me.

And I still don't know the freaking result of that test.

I look around as everyone jokes and laughs while finishing their desserts, the drinks flowing easier than they were before.

Leaning over, I whisper in Alex's ear.

"What's happened?"

"Everything has gone well with... yeah," he says, guilt washing through his features in apology for his vagueness.

"And we're safe here now?"

"As safe as we ever are."

"How reassuring," I mutter.

"Are you sure you're okay? You've barely eaten anything toni—" Alex's words are cut off as the ground rocks with what I can only assume is an explosion before gunfire cuts through the air.

"Motherfuckers," someone booms before women start screaming and men begin barking orders.

Everything happens in a blur as someone grabs my upper arm and drags me behind our table that has suddenly been upended so we can hide behind it.

"I fucking knew this was a bad idea," Daemon barks before taking off behind Theo and Nico.

"No, wait. Come back," I scream, fear like I've never known pressing down on me until I'm barely able to breathe.

"Trust us to do our jobs, Cal." Alex grabs my face and kisses my brow before he takes off as well, just as another round of gunfire echoes through the room.

Things shatter and break, and explosions rock the ground beneath our feet as chaos ensues.

"Fuck," someone cries from behind me, and when I look back, I find Jerome with blood pouring from his thigh.

"Shit, have you been shot?" I ask, adrenaline kicking in as I rush over to help him.

"N-no," he stutters, staring down at the wound with wide eyes. "It was glass."

"Okay, good. You got a gun?" I ask, slipping my hand into his jacket in the hope I find one tucked into his waistband.

Wrapping my fingers around the cool metal, I pull it free and place it in his hand.

When I find his eyes again, I can't help but swallow nervously. He looks fucking terrified.

"You've got this, J. Anyone who isn't one of us, shoot them, yeah? We're gonna get out of here."

But as I say that, another ominous crash sounds out as something collapses.

"They've blown the entrance," a familiar voice shouts. "We need to find a way out."

"They're coming in through the back," someone else calls.

"Find cover. Take those motherfuckers out."

My heart beats at a million miles a minute as I listen to the chaos from the safety of our table. But that's not going to be the case for long.

I glance at Jerome again, seeing more blood draining from his face in favour of flooding the carpet.

"Fuck."

Pushing forward, I peek around the table and my eyes widen at the carnage.

The far end of the building has completely collapsed, the room is destroyed, the windows all shattered and there are... I gag when I find a pair of legs sticking out from beneath a chair.

Oh fuck.

"Jerome, we need to get out of here."

Footsteps thunder somewhere on the other side of the table, followed by close-range shots, and I panic, pulling my gun from its holster.

I raise it, but when the person belonging to the footsteps emerges behind the table, I breathe a sigh of relief when I discover it's just Jodie.

"What the fuck is going on?" I hiss, although I'm not really expecting an answer I don't already know.

It's the Italians.

Pieces of my missing puzzle begin to slot into place.

They thought they'd tricked them.

They thought they'd taken them out elsewhere and that we were safe. How fucking wrong, and how fucking stupid were they?

"Emmie and Stella are fine, they're over there. They're gonna head out the side door. They told me to tell you that they'll meet us at your house."

"What about the boys?"

Worry darkens Jodie's eyes before she swallows it down and drags up some strength I really need to fucking latch onto right now.

"This is what they're trained for, Calli. They've got this."

"And if they don't?"

"There's a door over there," she says, jerking her chin toward the table that's hiding our sight of it.

We're trapped in a corner, which might be safe right now, but we're screwed if the guys don't manage to get this under control. We're sitting ducks.

"What about Jerome?"

"Can you walk?" Jodie asks him.

"I don't know," he says weakly.

"Let's just go with no," I say pessimistically.

A ripple of fear goes between us as the shouts and gunfire get louder.

"We need to do something," Jodie says.

The three of us jump a freaking mile when something suspiciously close to us explodes.

My hands tremble and sweat trickles down my spine as I try to get my head straight.

What would Dad do?

Fuck that, he got us into this fucking mess.

What would Daemon do?

"We need a distraction, then we need to run for it."

"I'm down. What's the distrac—"

Gunfire slams into the table hiding us, and both our eyes are wide with our impending death as they meet.

Fuck. I can't die tonight. I need to look at that goddamn test.

I can't die before I know the truth.

When it calms down, I peek out again, finding men with balaclavas covering their faces.

Fuck. I really fucking hope one of them is Ant, who can get me out of this.

"Take Jerome's gun. We fire and run. We've just got to pray their shots are shit."

"That's suicide," Jerome says.

"Do you have a fucking better idea?" Jodie snaps, making him pale further.

"No, I—" Something cracks before the wall beside us crumbles.

"Oh shit."

Explosions go off one after the other, gunfire rains down, and the heart-sinking realisation that we're too slow seeps deep into my bones.

We're gonna die here.

And it's all my parents' fault.

My eyes burn with tears, my hope dwindling as my hand rests against my belly.

A scream pieces the air as a body comes flying over the table, bullets still hitting it every few seconds.

"What the—"

"Daemon," I cry, relief overwhelming me as I fly into his arms.

"It's okay, Angel. I'm gonna get you out of here, okay?"

I pull back and look at his face.

His eyes are as dark as the dead of night, and he's got blood sprayed over almost every inch of him.

He's got a gun in one hand and a red-tinged knife in the other.

"You need to come too. I won't go without you."

"There's no time for an argument, Calli."

The gunfire lessens, leaving my ears ringing.

"When I say go, you're going to drag his bleeding arse out toward that door, and you're not going to stop running until you're in the SUV that dropped you here. It's waiting for you. Stella and Emmie too."

"But—"

"I'll meet you back at yours."

"You promise?"

"I fucking promise, Angel."

Dropping his knife to the floor, he twists his bloody fingers in my hair and slams his lips down on mine.

Just for those few seconds, everything fades away, and it's just the two of us on that beach again. But the second he pulls back, it's lost.

"Ready?" he asks.

He lifts my arm, raising my gun as if I'm going to need to shoot someone.

Hauling Jerome from the floor, Daemon encourages us to help him before reloading his gun and getting ready.

"Three. Two." My heart beats out of rhythm as I try and focus, blood rushing past my ears and making everything blur. "One. Fucking run."

I do as I'm told because it's Daemon. I'd be stupid to do anything but what he says in a situation like this.

Gunfire explodes behind us as Jodie and I half drag Jerome toward the doors.

"Are you all okay?" I shout as we spill out into the darkness of the gardens beyond.

"Yeah," Jodie agrees while Jerome just groans. I take that as agreement, because I can't cope with anything else right now.

We continue to run as fast as we can with the almost dead weight between us as the carnage continues behind us.

The ground rocks with another explosion, and I stupidly risk a look back.

A scream rips from my throat as I watch the part of the building we were just in collapse.

"He'll be okay, Calli," Jodie assures me, reminding me that she witnessed that kiss. "We gotta keep going."

We spill through the trees, leaving the barely standing building behind us.

The SUV is at the end of the driveway with the lights on.

The second we're spotted, both Stella and Emmie jump out and rush toward us, taking Jerome's weight from me.

"Calli, get in the fucking car," Emmie screams when I come to a stop and turn around, watching the dark smoke pluming into the sky.

I'm just about to move when a body explodes through the trees. I raise my gun on instinct when I see his face covering, my finger on the trigger and ready to shoot.

But our eyes collide and my heart sinks into my feet.

He pulls his balaclava off and a sob erupts as I stare at the boy I foolishly trusted.

My own stupidity slams into me.

"Calli," Ant breathes. "I'm sorry. I'm so fucking sorry."

Burning hot tears flood my cheeks as I stare at him with my gun still raised.

"I'll get them out, all of them. I fucking promise you."

It's stupid. But as he says the words, I have no choice but to believe him, even in the middle of this bloody war.

"You fucking better, or this won't be the last time you're staring down the barrel of my gun, Antonio Santoro." The conviction behind my words shocks me.

He nods once before shouting for me to get the fuck out of here and running toward the building.

Hands grab my upper arms and I'm dragged back and damn near thrown into the back of the SUV by my two best friends.

"GO," Emmie shouts.

"No," I scream, scrambling around so I'm looking out the back window. "NOOOOOO."

Arms wrap around me and I'm dragged down onto Stella's lap as they all hold me, stopping me from completely shattering into a million pieces all over the floor.

"They'll be okay. This is just a normal day's work for them," Stella whispers in my ear before pressing her brow to mine. "They're better than the Italians."

The image of Ant standing there, still making me promises after everything we've been through fills my mind, and I cry harder.

I could be about to lose everyone.

On one hand, the drive back to the house seems to pass me by in a flash, but the second I'm dragged out and held up by Stella, it feels like a million years since I watched that building implode on Daemon.

Another sob rips from my throat as the front door is thrown open and Jocelyn runs toward us.

"Calli," she cries, gathering me up in her arms and helping Stella get me inside.

She directs us to the kitchen where we find Mum, Selene, Iris, Clio, Isla, and... Gianna.

Finding some strength from somewhere deep inside me, I shake off my supports and surge forward.

"This is all your fault," I scream in Mum's pale face. "If you didn't feel the need to show off, this never would have happened." My voice doesn't even sound like my own as I continue to rail on her. "We could lose all of them, and it's all your fault."

"Can you three take her somewhere?" Jocelyn demands, leaving little room for argument.

"Gianna, can you look at Jerome, please," Jodie asks, as she and Emmie lower a passed-out Jerome to the sofa.

She rushes over as I'm once again manhandled out of the room.

"I can't lose them. I can't. I can't lose them," I wail before I'm forced onto the sofa in the den.

Images of my dad, Nico, Daemon, Alex, Theo... fuck. I glance at Jodie as she joins us, and the devastation on her face guts me all over again.

She's been through too much to lose Toby.

My sobs get louder once more before the sofa dips on both sides of me.

"Drink this," Emmie demands, shoving a glass of some amber liquid in front of me.

"I can't," I whisper.

"You can. Swallow it in one go. It'll help."

"I can't. I might—"

"Fuck your hangover, Calli. Jodie will just have to cope if you puke over her," Stella says, forcing me to look up and finding Jodie sitting on the coffee table before me, her hands on my knees in support.

I cave, taking the glass from Emmie and throwing it back.

Guilt floods me the second I do, but as the liquid burns down my throat and then begins to warm my belly, I can't deny that it did help.

"What the fuck are we going to do?" I ask after the longest silence as we all lose ourselves in our fears.

"We wait for them to return and then give them all the best night of their goddamn lives," Emmie announces.

"Alex is shit out of luck tonight then," Jodie says, making me look up in a panic. "I'll call Bri in for Nico." I don't even have it in me to wince at that thought.

"And Daemon," Stella adds.

"Maybe Calli can have her mind blown by the Deimos twins at last," Emmie jokes while Jodie stares at me with understanding eyes.

Reaching forward, I take her hand in mine and squeeze, silently thanking her for keeping quiet.

Jocelyn rushes in with a tray of drinks and snacks, but none of us touch them.

We're all too worried about our boys.

The clock above the fireplace continues to tick ominously, counting down every second they're not here. And as the minutes turn into an hour, and then two, I start to lose hope. Glancing at the girls, I find the same expression etched into their features.

"Headlights," Stella suddenly announces before jumping from the sofa and rushing toward the window. "Fuck. They're here. They're here," she damn near screams as she runs for the door.

We all follow as the front door slams and footsteps fill the hallway.

The three of us spill out of the room as hope fills my heart that I'm about to lay eyes on Daemon. Fuck what everyone thinks, because I'm going to run straight into his arms and shatter everyone's illusions that I'm still their innocent princess.

Only when I look up, I only find four of them.

Theo, Toby, Seb, and Alex all stand before us with grim expressions on their faces.

Movement behind me gives me hope once more, but only Uncle Damien and Galen appear.

"Where are the others?" I demand.

Where's my dad, my brother, my— I swallow down that thought as tears flood my eyes once more and my heart breaks for the millionth time in the past few days.

"I'm sorry, Calli. They're not with us."

"No." I shake my head, refusing to believe that tonight was my last night with the most important men in my life. "No."

My knees buckle, but just before I hit the floor, strong arms catch me and pull me into his chest.

I blink away my tears and find Alex's glassy ones staring back at me.

"I've got you, Calli. Okay? I've fucking got you."

His arms engulf me, cutting me off from the others as I shatter, disbelief, grief, and bone-chilling fear taking hold of every inch of me.

I sob until my eyes burn and my throat aches from screaming, but Alex never once lets me go.

When I finally feel able to pull away from him, I find the hallway empty around us and tears staining Alex's cheeks just like they are mine.

"I found this," he says, his voice rough with emotion as he holds my clutch up.

I stare at it in disbelief.

Oh God.

I reach for it with shaky hands as his eyes burn into the top of my head, probably wondering why I'm reaching for it as if it's the holy grail.

I forget that he's watching me, pushing aside any concerns for what I'm potentially about to reveal to him. None of it matters. Nothing other than the truth matters.

I flip my bag open, finding the little packet exactly where I left it sitting beside my phone.

"Calli?" Alex asks, watching my every move.

Reaching inside, I pull the stick out from the open end of the foil and stare down at the screen with my answer.

"Holy fuck, Calli. Is that—"

Calli & Daemon's story continues in Dark Legacy...

ABOUT THE AUTHOR

Tracy Lorraine is a *USA Today* and *Wall Street Journal* bestselling new adult and contemporary romance author. Tracy has recently turned thirty and lives in a cute Cotswold village in England with her husband, baby girl and lovable but slightly crazy dog. Having always been a bookaholic with her head stuck in her Kindle, Tracy decided to try her hand at a story idea she dreamt up and hasn't looked back since.

Be the first to find out about new releases and offers. Sign up to my newsletter here.

If you want to know what I'm up to and see teasers and snippets of what I'm working on, then you need to be in my Facebook group. Join Tracy's Angels here.

Keep up to date with Tracy's books at
www.tracylorraine.com

ALSO BY TRACY LORRAINE

<u>Falling Series</u>

<u>Falling for Ryan: Part One</u> #1

<u>Falling for Ryan: Part Two</u> #2

<u>Falling for Jax</u> #3

<u>Falling for Daniel</u> (A Falling Series Novella)

<u>Falling for Ruben</u> #4

<u>Falling for Fin</u> #5

<u>Falling for Lucas</u> #6

<u>Falling for Caleb</u> #7

<u>Falling for Declan</u> #8

<u>Falling For Liam</u> #9

<u>Forbidden Series</u>

<u>Falling for the Forbidden</u> #1

<u>Losing the Forbidden</u> #2

<u>Fighting for the Forbidden</u> #3

<u>Craving Redemption</u> #4

<u>Demanding Redemption</u> #5

<u>Avoiding Temptation</u> #6

<u>Chasing Temptation</u> #7

<u>**Rebel Ink Series**</u>

Hate You #1

Trick You #2

Defy You #3

Play You #4

Inked (A Rebel Ink/Driven Crossover)

<u>**Rosewood High Series**</u>

Thorn #1

Paine #2

Savage #3

Fierce #4

Hunter #5

Faze (#6 Prequel)

Fury #6

Legend #7

<u>**Maddison Kings University Series**</u>

TMYM: Prequel

TRYS #1

TDYW #2

TBYS #3

TVYC #4

TDYD #5

TDYR #6

Knight's Ridge Empire Series

Wicked Summer Knight: Prequel (Stella & Seb)

Wicked Knight #1 (Stella & Seb)

Wicked Princess #2 (Stella & Seb)

Wicked Empire #3 (Stella & Seb)

Deviant Knight #4 (Emmie & Theo)

Deviant Princess #5 (Emmie & Theo

Deviant Reign #6 (Emmie & Theo)

One Reckless Knight (Jodie & Toby)

Reckless Knight #7 (Jodie & Toby)

Reckless Princess #8 (Jodie & Toby)

Reckless Dynasty #9 (Jodie & Toby)

Dark Halloween Knight (Calli & Batman)

Dark Knight #10 (Calli & Batman)

Dark Princess #11 (Calli & Batman)

Dark Legacy #12 (Calli & Batman)

Corrupt Valentine Knight (Nico & Siren)

Ruined Series

Ruined Plans #1

Ruined by Lies #2

HATE YOU SNEAK PEEK
PROLOGUE

Tabitha

I stare down at my gran's pale skin. Her cheeks are sunken and her eyes tired. She's been fighting this for too long now, and as much as I hate to even think it, it's time she found some peace.

I take her cool hand in mine and lift her knuckles to my lips.

"It's Tabitha," I whisper. I've no idea if she's awake, but I don't want to startle her.

Her eyes flicker open. After a second they must adjust to the light and she looks right at me. My chest tightens as if someone's wrapping an elastic band around it. I hate seeing my once so full of life gran like this. She was always so happy and full of cheer. She didn't deserve this end. But cancer doesn't care what kind of person you are, it hits whoever it fancies and ruins lives.

Pulling a chair closer, I drop onto it, not taking my eyes from her.

"How are you doing today?" I hate asking the question, because there really is only one answer. She's waiting, waiting for her time to come to put her out of her misery.

"I'm good. Christopher upped my morphine. I'm on top of the world."

She might be living her last days, but it doesn't stop her eyes sparkling a little as she mentions her male nurse. If I've heard the words 'if I were forty years younger' once while she's been here, then I've heard them a million times. She's joking, of course. My gran spent her life with my incredible grandpa until he had a stroke a few years ago. Thankfully, I guess, his end was much quicker and less painful than Gran's. It was awful at the time to have him healthy one moment and then gone in a matter of hours, but this right now is pure torture, and I'm not the one lying on the hospital bed with meds constantly being pumped into my body.

"Turn the frown upside down, Tabby Cat. I'm fine. I want to remember you smiling, not like your world's about to come crashing down."

"I know, I'm sorry. I just—" a sob breaks from my throat. "I don't know how I'm going to live without you." Dramatic? Yeah. But Gran has been my go-to person my whole life. When my parents get on my last nerve, which is often, she's the one who talks me down, makes me see things differently. She's also the only one who's encouraged me to live the life I want, not the one I'm constantly being pushed into.

That's the reason I'm the only one visiting her right now.

When my parents discovered that she was the one encouraging my 'reckless behaviour', as they called it, they cut contact. I can see the pain in her eyes about that every time she looks at me, but she's too stubborn to do anything about it, even now.

"You're going to be fine. You're stronger than you give yourself credit for. How many times have I told you, you just need to follow your heart. Follow your heart and just breathe. Spread your wings and fly, Tabby Cat."

Those were the last words she said to me.

HATE YOU SNEAK PEEK
CHAPTER ONE

Tabitha

The heavy bass rattles my bones. The incredible music does help to lift my spirits, but I find it increasingly hard to see the positives in my life while I'm hanging out with my friends these days. They've all got something exciting going on—incredible job prospects, marriage, exotic holidays on the horizon—and here I am, drowning in my one-person pity party. It's been two months since Gran left me, and I'm still wondering what the hell I'm meant to be doing with my life.

"Oh my god, they are so fucking awesome," Danni squeals in my ear as one song comes to an end. I didn't really have her down as a rock fan, but she was almost as excited as James when he announced that this was what we were doing for his birthday this year. Although I do wonder if it's the music or the frontman who's really captured her attention. She'd never admit it, but she's got a thing for bad boys.

I glance over at him with his arm wrapped around Shannon's shoulders and a smile twitches my lips. They're so cute. They've got the kind of relationship everyone craves. It seems so easy yet full of love and affection. Ripping my eyes from the couple, I focus back on the stage and try to block out that I'm about as far away from having that kind of connection with anyone as physically possible.

I sing along with the songs I've heard on the radio a million times and jump around with my friends, but I just can't quite totally get on board with tonight. Maybe I just need more alcohol.

"Where to next?" Shannon asks once we've left the arena and the ringing in our ears has begun to fade.

"Your choice," James says, looking down at her with utter devotion shining in his eyes. It wasn't a great surprise when Shannon sent a photo of her giant engagement ring to our group chat a couple of months ago. We all knew it was coming—Danni especially, seeing as it turned out that she helped choose the ring.

Shannon directs us all to a cocktail bar a few streets over and I make quick work of manoeuvring my way through the crowd to get to the bar, my need for a drink beginning to get the better of me. The others disappear off somewhere in the hope of finding a table

"Can we have two jugs of..." I quickly glance at the menu. "Margaritas please."

"Coming right up, sweetheart." The barman winks

at me before his eyes drop to my chest. Hooking up on a night out isn't really my thing, but hell if it doesn't make me feel a little better about myself. He's cute too, and just the kind of guy who would give both my parents a heart attack if I were to bring him home. Both his forearms are covered in tattoos, he's got gauges in both his ears, and a lip ring. A smile tugs at the corner of my mouth as I imagine the looks on their faces.

My gran's words suddenly hit me.

Just breathe.

My hand lifts and my fingers run over the healing skin just below my bra. My smile widens.

I watch the barman prepare our cocktails, my eyes focused on the ink on his arms. I've always been obsessed by art, any kind of art, and that most definitely includes on skin.

I'm lost in my own head, so when he places the jugs in front of me, I startle, feeling ridiculous.

"T-Thank you," I mutter, but when I lift my eyes, I find him staring intently at me.

"You're welcome. I'm Christian, by the way."

"Oh, hi." A sly smile creeps onto my lips. "I'm Biff."

"Biff?" His brows draw together in a way I'm all too used to when I say my name.

"It's short for Tabitha."

"That's pretty. So... uh... how do you feel about—"

"Christian, a little help?" one of the other barmen shouts, pulling Christian's attention from me.

"Sorry, I'll hopefully see you again later?"

I nod at him, not wanting to give him any false hope. Like I said, he's cute, but after my last string of bad dates and even worse short-term boyfriends, I'm happy flying solo right now. I've got a top of the range vibrating friend in my bedside table; I don't need a man.

Picking up the tray in front of me, I turn and go in search of my friends. It takes forever, but eventually I find them tucked around a tiny table in the back corner of the bar.

"What the hell took so long? We thought you'd pulled and abandoned us."

"Yes and no," I say, ensuring every head turns my way.

"Tell us more," Danni, my best friend, demands.

"It was nothing. The barman was about to ask me out, but it got busy."

"Why the hell did you come back? Get over there. We all know you could do with a little... loosening up," James says with a wink.

"I'm good. He wasn't my type."

"Oh, of course. You only date posh boys."

"That is not true."

"Is it not?" Danni asks, chipping in once she's filled all the glasses.

"No..." I think back over the previous few guys they met. "Wayne wasn't posh," I argue when I realise they're kind of right.

"No, he was just a wanker."

Blowing out a long breath, I try to come up with an argument, but quite honestly, it's true. My shoulders slump as I realise that I've been subconsciously dating guys my parents would approve of. It's like my need to follow their orders is so well ingrained by now that I don't even realise I'm doing it. Shame that their ideas about my life, what I should do, and whom I should date don't exactly line up with mine.

Glancing over my shoulder at the bar, I catch a glimpse of Christian's head. Maybe I should take him up on his almost offer. What's the worst that could happen?

Deciding some liquid courage is in order, I grab my margherita and swallow half down in one go.

I'm so fed up of attempting to live my parents' idea of a perfect life. I promised Gran I'd do things my way. I need to start living up to my promise.

By the time I'm tipsy enough to walk back to the bar and chat up Christian, he's nowhere to be seen. I'm kind of disappointed seeing as the others had convinced me to throw caution to the wind (something that I'm really bad at doing), but I think I'm mostly relieved to be able go home and lock myself inside my flat alone and not have to worry about anyone else.

With my arm linked through Danni's, we make our way out to the street, ready to make our journeys home, and Shannon jumps into an idling Uber while Danni waits for another to go in the opposite direction.

"You sure you don't want to be dropped off? I don't mind."

"No, I'm sure. I could do with the fresh air." It's not a lie—the alcohol from one too many cocktails is making my head a little fuzzy. I hate going to sleep with the room spinning. I'd much rather that feeling fade before lying down.

"Okay. Promise me you'll text me when you're home."

"I promise." I wrap my arms around my best friend and then wave her off in her own Uber.

Turning on my heels, I start the short walk home.

I've been a London girl all my life, and while some might be afraid to walk home after dark, I love it. I love seeing a different side to this city, the quiet side when most people are hiding in their flats, not flooding the streets on their daily commutes.

My mind is flicking back and forth between my promise to Gran and my missed opportunity tonight when a shop front that I walk past on almost a daily basis makes me stop.

It's a tattoo studio I've been inside of once in my life. I never really pay it much attention, but the new sign in the window catches my eye and I stop to look.

Admin help wanted. Enquire within.

Something stirs in my belly, and it's not just my need to do something to piss my parents off—although getting a job in a place like this is sure to do that. I'm pretty sure it's excitement.

Tattoos fascinate me, or more so, the artists.

I'm surprised to see the open sign still illuminated, so before I can change my mind, I push the door open. A little bell rings above it, and after a few seconds of standing in reception alone, a head pops out from around the door.

"Evening. What can I do you for?" The guy's smile is soft and kind despite his otherwise slightly harsh features and ink.

"Oh um…" I hesitate under his intense dark stare. I glance over my shoulder, the back of the piece of paper catching my eye and reminding me why I walked in here. "I just saw the job ad in the window. Is the position still open?"

His eyes drop from mine and take in what I'm wearing. Seeing as tonight's outing involved a rock concert, I'm dressed much like him in all black and looking a little edgy with my skinny black jeans, ripped AC/DC t-shirt and heavy black makeup. I must admit it's not a look I usually go for, but it was fitting for tonight.

He nods, apparently happy with what he sees.

"Experience?" he asks, making my stomach drop.

"Not really, but I'm studying for a Masters so I'm not an idiot. I know my way around a computer, Excel, and I'm super organised."

"Right…" he trails off, like he's thinking about the best way to get rid of me.

"I'm a really quick learner. I'm punctual, methodical and really easy to get along with."

"It's okay, you had me sold at organised. I'm Dawson, although everyone around here calls me D."

"Nice to meet you." I stick my hand out for him to shake, and an amused smile plays at his lips. Stretching out an inked arm, he takes my hand and gives it a very firm shake that my dad would be impressed by—if he could look past the tattoos, that is. "I'm Tabitha, but everyone calls me Biff."

"Biff, I like it. When can you start?"

"Don't you want to interview me?"

"You sound like you could be perfect. When can you start?"

"Err... tomorrow?" I ask, totally taken aback. He doesn't know me from Adam.

"Yes!" He practically snaps my hand off. "Can you be here for two o'clock? I can show you around before clients start turning up. I'll apologise now for dropping you in the deep end, we've not had anyone for a few weeks and things are starting to get a little crazy."

"I can cope with crazy."

"Good to know. This place can be nuts." I smile at him, more grateful than he could know to have a distraction and a focus.

My Masters should be enough to keep my mind busy, but since Gran went, I can't seem to lose myself in it like I could previously. Hopefully, sorting this place's admin out might be exactly what I need.

"Two o'clock tomorrow then," I say, turning to

leave. "I'll bring ID. Do you need a reference? I've done some voluntary work recently, I'm sure they'll write something for me."

"Just turn up on time and do your job and you're golden."

I walk out with more of a spring in my step than I have in a long time. I'm determined to find something that's going to make me happy, not just my parents. I've lived in their shadow for long enough.

I look myself over before leaving my flat for my first shift at the tattoo studio. I'm dressed a little more like myself today in a pair of dark skinny jeans, a white blouse and a black blazer. It's simple and smart. I'm not sure if there's a dress code—D never specified what I should wear. With my hair straightened and hanging down my back and my makeup light, I feel like I can take on whatever crazy he throws at me.

With a final spritz of perfume, I grab my bag from the unit in the hall and pull open my door. My home is a top floor flat in an old London warehouse. They were converted a few years ago by my father's company, and I managed to get myself first dibs. They might drive me insane on the best of days, but at least I get this place rent-free. It almost makes up for their controlling and stuck-up ways... almost.

Ignoring the lift like I always do, I head for the stairs. My heels click against the polished concrete until I'm at the bottom and out to the busy city. I love London. I love that no matter what the time, there's always something going on or someone who's awake.

The spring afternoon is still a little fresh, making me regret not grabbing my coat, or even a scarf, before I left. I pull my blazer tighter around myself and make the short journey to the shop.

The door's locked when I get there, and the bright neon sign that clearly showed it was open last night is currently saying closed.

Unsure of what to do, I lift my hand to knock. Only a second later, the shop front is illuminated, and the sound of movement inside filters down to me, but when the door opens it's not the guy from last night.

"Oh... uh... hi. Is... uh... D here?"

The guy folds his arms over his chest and looks me up and down. He chuckles, although I've no idea what he finds so amusing.

"D," he shouts over his shoulder, "there's some posh bird here to see you."

My teeth grind that he's stereotyped me quite so quickly, but I refuse to allow him to see that his assumptions about me affect me in any way.

"Ah, good. I was worried you might change your mind."

"Not at all," I say, stepping past the judgemental arsehole and into the studio reception-cum-waiting room.

"That's Spike. Feel free to ignore him. He's not got laid in about a million years, it makes him a little cranky." I fight to contain a laugh, especially when I turn toward Spike to find his lips pursed and his eyes narrowed in frustration. All it does is confirm that D's words are correct.

"Is that fucking necessary? Posh doesn't need to know how inactive my cock is, especially not when she's only just walked through the fucking door. Unless..." He stalks towards me and I automatically back up. I can't deny that he's a good looking guy, but there's no way I'm going there.

"I don't think so."

"You sure? You look like you could do with a bit of rough." He winks, and I want the ground to swallow me up.

"Down, Spike. This is Tabitha, or Biff. She's our new admin, so I suggest you be nice to her if you want to stop organising your own appointments and shit. I don't need a sexual harassment case on my hands before she's even fucking started."

I can't help but laugh at the look on Spike's face. "Don't worry. I'm sure you'll find some desperate old spinster soon."

He looks me up and down again, something in his eyes changed. "Appearances aside, I think you're going to get on well here."

I smile at him. "Mine's a coffee. Milk, no sugar. I'm already sweet enough." His chin drops.

"I thought you were our new assistant. Why am I still making the coffee?"

"Know your place, Spike. Now do as the lady says. You know my order."

"Yeah, it comes with a side of fuck off!" He flips D off before disappearing through a door that I can only assume goes to a kitchen.

"I probably should have warned you that you've agreed to work around a bunch of arseholes."

"I know how to handle myself around horny men, don't worry."

After finishing my A levels, before I grew any kind of backbone where my parents were concerned, I agreed to work for my dad. I was his little office bitch and spent an horrendous year of my life being bossed around by men who thought that just because they had a cock hanging between their legs it made them better than me. I might have fucking hated that year, but it taught me a few things, not just about business but also how to deal with men who think they're something fucking special just because they're a tiny bit successful and make more money than me. I've no doubt that my time at Anderson Development Group gave me all the skills I'm going to need to handle these artists.

"So I see. So, this is your desk. When you're on shift you'll be the first person people see when they're inside, so it's important that you look good. But from what I've seen, I don't think we'll have an issue. I've sorted you out logins for the computer and the software we use. Most of it is pretty self-explanatory.

I'm pretty IT illiterate and I've figured most of it out, put it that way."

D's showing me how they book clients in when someone else joins us. This time it's someone I recognise from my previous visit, although it's immediately obvious that he doesn't remember me like I do him. But then I guess he was the one delivering the pain, not receiving it.

"Biff, this is Titch. Titch, this is Biff, our new admin. Be nice."

"Nice? I'm always nice. Nice to meet you, Biff. You have any issues with this one, you come and see me. He might look tough, but I know all his secrets." Titch winks, a smile curling at his lips that shows he's a little more interested than he's making out, and quickly disappears towards his room.

It's not long until the first clients of the afternoon arrive, and I'm left alone to try to get to grips with everything.

Between clients, D pops his head out of his room to check I'm okay, and every hour I make a round of coffee for everyone. That sure seems to get me in their good books.

"I think I could get used to having you around," Spike says when I deliver probably his fourth coffee of the day. "Only thing that would make it better is if it were whisky."

"Not sure the person at the end of your needle would agree." He chuckles and turns back to the design he was working on when I interrupted.

My first day flies by. D tells me to head home not long after nine o'clock. They've all got hours of tattooing to go yet, seeing as Saturday night is their busiest night of the week, but he insists I get a decent night's sleep.

Continue reading Tabitha and Zach's story
HATE YOU!

www.ingramcontent.com/pod-product-compliance
Lightning Source LLC
Chambersburg PA
CBHW030143200726
48285CB00004BC/1403